They were the eyes of a dragon, hungry and superior

She wanted to run, to hide away. Every cell in her body recoiled, every instinct blindly backed away in a xenophobic cringing.

Sam spoke to her, his voice soft and sibilant. "Not yet, Mother, I have yet to make the change. When that happens, you may look at me."

Erica realized he was manipulating the timbre and pitch so the vibrations would resonate sympathetically to the inner ear and stimulate the neuroenergy system. "Make the change to what?"

"I'm not sure yet of what I will be. A child of the hidden places, the perfect offspring of another great order of life, the living legacy of the Serpent Kings...the last of which enters into extinction this night."

Other titles in this series:

James Axler
Outlanders

DRAGONEYE

A GOLD EAGLE BOOK FROM
WORLDWIDE.

TORONTO • NEW YORK • LONDON
AMSTERDAM • PARIS • SYDNEY • HAMBURG
STOCKHOLM • ATHENS • TOKYO • MILAN
MADRID • WARSAW • BUDAPEST • AUCKLAND

First edition August 2002

ISBN 0-373-63835-3

DRAGONEYE

Special thanks to Mark Ellis for his contribution to the
Outlanders concept, developed for Gold Eagle Books.

DRAGONEYE

The Road to Outlands—
From Secret Government Files to the Future

Almost two hundred years after the global holocaust, Kane, a former Magistrate of Cobaltville, often thought the world had been lucky to survive at all after a nuclear device detonated in the Russian embassy in Washington, D.C. The aftermath— forever known as skydark—reshaped continents and turned civilization into ashes.

Nearly depopulated, America became the Deathlands— poisoned by radiation, home to chaos and mutated life forms. Feudal rule reappeared in the form of baronies, while remote outposts clung to a brutish existence.

What eventually helped shape this wasteland were the redoubts, the secret preholocaust military installations with stores of weapons, and the home of gateways, the locational matter-transfer facilities. Some of the redoubts hid clues that had once fed wild theories of government cover-ups and alien visitations.

Rearmed from redoubt stockpiles, the barons consoli- dated their power and reclaimed technology for the villes. Their power, supported by some invisible authority, extended beyond their fortified walls to what was now called the Outlands. It was here that the rootstock of humanity survived, living with hellzones and chemical storms, hounded by Magistrates.

In the villes, rigid laws were enforced—to atone for the sins of the past and prepare the way for a better future. That was the barons' public credo and their right-to-rule.

Kane, along with friend and fellow Magistrate Grant, had upheld that claim until a fateful Outlands expedition. A displaced piece of technology…a question to a keeper of the archives…a vague clue about alien masters—and their world shifted radically. Suddenly, Brigid Baptiste, the archivist, faced summary execution, and Grant a quick termination. For Kane there was forgiveness if he pledged his unquestioning allegiance to Baron Cobalt and his unknown masters and abandoned his friends.

But that allegiance would make him support a mysterious and alien power and deny loyalty and friends. Then what else was there?

Kane had been brought up solely to serve the ville. Brigid's only link with her family was her mother's red-gold hair, green eyes and supple form. Grant's clues to his lineage were his ebony skin and powerful physique. But Domi, she of the white hair, was an Outlander pressed into sexual servitude in Cobaltville. She at least knew her roots and was a reminder to the exiles that the outcasts belonged in the human family.

Parents, friends, community—the very rootedness of humanity was denied. With no continuity, there was no forward momentum to the future. And that was the crux— when Kane began to wonder if there *was* a future.

For Kane, it wouldn't do. So the only way was out— way, way out.

After their escape, they found shelter at the forgotten Cerberus redoubt headed by Lakesh, a scientist, Cobaltville's head archivist, and secret opponent of the barons.

With their past turned into a lie, their future threatened, only one thing was left to give meaning to the outcasts. The hunger for freedom, the will to resist the hostile influences. And perhaps, by opposing, end them.

Prologue

Domi returned the red-eyed glare of the slavering three-headed hound on the wall. She wondered briefly if their fangs were bared in snarls or grins. At the moment, she felt like doing both.

Grasping the green lever set into the wall beside the illustration of Cerberus, she pulled it to a midpoint position. With a rumble and whine of buried hydraulics and gears, the massive sec door began folding aside, opening like an accordion. The door was so heavy, it took nearly half a minute for it to open just enough to allow her to step out onto the mountain plateau.

Sunrise flooded the broad plateau with a golden radiance, striking highlights from the scraps of the chain-link fence enclosing the perimeter. The air smelled fresh, rich with the hint of spring growth wafting up from the foothills far below. It still carried a chill and she shivered.

Domi turned at the sound of a footfall behind her. Lakesh stepped through the opening in the sec door, smoothing down his hair, still disheveled from sleep. He gazed reproachfully at her with bleary eyes.

"Darlingest one," he said severely, "you could

have waited for me. I'm not my best this early in the morning. Besides, what can be so important that you rouse me literally at the crack of dawn and tell me to follow you out here?''

Quietly, as if she feared waking the other residents of the redoubt, she said, ''We have guests arriving.''

Lakesh's eyes went wide in surprise, then narrowed with a wary skepticism. ''How can you possibly know that?''

''A trans-comm call came in a little while ago,'' she replied. ''Farrell received it. He woke me up to tell me he couldn't find you.''

''A trans-comm call?'' Lakesh echoed incredulously. ''From whom?''

''Sky Dog.''

Lakesh nodded in understanding. Sky Dog and his band of Sioux and Cheyenne were the Cerberus redoubt's nearest neighbors—its only neighbors for that matter. Only a year or so before, direct contact had been established between the redoubt's personnel and the tribespeople. Kane had managed to turn a potentially tragic misunderstanding into an alliance with Sky Dog.

Not so much a chief as a shaman, a warrior priest, Sky Dog was Cobaltville-bred like Kane, Grant and Brigid. Unlike them, he had been exiled from the ville while still a youth, due to his Lakota ancestry. He joined a band of Cheyenne and Sioux living in the foothills of the Bitterroot Range and eventually earned a position of high authority and respect among them.

Kane, on one of his visits, had entrusted the man with one of the trans-comm units. Though its range was limited to a couple of miles, it was better than no means of communication at all.

"So when Sky Dog made the call," Lakesh said, "he was already in sight of our front door."

"Yeah."

"Why is he coming here at such an ungodly hour?"

"He's bringing…" Domi paused as if groping for the proper term. "Something that belongs to Kane."

Lakesh frowned, becoming annoyed at the vague information Domi was supplying. "Something he left in the village during one of his trips down there? That makes no sense. Whatever it was, it couldn't have been that important."

Domi turned to favor him with an intense stare he found discomfiting. "No, Lakesh," she said softly, "it's not something he left in the village. It's something Kane never talked about with anybody here. He never talked about it with me, either, but that's because I already knew about it. Or I knew that possibly this day might come."

Lakesh shivered, but it wasn't due to the chill in the air. Fingers of dread knotted in his stomach. "This involves your captivity in Area 51, doesn't it?"

She nodded once, a short jerk of her white-haired head, and she fell silent. Lakesh waited for her to say more. He was on the verge of demanding further explanation, when the steady clop-clop of hooves on asphalt reached his ears.

Domi tensed, watching the point where the plateau narrowed down into the road. The sound grew louder and Lakesh realized two horses were approaching, coming up the incline. Silhouetted against the rising sun, two figures mounted on horseback appeared at the edge of the plateau.

"Sky Dog," Domi murmured.

Lakesh had never met the shaman, permitting Kane to act as both ambassador and liaison. He squinted at the second figure astride a pony. Even in the uncertain light, he could see the figure was very slight of build, almost childlike. A blanket lay draped over the head and shoulders.

"Who is that other one?" Lakesh asked.

Domi didn't answer. She strode quickly forward to meet them. Sky Dog reined his horse to a halt and gestured to her. *"Hou, mita cola,* Domi. It's been a while."

Domi acknowledged the comment with a jittery smile. She moved swiftly to the other mounted person and spoke in such low murmurs, Lakesh couldn't catch a single word. He glanced up at Sky Dog. The man's face was lean and sharply planed with wide cheekbones and narrow eyes the color of obsidian. Shiny black hair plaited in two braids fell almost to his waist. Behind his right ear a single white eagle feather dangled.

"I'm Sky Dog," he said pleasantly. "I don't believe I've had the pleasure."

Lakesh stepped forward, extending a hand. "My name is Lakesh. I've heard a lot about you, sir."

Sky Dog's eyes flashed with surprise. "Same here, Lakesh. I have to confess you don't look anything like the man I expected."

He clasped Lakesh's hand tightly. Lakesh winced a bit at the strength of the man's grip and replied, "I've had what used to be called a makeover. What brings you here?"

Sky Dog's face registered surprise a second time. "You mean you don't know?"

He jerked his head toward the blanket-swathed figure whom Domi was helping dismount. "She showed up in my village two days ago, begging to be brought here. She claimed she knew all of you, particularly Kane. She said it was a matter of life and death."

Lakesh gazed suspiciously at the figure. "Whose life?"

When the blanket dropped, his suspicious gaze became a gape of goggle-eyed shock. The hybrid female was small, smaller even than Domi. Her huge, up-slanting eyes of clear crystal blue gave Lakesh a silent appraisal. They looked haunted. White hair the texture of silk threads fell from her domed-shaped skull and curled inward at her slender shoulders.

Her compact, tiny-breasted form was encased in a silvery-gray, skintight bodysuit, which only accentuated the distended condition of her belly. Lakesh's experience with pregnant women was exceptionally slight, but he guessed she was at least six months along.

Holding her belly with both long-fingered hands, she said in a high, almost childlike voice, "*This* life. My name is Quavell, and I have traveled a very long way in order to save it."

Lakesh stared at the woman's interlinked fingers and the belly swelling beneath them as if he had never seen anything like either before. Distantly, he realized that not only had he never seen a pregnant hybrid, but also the possibility that one might exist never occurred to him, so his fascination was understandable if a bit rude.

Domi cleared her throat peremptorily, and Lakesh's eyes flicked toward her. Standing beside Quavell, he was struck by the resemblance between the two women. A curvaceous white wraith, barely five feet tall, Domi's flesh was the color of a beautiful pearl and her ragged mop of hair the hue of bone. Although petite, she was exquisitely formed.

On either side of a high-bridged nose, her eyes gleamed like polished rubies. She wore a black T-shirt and a pair of red, high-cut shorts that showed off her pale, gamin-slim legs.

In a halting voice, Lakesh said to Quavell, "Forgive me staring. I've never seen a hybrid in your condition. You look like a child."

The corners of Quavell's lips quirked in what he interpreted as a patronizing smile. "I am sixty-seven of your years old, Mohandas Lakesh Singh. You do not look your age, either."

Lakesh's hand reflexively went up to touch his glossy black hair. His restored youth—or more accurately, his restored early middle age—was the only tangible result of his encounter with Sam, the self-proclaimed imperator of the baronies. He still remembered with vivid clarity how Sam, who resembled a ten-year-old boy, had accomplished the miracle by the simple laying on of hands.

Lakesh knew the process was far more complex than that, but he could engage only in fairly futile speculation as to how it had been accomplished. He assumed Sam possessed the ability to transfer his biological energy to other organic matter, which in turn stimulated the entire human cellular structure. Beyond that, Lakesh could only guess. He theorized the energy transfer might have rejuvenated the MHC in the six chromosomal structures, which resulted in turning back the hands of the metabolic clock persuading the cells to reproduce and repair themselves.

Regardless of how Sam had done it, Lakesh knew his youth and vitality was not bestowed without a price. At this juncture he didn't know what he would eventually have to pay out. So far, the restoration had been beneficial, particularly since his sex drive had also been stimulated—kicked into overdrive, actually, if Domi's opinion was to be taken seriously.

Sky Dog swung off his horse, commenting, "Apparently nothing and no one up here in the Darks is

what they appear to be." He nodded toward Domi.
"The last time I saw you, you were only a black
scorch mark."

Domi acknowledged the observation with a wry
grin. "I got better."

"So Unktomi Shunkaha told me." Sky Dog used
Kane's Lakota name, which meant "Trickster Wolf."

Hands on his hips, Sky Dog surveyed the plateau
and the great gray peak towering over it. "From below, this looks nothing like the Cerberus redoubt."

"It's not supposed to," Lakesh replied distractedly.

When the Cerberus facility was built in the late
twentieth century, it was designed with maximum im-
penetrability and secrecy in mind. Although they
couldn't be noticed from the plateau, an elaborate system of heat-sensing warning devices, night-vision vid
cameras and motion-trigger alarms surrounded the
mountain peak.

Planted within rocky clefts of the peak and con-
cealed by camouflage netting were the uplinks with
an orbiting Vela-class reconnaissance satellite and a
Comsat. It could be safely assumed that no one or
nothing could approach Cerberus undetected by land
or by air—not that there was much reason to do so.

The few people who lived in the region held the
Bitterroot Range, colloquially known as the Darks, in
superstitious regard. Due to their mysteriously shadowed forests and deep, dangerous ravines, a sinister
body of myths had grown up around the Darks. Every
exile in the redoubt went to great pains to maintain

the enduring myths about evil spirits that lurked in the mountain passes to devour body and soul.

The redoubt was constructed primarily of vanadium alloy, and all design and construction specs had been aimed at making the seat of the Totality Concept's Project Cerberus a self-sufficient community of at least a hundred people, although Lakesh preferred to think of the trilevel, thirty-acre facility as a sanctuary. The redoubt contained a frightfully well-equipped armory and two dozen self-contained apartments, a cafeteria, a decontamination center, an infirmary, a swimming pool and even detention cells on the bottom level.

The Cerberus redoubt had weathered the nukecaust of January 20, 2001 and all the earth changes that came after. Its radiation shielding was still intact, and its nuclear generators still provided an almost eternal source of power. The facility also had a limestone filtration system that continually recycled the complex's water supply.

Blue eyes still fixed on Quavell, Lakesh asked, "How did you get to Sky Dog's village—and from where?"

Matter-of-factly, Quavell answered, "I drove in an overland conveyance you refer to as a Sandcat. I came from Nevada."

"Groom Lake?" Lakesh's tone was a mixture of surprise and incredulity. "You drove from Area 51 all by yourself in your condition?"

Quavell shrugged as if the matter were of little importance. "I must speak with Kane."

Lakesh hesitated a moment before replying, "He is not here at present."

She cocked her head at him, a quizzical gesture he found eerily familiar. "When will he return?"

"I couldn't say, madam."

"Where is he?" A touch of impatience, a hint of the hybrid arrogance he had grown to know and despise, edged her voice.

Lakesh didn't know what to say or even how much to tell her, so he elected to stay silent. To his surprise, Domi stated, "The Moon."

Quavell's mild expression showed no more reaction to Domi's declaration than if she had said, "In the shower."

Sky Dog's response was not so restrained. He swept Domi with a slit-eyed stare, then tilted his head back, scanning the orange-pink tapestry of the dawn sky. "Did I hear you right?" he demanded. "Did you say the *Moon?*"

Lakesh shrugged. "She did. He, Grant and Brigid are on the Moon. Or at least I hope they are, since that was their intended destination."

Sky Dog's normally stoic expression molded itself into one of disbelief. "How did they get there?"

"It's a long story."

Lakesh extended a hand toward Quavell. "Please come inside. It probably wouldn't be out of order to schedule an examination with DeFore, our resident expert in medical matters."

Quavell didn't remove her hands from her belly, but she stepped forward. "I am in perfect health, else I would not have been able to make the cross-country journey. I would like something to eat, however."

Sky Dog grunted disapprovingly. "She didn't care for my people's cuisine."

"As I told you," Quavell said, crossing the tarmac toward the open sec door, "my refusal to partake of your food had little if anything to do with matters of palate. It has to do with differing metabolisms."

Lakesh caught the shaman's eye. "You're welcome, too, of course. Give me a few minutes, and I'll arrange the fifty-cent tour of the installation. You've certainly earned it."

Sky Dog nodded gravely. "Thank you. I'll put the animals out to graze and hobble them. I'll join you in a bit."

Lakesh escorted Quavell and Domi through the sec door and into the redoubt. Quavell eyed the lurid illustration of the three-headed black hound painted on the wall. Fire and blood gushed between yellow fangs, the crimson eyes glared bright and baleful. Underneath it, in ornate Gothic script was written one word: Cerberus.

"The guardian of the gates of Hell," she said quietly. "Appropriate symbolism inasmuch as Project Cerberus was devoted to ripping asunder the gates of the quantum stream."

Lakesh felt his eyebrows crawling toward his hairline at the woman's casual encapsulation of what was once one of the most deep, dark secrets of the twentieth century. He had assumed that only the elite of the ville societies, the barons, their personal staffs and members of the Trust were even aware of the project's code name, much less what it entailed.

Domi took Quavell by the elbow and guided her down the twenty-foot-wide, vanadium-sheathed corridor. "To the cafeteria or the infirmary first?" she asked Lakesh over her shoulder.

Lakesh caught up with the two women and put himself in front of them. He put out a hand and they came to sudden halts. In a soft, grim voice he said, "I didn't want to show bad manners in front of Sky Dog, but now that we're alone I demand some answers."

Quavell looked up into his face, her crystal blue eyes as placid as the surface of a frozen-over lake. "Actually, you want only one. Am I carrying Kane's child?"

"Are you?"

Quavell smiled in way that was almost pitying. "That's one reason I am here, Mohandas Lakesh Singh. We'll find out together, if your resident expert in medical matters is truly an expert."

Lakesh's eyebrows knitted at the bridge of his nose. "You didn't make a long, dangerous journey by yourself to settle an issue of patrimony, Quavell. What are the other reasons?"

The smile fled Quavell's lips. "The old ways die slow and hard." Her voice was scarcely above a rustling whisper. "But they die at last. I am here to make sure the child I carry does not perish with them."

Chapter 1

The Moon, The Great North Chasm

With one hand on the rock wall, Grant moved through the cavern. The wall curved gradually to the left, and he saw the source of the light. A misty blue glow permeated a gallery, seeming to emanate from the walls like fog. He entered cautiously, noting the glow was a kind of phosphorescence.

As he walked deeper into the gallery, he saw droplets of condensation beading his helmet's faceplate. It took his oxygen-starved brain a moment to understand the implications, and he came to a sudden halt.

He gazed around, seeing the gleam of moisture on stone and vaporous steam arising from points all over the Blue Gallery, as he had named it. The steam wafted up from what appeared to be a peat bog at the far end of the gallery, and the sight rooted him in his tracks. Grant recalled what Philboyd had said about volcanism in the Moon, and he wondered if he had stumbled into a little pocket of such activity, like a hot spring.

Grant realized if there was steam, then there was some sort of atmosphere. After a few seconds of trying to ponder the pros and cons, he undid the seals on his helmet and tentatively lifted it off. He sniffed the air experimentally and despite his impaired sense of smell, a stench like a thousand open cesspits assaulted his nostrils. The air was thick, clammy and fetid, but it was breathable. However, the stench was so repulsive he wasn't sure if he didn't prefer suffocating inside his helmet.

Nevertheless, he stood there and inhaled slowly through his mouth, enriching his lungs. By degrees, his fierce headache ebbed, even though a sulfurous taste coated his tongue. He had no idea how there could be an atmosphere of any sort within the Moon, but he wasn't inclined to investigate the mystery. He would leave that up to Brigid. A muted, stealthy sound reached his ears. A breathable atmosphere also conducted sound, and he tried to quiet his respiration.

Dim shapes came into view, moving out through the haze from the right. Dropping to his hands and knees, Grant crawled headlong into the peat bog, algae occluding his vision. He struck out for the far side, moving through the muck as quietly as he could. His boots struck solid footing, and he pushed himself across the pond. The bottom rose beneath him, slanting upward, and he lifted his head onto the bank.

The patrol was behind him, and they were also turned away. Grant crawled up onto the cavern floor and kept to the shadows as much as possible. Stealthily, he slipped through the haze-shrouded gallery. Keeping always within the shadows of the outcroppings, he crept soundlessly over the cavern floor. He breathed more easily when he couldn't see so much as an outline of the patrol.

He stood up—just as the carnobot sprang at him. Grant had no time to bring his Sin Eater to bear. The torrent of flame that washed over its alloyed hide seemed to come from nowhere. The robot rose up on its hind legs, wrapped in a wreath of fire, then its body exploded outward. Seams split, spewing sparks and smoke. Bits of metal pattered down around him.

Grant, too numbed to do more than gape at the wreckage clattering over the rock floor, didn't immediately respond to the male voice saying, "Come on! We don't have much time!"

Turning slightly, he saw a medium-sized man stepping out of a fissure in the gallery wall, brandishing a plasma rifle. His hair was cut short like Neukirk's, only it was black. He wore a one-piece zippered coverall like the people Grant had met at the base. "Who the hell are you?" he demanded.

The man said with an angry impatience, "That doesn't matter right now. We both have limited time to reach the citadel."

Grant stepped closer to him. A small circular body, gleaming like brushed aluminum, was attached to his mastoid bone. From it stretched ten tiny wires, like spider legs made of jointed alloy, each one tipped with a curving claw. Each of the claws appeared deeply embedded in the man's flesh.

His belly turned a cold flip-flop. "You've been tagged by the Furies."

The man nodded grimly. "That's why my time is limited. Once she—"

The man jerked convulsively, dropping the plasma rifle. He clawed at the silver spider on the side of his neck. A halo of pale blue light sprang up and shimmered around it.

The man's body swayed, the sway became a tremble and the tremble turned into a spasm. His eyes remained open, but they didn't see. His mouth gaped wide, but no words came out. He croaked a sound blended of pain, terror and agony.

Grant took a hasty step back, horror filling his mind.

With a faint crackling sound similar to that of burning wood, a gray pallor suddenly swept over the man's body, spreading out from the device attached to his neck. Before Grant's eyes, his flesh and clothes were transmuted to an ash-gray substance. It swiftly darkened, becoming like a layer of anthracite between one eye blink and another.

The man's back arched violently, as if he had received a heavy blow between the shoulders. His arms contorted and drew up like the gnarled branches of a leafless tree as the blanket of dark gray petrifaction crept over his torso and down his legs.

A ghastly dry gargling came from his mouth, then the gray tide covered his lips, smothering his voice. Within another pair of eye blinks, a coal-black calcified statue knelt before the podium. The silver spider seemed to have dissolved, absorbed by the same process that turned flesh to carbon.

A ghostly voice caressed his ears. "He thought to escape my judgment. Like so many others, he was deluded."

Grant recognized the voice as Megaera's. She stepped out of the fissure and around the black statue. Grant's finger touched the trigger stud of his Sin Eater, then he became aware of movement in the fog around him.

Half a dozen tall, lean men as gaunt as cadavers closed in on him, moving with deliberation. From throat to fingertip to heel they were clad in one-piece black garments that fit as tightly as doeskin gloves. Even their heads were hooded in tight black cowls. They bore Oubolus rods in their hands. Beneath the cowls their visages were smooth featureless ovals.

Megaera lovingly caressed the gems on the band encircling her right wrist. "But as for you," she said in a low croon, "on you the great god Enki himself will pass judgment."

Grant had found himself in too many similar situations over the past couple of years to allow his surge of fear to show on his coffee-brown face. Instead, he almost negligently aimed his Sin Eater at Megaera, framing her deeply seamed face in the sights. In a studiedly dismissive tone, he said, "I can arrange it so he will pass judgment on us both."

Megaera's black-clad Furies didn't move. The blank masks concealing their features were molded to fit closely to long-jawed, narrow-chinned, high-cheekboned faces. Although Grant knew the men could not only see through the masks, but also use them as range finders and thermal imagers, they still sent a chill of dread up his spine, as did the Oubolus rods in their gloved hands. Rods of sleek, gleaming black alloy more than two feet long, they were tipped with spherical knobs of a dull, silvery metal, slightly smaller than fowl's eggs. As Grant had reason to know, the knobs were far more deadly than eggs.

Megaera gazed at him with a dispassionate haughtiness. Long, stringy hair streamed out like a gray mop from the woman's head. The hem of her ankle-length, sky-blue robe was frayed and showed wet stains, indicating she had walked through standing water. She was old and withered, but the placid malice of her gaze exuded a frightening force of personality. "You are the interloper here, not I. You have brought down the judgment on yourself."

Grant drew himself up to his full six feet four inches, squaring his massive shoulders and thrusting out his broad chest. His dark skin gleamed with a sheen of perspiration. Gray threaded his short, curly black hair, and a gunfighter's mustache swept fiercely around the corners of his mouth. Smiles didn't come easily to him, so he had to force a contemptuous smirk to his lips to show Megaera and her Furies he was not in the least intimidated by them.

"What's good for the goose," he declared flatly. He wasn't exactly sure of the meaning of the old bromide he had heard Lakesh employ on occasion, but it sounded appropriately challenging. "You were an interloper on Earth, remember? But from what I've seen of it so far, you can keep the Moon. I'd trade you the hottest hellzone around Washington Hole for it."

While he spoke, Grant kept alert for the sounds of the pursuing patrol, his skin crawling beneath his EVA suit in anticipation of being sandwiched between two slices of blood-mad insanity.

Megaera's eyes of icy blue glinted with anger. "This is a holy place."

"And all I want to do is leave it."

"To do that, you must come with us."

"I'll find my own way, thanks."

Megaera gestured with one bony hand. The Furies slowly lowered their silver-knobbed batons. "Yield up your weapon and you will not be harmed. Enki's command is that neither you nor your friends will be harmed by us."

No flicker of emotion touched Grant's face. "My friends are alive?"

"Enki says you may be of use," she said calmly as if he had not spoken. "I myself do not understand how sinners may be of any use, other than as object lessons. But as he wills it, so shall I obey."

Grant snorted in derision. At the far edges of his hearing he heard a faint sound from the tunnel behind him, but he didn't react to it. He took a menacing half step forward, blaster bore trained on Megaera's face.

"You should be more concerned about obeying me. Get the hell out of my way."

Megaera smiled patronizingly but didn't move. "I doubt not that you are brave as mortal men define bravery. But you are still only a man and a sinner at that. But Enki bade me to bring you to him unharmed and without weapons."

Grant's finger lightly brushed the trigger stud of his Sin Eater. "Step aside, lady. I won't tell you again."

Megaera's seamed face locked in a grim mask, her eyes glaring angrily into Grant's. He scowled back at her, his dark gaze glinting from beneath his heavy brows. Her cold, piercing stare intensified. His own unblinking gaze did not falter.

The eye-wrestling match was broken by the swift scraping of running feet behind him. Grant resisted the urge to turn, but he saw Megaera's gaze flit from his face, her eyes widen and fix on a point in the darkness behind him. Her gaunt body stiffened. Her thin lips worked and she screeched, *"Di-ku!"*

Grant knew the meaning of the ancient Sumerian term and he reacted instantaneously, finger depressing the firing stud of the Sin Eater. But Megaera reacted just as swiftly, lunging behind one of her Furies as the cavern walls beat back the thunderous reports.

A 9 mm hollowpoint slammed into the Fury's shoulder, spinning him in an arm-flailing dervish dance amid a misting of blood. His hand clutched convulsively around the firing mechanism of his Oubolus rod. The wand emitted a small click, as if a piece of wire had broken loose inside of it. Light glinted dully from the round object that sprang from the end of the rod. Grant caught a brief glimpse of spindly silver spider legs unfolding as it flashed over his head.

Leading with his Sin Eater, Grant pivoted on his heel, following the trajectory of the Oubolus. He saw helmeted figures in bulky EVA suits swarming into the area, brandishing plasma rifles. To Grant's shock the patrol ignored him and focused their attention and fire on Megaera and her group of Furies.

Sliding sideways, Grant twisted his body out of the path of a stream of blue-white energy that whiplashed from the bell-shaped muzzle of a plasma rifle. The torrent of incandescence engulfed two of the Furies. Instantly, they burst into flame, transformed into capering, fire-wreathed scarecrows.

They didn't cry out, nor did they fall. Instead, they staggered drunkenly, arms windmilling as if they were hoping to fly away from their pain. Then, like the effect of the plasma energy on the carnobot, their bodies exploded from within and viscera splattered the cavern for twenty feet all around. Grant recoiled when he felt something hot and slippery slap the left side of his face.

The patrol of EVA-suited men fanned out, the muzzles of their weapons swinging toward him. Grant fired his Sin Eater again, the burst of rounds tearing into a man's upper chest and helmeted head. The visor shattered and the multiple impacts sent him sprawling.

Moving swiftly, he jammed the toe of his boot beneath the plasma rifle Megaera's victim had dropped and gave it an upward kick. In the lesser gravity, the weapon flew straight up as if jerked by a wire. Grant snatched it out of the air with his left hand, then dived headlong to avoid a crackling stream of lethal energy.

Knowing that expending the time required to figure out how to fire the weapon would only get him killed by one group or the other, Grant rolled across the floor toward the man turned into a black statue by the Oubolus. He struck the figure with the barrel of his Sin Eater, and hairline cracks immediately appeared in the black body. From the cracks spewed tendrils of sepia-hued smoke. At the same time, an astringent stench filled Grant's nostrils, an odor of hot sulfur mixed with ammonia.

The cracks in the statue's body expanded into deep splits, and more of the oily vapor plumed out. The smoke spread quickly and the man seemed to unravel at the edges, twists of mist rising like a multitude of loose black threads. Clothing, flesh, bones and hair dissolved into a foul-smelling fog.

As thick, blinding smoke boiled out, Grant heard Megaera's raucous voice screeching incomprehensible words. He shifted sideways as foul-smelling ash showered down and black clouds of thick smoke mushroomed up. Having seen the phenomenon before, Grant knew what to expect. He kept his mouth tightly closed to avoid inhaling the vapor and succumbing to a coughing fit. He squeezed his eyes shut.

He could see nothing through the obsidian fog anyway, but he doubted the EVA-suited patrol could, either. He hoped the thermal-imaging function of the Furies' visors was impaired by his own environmental suit, but it really didn't matter. As far as Grant was concerned, everybody in the cavern was a legitimate target.

After a second of fumbling, he found the trigger switch of the plasma rifle and squeezed it, firing from a prone position. He sprayed the wave of blue-white light as if it were water from a hose, swinging the muzzle in a wide arc. Even through his closed eyelids, he could see impressions of the bright flares of energy.

He heard brief, gargling cries. Grant kept his finger on the trigger, sending raw power bluing out in a crackling torrent. Although he had never fired one before, he knew energy weapons weren't subject to the effects of wind or gravity, but they didn't pack much of a kinetic punch, either. However, in the rarefied atmosphere of the Moon's Great Chasm, the plasma rifle was ideal. The beam cut through anything in its path.

Opening his eyes to a slit, he saw the plasma charge slice through a Fury, carving him open diagonally from right shoulder to his left hip. The two halves of the body separated in a bright shower of blood. His eardrums registered two mushy explosions from behind him, and he rolled in that direction. The rifle in his hands emitted a sputter, and the beam of plasma energy disappeared.

Carefully, he opened his eyes fully. Flat planes of

smoke hung in the air like streamers of filthy lace. The foul tang of sulfur was sharp on his tongue. He turned his head and spit as he pushed himself to a crouch and listened. He heard nothing but moist, bubbling sounds as of raw meat on a hot griddle. The stink of blistered, seared flesh and scorched hair overpowered the fetid miasma rising from the peat bog. The fact he could smell it at all was a testimony of how strong the effluvium really was. His nose had been broken three times in the past, and always poorly reset. Unless an odor was extraordinarily pleasant or virulently repulsive, he was incapable of detecting subtle scents unless they were right under his nostrils. A running joke during his Mag days had been that Grant could eat a hearty dinner with a dead skunk lying on the table next to his plate.

Fanning the foul air away from his face, he rose and saw the pulsing husks that had been men a moment before. He choked down the bile rising in his throat as he did a quick body count. There were five, possibly six burst-open corpses on the cavern floor. He couldn't be sure if one litter of smeared organs was really a man or just a heap of viscera that had exploded outward from the others. He didn't understand why the patrol had seemingly forgotten about him upon seeing Megaera and her Furies. He had been told both groups served Enki, but he wasn't inclined to spend much time trying to reason out the whys and wherefores behind the hostilities. Survivors of either faction could return to the cavern at any second.

Grant did not see Megaera's body among the dead,
but that meant nothing. Even if she had been caught
in the spray of plasma, he doubted he would be able
to identify her. He examined the plasma rifle and
found a small LCD window near the trigger plate.
Three zeroes glowed redly against a black background. The weapon was drained of energy, and he
tossed it aside.

He glanced briefly at the layer of ash that was all
that was left of the man who had wielded the weapon
and wondered what his name had been. Then he wondered about the citadel the man had mentioned, its
location and how far it was. He started to wonder if
he would ever see Earth and Shizuka again, then decided it was best not to think about it.

Despite the threat of more lurking carnobots, Grant
entered the fissure from which Megaera and the Furies
had emerged. It was a true passageway about three
yards wide, with the lunar stone of the walls and floor
ground down and beautifully polished. He kept his
body pressed against the left-hand wall. He wasn't
certain if the little silver spiders fired by the Oubolus
rods could penetrate his EVA suit's ten layers of alu-
minized Mylar insulation interlaced with six layers of
Dacron and tough outer facings of Kevlar. And even
if the devices could do so, they would then encounter
his shadow suit.

Composed of a weave of spider silk, Monocrys and
Spectra fabrics, the black one-piece garments were essentially a single crystal metallic microfiber with a

very dense molecular structure. The outer Monocrys sheathing went opaque when exposed to radiation, and the Kevlar and Spectra layers provided protection against blunt trauma.

They were the same kind of garments worn by the Furies, and Grant guessed they probably were resistant to the Oubolus, intentionally designed to protect a Fury from a carelessly fired silver spider.

The tunnel seemed to be dimly illuminated with the same kind of waxy blue light as the cavern. The source was more than likely the lumen panels, self-perpetuating light sources that appeared to need no batteries or recharging. The illumination wasn't bright enough to read by, but the light was strong enough so he could see when the tunnel curved and bent.

Grant hadn't walked more than a hundred feet when he heard a faint repetitive murmur ahead of him. He paused, squinted and just barely made out a dark shape huddled on the tunnel floor a few yards beyond him. Sin Eater stretched out at the end of his right arm, he instinctively walked heel-to-toe as his Magistrate training had instilled in him.

As he drew closer to the shape, he recognized the murmur as a whimpering chant. Megaera sat on the tunnel floor, rocking back and forth, keening and whispering.

Grant kept his pistol trained on her head as he sidled up beside her. She paid no attention to his approach, despite the fact the heavy treads of his boots scraped against the stone floor. The stink of burned hair and seared flesh tickled his nostrils, and he realized the woman had only one arm.

Her right arm was amputated at the bicep. The plasma rifle had vaporized it and the wrist-band controls for the Oubolus. The stump was cauterized, so there would be no infection or bleeding.

Still chanting, Megaera lifted her face and Grant nearly gagged at the sight. Not only was she missing an arm, but both her eyes, as well. They had been cooked in their sockets like eggs left too long on a high boil. Gelatinous slime oozed between her eyelids. The woman's face was a blistered, peeled travesty.

Grant gazed down at her, astonished and little horrified that she was even alive, much less conscious. He didn't know if he was responsible for her injuries, and at the moment the matter wasn't particularly relevant.

He needed a guide to the citadel, a source of information, and even crippled and blind, Megaera was the only candidate available. The woman seemed completely unaware of his presence, even after he deliberately clinked the barrel of his Sin Eater against the wall. She continued rocking and chanting in the language Grant had been told was a dialect derived from Sumerian.

Pitching his voice low, he muttered bleakly, *"Diku."*

It was an ancient Sumerian term that meant "to judge" or "judgment determiner" and was the equivalent of Megaera's war cry.

The priestess affected not to have heard him. The unintelligible words continued to issue from her cracked and leaking lips. Grant repressed a profanity-salted sigh.

The mystery of Megaera and her shadow-suited Furies was what brought him, Kane and Brigid to the Moon from the Cerberus redoubt in Montana. They had first encountered the Furies a few months before, while following up on sensor link activity in the gateway unit in Redoubt Echo. That in itself wasn't unusual. Over the past year and a half, the sensor link had registered an unprecedented volume of mat-trans traffic. Most of it was due to the concerted search for the renegade Magistrates from Cobaltville, but there had also been the appearance of anomalous activities, signatures of jump lines that could not be traced back to their origin points.

However, the signal from the gateway in Redoubt Echo wasn't anomalous. The unit was an indexed part of the Cerberus network, and Lakesh believed the activity was connected to the Totality Concept's Operation Chronos—primarily because Chronos had been headquartered in a subterranean facility in Chicago, at least for a time.

They couldn't open a jump line to the gateway in Redoubt Echo, so Kane, Brigid, Domi, Grant and DeFore had embarked on a long overland journey to Chicago. There, they encountered the bizarre group of Furies led by Megaera, who meted out their own terrible form of justice with the Oubolus rods.

In ancient Greek mythology, Megaera was a Fury, one of three sisters charged by the gods to pursue sinners on Earth. They were inexorable and relentless in their dispensation of justice. A bit of old verse about them claimed that "Not even the sun will transgress his orbit lest the Furies, the ministers of justice, overtake him."

The Oubolus was the collective name for the payment given by souls on their way to the underworld, a form of coin given to Charon, the ferryman for passage across the River Acheron. According to myth, if payment was not made, a soul had to wander the riverbank throughout eternity.

Megaera's version of the Oubolus was a little device fired from the hollow baton. It attached itself to a target, a sinner, and delivered an incapacitating jolt of voltage. Once judgment was levied against the sinner, the wristband control mechanism initiated a horrifying process by which the skeletal structure and internal organs were dissolved, leaving only an empty, carbonized husk in the shape of the sinner.

Megaera and a contingent of Furies had stalked a group of Farers in Chicago, bringing to terrifying life old folk tales about soul-stealing demons called night gaunts. They never spoke or laughed and never smiled, because they had no faces at all to smile with.

Despite the circumstances, Grant couldn't help but note the irony in the fact that Megaera no longer had much of a face to smile with, either.

Bending, he took her by the left arm and lifted her

to her feet. She didn't resist, but her prayers trailed off long enough for him to interject in a flat tone, "You're hurt but I can help you—if you help me. I'll take you to a place where you can get medical attention, but you'll have to be my guide. I'll be your eyes."

In a thin, aspirated whisper Megaera said, "I am of no use to the great god now. I have failed him too many times, and so I will meet my judgment here. Already I hear the Thunder of Enki. Leave me to die."

Grant heard a steady whine, so high in pitch it was nearly beyond his range of hearing. He increased the pressure of his grasp on the woman's arm but relaxed it almost immediately. The old priestess was in agony, and any pain he could inflict would be tantamount to a gnat bite.

"You don't die till I tell you to die," he growled. "As far as your life and death are concerned, *I'm* your great god now. You understand me?"

Megaera didn't respond, didn't react. Grant pulled her forward. "Take me to the citadel."

Slowly, Megaera began shuffling down the corridor, groping her way with her left hand. Shuddering, Grant followed her.

Chapter 2

Brigid Baptiste's helmet light flashed its bright beam along the gloomy passage. It disclosed a maze of squared chambers and galleries that long, long ago had been hewn out of the citadel's base. The first chamber they looked into held the wreckage of an ancient chemical laboratory. There had been racks of instruments and receptacles, but they were smashed and scattered.

Kane and Brigid moved on from one great chamber to another. They saw a battery of what seemed to have once been a series of generators. Another chamber held the ruins of a pump apparatus that she guessed had been used for oxygenation. Other, smaller chambers seemed to have been living quarters.

"This is the place of the Annunaki," Brigid breathed in a hushed voice.

They moved on along the passageway and saw the vague outlines of towering metal shapes rising out of the dimness ahead. They were big mechanisms of such an unfamiliar design their purpose was unfathomable. One was a complex arrangement of cogged wheels of silver metal, geared to a sliding hollow cylinder that suggested the barrel of an artillery piece. Another was a massive upright metal bulb that suggested nothing. Upon the base of each machine was a lengthy inscription in Sumerian.

"If I could only read those," Brigid said in angry frustration.

Kane knew she was feeling the strain of apprehension. Somewhere ahead of them waited the last of the Serpent Kings, and behind them was Grant's unknown fate.

Suddenly, a high-pitched whine reverberated through his helmet. He came to a sudden halt, lifting his Sin Eater. "Do you hear that?" he demanded.

Brigid stopped and looked around. "I hear something," she admitted at length. "Like the vibrations of machinery we heard before."

"How can we hear it through our helmets?"

"Maybe we're passing through a sonic field of some sort."

Standing motionless and listening intently, he cast his eyes quickly around. He could see nothing but the mysterious, silent machines towering about him in the red-lit murk. They crept forward, both people moving soundlessly. Kane took point, walking heel to toe as he always did in a potential killzone.

"There's a legend associated with Enki," Brigid said quietly, almost reluctantly. "Something about his command of the thunder. It was so powerful, it crushed his enemies."

Kane said dismissively, "Whatever we're hearing, it isn't thunder, Baptiste."

"Not yet, anyway," she retorted.

The whine seemed to rise in pitch with every step they took, straining to hit an ultrahigh frequency and put it out of the range of audibility. He almost wished it would happen. A cry of pain from Brigid galvanized him, caused him to skip around, heart pounding.

She clutched futilely at the sides of her helmet. Through clenched teeth, she said, "Whatever the sound is, it's feeding through our helmet comms, turning them into receivers."

Kane said, "Maybe we can disconnect them."

A white-hot wire seemed to lance through his head, passing into one ear and out the other. He was only dimly aware of crying out. Over the humming sleet storm of agony in his head, he heard Brigid blurt, "The Thunder of Enki!"

Sound could grow too deep, too high or simply too loud for the human ear to record. But the Thunder of Enki had an unbearable depth, an intolerable volume, yet the ear and the mind were keenly responsive to its resonance and didn't grow numb or dulled.

Its terrible sweetness was beyond human endurance. Kane gasped and struggled. He was aware that Brigid held her hands over the sides of her helmet, but he didn't realize he was writhing on the floor, too consumed with agony even to scream.

Thrashing wildly in a vain attempt to get up, Kane shouted a curse as the agony building within the walls of his skull increased. His helmet reverberated with his hoarse cry. He glimpsed Brigid falling onto her side, knees drawing up in a fetal position. Her own primal shriek of pain fed through his UTEL receiver and filled his ears with a deafening cacophony of torment.

Kane set his teeth on a scream and tried to force himself to act, to think. He felt bathed in continuous, rippling rhythms of fiery pain, but he had felt pain before. A dark, cobwebby corner of his mind still harbored lucid thoughts, and it told him he had to get his and Brigid's helmets off before they both died or went completely mad. Exposing themselves to a hard, airless vacuum could be no worse than dying in shrieking, nerve-shredded agony. Summoning all of his Magistrate-bred resolution, he fought his way to his knees—and fell down again.

Kane's gloved fingers, feeling somehow removed from the rest of his body, frantically explored and fumbled with the seals and latch of his helmet. He clawed desperately at the collar of his EVA suit, red rage mounting and fighting against the pain. He swore he would pay back whoever was responsible for the torture, but to exact revenge he had to survive. Survival first, then revenge.

His lips formed the words as he found a catch lock at the base of the helmet. "Survival first, then revenge." He repeated the four words like a mantra.

The first spring lock snapped open under the pressure of his thumb, and his hands found another one. It popped loose and faintly he heard the hissing puff of air escaping from his helmet. He started to hold his breath, then refused to follow the impulse. Even if his lungs collapsed, it would be a death of his own choosing, not one decided by a remote and invisible tormentor.

Twisting the helmet counter clockwise, he heard the sucking pop of gaskets releasing. He pulled it up and off of his head, tossing it aside. Survival first, then revenge—

As though a switch had been thrown, the sleet storm of agony sweeping through every molecule of Kane's body suddenly stopped. It didn't abate gradually or ebb by degrees; it simply stopped. He gasped in relief, then almost gasped in surprise when he realized he was able to breathe. The air was thin and bitingly cold on his exposed cheeks, but he filled his lungs with it nevertheless.

Crawling on all fours, he scrambled over to Brigid, his nerve endings still twitching and flinching with the fresh memory of the torture inflicted on them. Brigid continued to thrash about, but the wild flailing of her limbs had become fitful and intermittent. Throwing himself over her body to keep her immobilized, he struggled to remove her helmet. Her hands struck out blindly at him, fingers curling and crooking in spasms.

Swiftly, he opened all the seals on her helmet, put his hands around it and gave it a fierce sideways twist and upward yank at the same time. Beneath the wild tangle of her red-gold mane, Brigid's eyes were tightly closed, and her chest rose and fell in a convulsive, uneven rate of respiration.

Cradling her in his arms, refusing to acknowledge the dread rising in him, Kane brushed back the hair from her face and slapped her sharply on both cheeks with his left hand. Brigid's head lolled back and forth, and he struck her again—hard. Her emerald eyes opened, glassy first with shock, then glinting hard with fear.

"You're all right," he told her with a confidence he didn't feel. "We're both all right."

She inhaled sharply through her nostrils, grimaced, then tried to sit up. Kane helped her, saying, "Yeah, there's a breathable atmosphere in here."

Putting hands to the sides of her head, she said, "That's debatable."

Kane silently agreed with her. The air carried with it a scent of burned motor oil that made the process of respiration unpleasant and labored. For a long moment they sat quietly, trying to get their shocked nervous systems back to normal. Little shudderings in their extremities was evidence that their bodies still suffered from the aftereffects.

Brigid intoned quietly, "We must be in a zone of infrasonics, attuned to cover the width of the passageway. It makes a perfect resonant cavity and our helmets' comms intersected with and amplified the band frequencies. If you hadn't gotten the helmets off..." Her words trailed away and a frown touched her lips.

Kane waited, then angled an eyebrow. "You're welcome, Baptiste."

She affected not to have heard the sarcasm. "We're

still in the zone, so I suggest we move along as quickly as possible.''

''Why? Without the helmets broadcasting the frequency—''

''I counted a seven-cycle note,'' she interrupted, slowly climbing to her feet. She tottered and would have fallen if Kane had not reached up a hand to steady her. Taking a breath, she continued, ''Seven cycles over a hundred decibels starts to break down organic cellular structures within a few minutes.''

Kane carefully rose, his temples throbbing, and he experienced a brief wave of vertigo. He stood an inch over six feet, a lean timber wolf of a man who carried most of his weight in his arms and shoulders. His longish dark hair showed sun-touched highlights. His steely blue-gray eyes were sunk above high cheekbones. A three-inch-long hairline scar stretched like a white thread against the pale bronze on the left side of his face.

''How do we know when we've reached maximum exposure?'' he asked. ''What will be the symptoms?''

Brigid tried to shrug, but it wasn't easy inside the EVA suit. Its bulky contours did little to conceal her tall, willowy, athletic figure. A curly mane of red-gold hair spilled over her shoulders and draped her upper back, framing a smoothly sculpted face dusted lightly with freckles across her nose and cheeks. The color of polished emeralds glittered in her big, feline-slanted eyes.

''Fairly straightforward,'' she answered brusquely.

"We'll just feel dizzy, fall over and die unless we have something to detect a seven-megahertz tone."

"I forgot to pack one this trip," Kane retorted.

Brigid gave him a wan smile and bent to retrieve her helmet. She almost stumbled in the attempt, but quickly regained her balance and picked it up. Holding it between her hands, she presented the interior to Kane. From within it issued an exceptionally high-pitched whistling whine, like a very distant pressure cooker straining to hit a note on the edges of audibility.

"The Thunder of Enki," he commented darkly. "So we just carry our headgear along with us and when the sound stops—"

"Or changes," she interjected.

"—we'll know we're out of the zone."

Brigid nodded. "Something like that. And by the way…thanks."

Kane nodded, stooped and lifted his own helmet. For an instant his vision blurred, and he tried to clear it by shaking his head. He discovered that was a mistake and didn't try it again a second time. "How do you know the infrasonic zone doesn't extend halfway around the Moon?"

"It's a matter of engineering," she told him, turning and walking along the corridor with her characteristic long-legged mannish stride. "Remember the study I made of the infrasound wand we picked up in Dulce a couple of years ago? They're not very precise weapons."

Kane tried to keep up with her, but found his lungs aching due either to the thin air or the sonic waves or a combination. "You could've fooled me," he commented sourly. "I was nearly killed by the damn things—more than once." He thought back to the incident in the facility beneath the New Mexico and to the harplike instrument played by Aifa in Ireland and a similar device Sindri claimed had been found on Mars, a relic of the Tuatha de Danaan. They all seemed related, devices operating on the same principle of sound manipulation. The infrasound wands wielded by the hybrids converted electricity to ultra-high sound frequencies powered by a miniature maser.

He recalled how Sindri had described the Danaan harp as producing energy forms with balanced gaps between the upper and lower energy frequencies. He explained if the radiation within particular frequencies fell on an energized atom—like living matter—it stimulated it in the same way a gong vibrated when its note was struck on a piano. Harmony and disharmony, healing and death.

Sindri went on to describe scientific precedents cloaked by myth and legend such as the Ark of the Covenant bringing down the walls of Jericho when the Israelites gave a great shout. He claimed the walls were bombarded and weakened by amplified sound waves of the right frequency transmitted from the Ark. Sindri also cited Merlin, who was reputed to be of half-Danaan blood and had "danced" the megaliths of Stonehenge into place by his music.

But then, Sindri was an egocentric blowhard, given to melodrama.

Brigid's impatient words broke his reverie. "Yes, but you were very close to the effect radii of the wands and the Danaan harp, remember? The problem with infrasonics is that you can't use them with any kind of precision on a small scale. That's what makes the wands and the harp ineffective for long range. Sound waves have to be of a certain size, and therefore whatever generates them has to be correspondingly big.

"For example, a seven-megahertz wave measures out to about 150 feet long and what's generating it is probably little more than a big whistle. I presume the generator is shielded against subsonic blow back, but if the thing could produce waves much bigger, it would trigger all sorts of seismic disturbances."

"So the fact that the ceiling of the citadel isn't caving in or the floor collapsing means that the infrasound zone has definite boundaries?"

"Exactly. It's more like a security system than a weapon. We probably tripped something when we entered."

"Do you think it'd affect any carnobots in the vicinity?"

Brigid nodded. "More than likely. Eduardo told us they derive power through a microbial fuel cell stomach, which is at least partially organic."

Kane recalled the description of how the killer machines operated. The stomach broke down food using

Escherichia coli bacteria and converted the chemical energy from the digestive process into electricity. The microbes from the bacteria decomposed the carbohydrates supplied by the food, which released electrons. The electrons in turn supplied a charge to the battery through a reduction and oxidation reaction that Eduardo referred to as the redox process. The robots possessed sensor chips that were programmed to detect perspiration and even pheromones.

As if sensing his thoughts, Brigid said, "I would imagine the sonic field would interfere with the carnobots' electronics, as well as their fuel cells. All their microprocessors would react as if exposed to an electromagnetic pulse, so we don't have to worry about them on top of everything else."

Kane forced a lopsided grin to his face. "I'll say this, Baptiste—no matter what else happens to me on these field trips of ours, whether I get shot, stabbed or blown up, I always have my science lesson to make all the suffering worthwhile."

"Glad I serve some function."

A wave of nausea turned his grin into a grimace. "I think I'm feeling it."

Brigid's eyes narrowed and she clenched her teeth. "Me, too. I think we should put our tried-and-true fallback strategy into use."

"Run for it?"

She nodded. "Run for it."

They broke into jogs but before they covered more than a score of feet, both people were gasping and reeling drunkenly. They passed beneath an archway above which was a plate-sized spiral glyph, the same kind of cup-and-circle design they had seen before both on Earth and on Mars.

Kane and Brigid became aware of a low hum ahead of them, almost like the bass register of a piano that continued to vibrate long after a key had been struck. From their helmets came a warbling, piping screech. Kane felt the pressure on his chest increase, as if heavy flat stones were being piled onto his sternum, one by one.

Sounding half-strangled, Brigid asked, "Does your chest hurt?"

"Yeah," he managed to husk out without coughing.

"I think we're getting closer to the generator."

At the end of the passageway they saw a narrow doorway. Carved into the rock above it was an inscription in the ancient Sumerian characters. Amoeba-like floaters swam across Kane's eyes, and his left shoulder banged painfully against the edge of the door as he and Brigid pushed through it at the same time and jammed themselves up for a couple of seconds. Under other circumstances, he might have laughed.

Beyond the door was a great stone chamber, the corners and ceiling swathed in deep shadows. Despite the dim light, they saw objects looming in the murk. Carefully fashioned out of complicated angles and curves of metal, they were instruments of mysterious purpose.

The biggest of them was a crystal wheel the size of

a dining table mounted horizontally atop a sphere of dull gray alloy. The globe looked to be at least ten feet in diameter, resting within a tripod type of contrivance. The wheel turned slowly, its rim glittering with crystalline points cut in precise polyhedrons. From it emitted the droning hum.

A notched cylinder seven feet tall extended from the top of the sphere. It resembled a ridiculously large flute. As they drew closer, their ears picked up a painfully high whistling note underscoring the hum. The sound seemed to tighten around his skull, squeezing and compressing it as if his head were trapped in a steel vise. Kane eyed the cylinder closely, forcing his vision back into focus.

"That's the generator and the whistle," Brigid panted as they circled it. "If we can get around it and out of range of the wave's circumference before we pass out—"

Kane came to a halt and reached into a pouch of his web belt. "I'd rather just plug up the source of the racket."

He pulled out a flat disk the size and shape of a saucer. A red button protruded from the top, and suction-cupped tabs extended from below. It was one of the demolition charges Grant had found a few hours earlier at an old excavation site. An expression of alarm crossed Brigid's face but before she could say anything, Kane slapped the disk onto the support sphere, the suction cups adhering tightly to the metal surface.

Although he had no idea of the length of the timer, he depressed the button until it clicked and held. Then he turned and ran, grabbing Brigid by the arms and hustling her ahead of him.

A flare of yellow light burst from behind them as a concussion pummeled Kane's back and the crumping explosion slammed against their eardrums. Kane staggered and fell, Brigid folding beneath him. Faintly he heard pieces of the machine clattering against rock.

They lay on the floor motionless for a long moment, their ears ringing. Kane's eyes slowly cleared of dancing yellow flecks. Just as slowly he realized that he and Brigid might be going to live for a while yet, and he pushed himself to a sitting position. After that, he didn't move for a short tick of time, waiting for his head to return to its normal size. He wasn't quite ready to stand, but his chest and stomach felt better.

Carefully turning his head, he saw the shattered shell of the metal sphere smoldering in the swiftly dying flame of the explosion. He stared at it, at the crystal shards glistening on the floor for yards all around. He didn't move until he was aware of Brigid saying something behind him. He turned toward her and asked, "What?"

Her face was screwed up in pain. "I said 'what kind of tactic was that?'"

Kane smiled coldly. "The Thunder of Kane." He didn't verbalize his true thoughts: We've survived—now it's time for revenge.

Brigid put a fingertip in her right ear and then

screwed it around. "If I lose my perfect pitch because of your thunder, you'll be responsible."

Kane grinned and climbed to his feet, extending a hand to help her rise. "Well," he said after a thoughtful moment, "if Enki didn't know we were here before, taking out his infrasound projector ought to announce us formally."

A hollow ghostly voice floated to them from out of the shadows. "That's a *very* certain thing, outlanders."

Chapter 3

Grant recalled his words when Lakesh first proposed the mission, and he repeated them now, in a growling mutter, "Moon, my ass."

The walls of the tunnel threw back mocking echoes of his voice. "My ass, my ass..."

Megaera murmured prayers beneath her breath without pause, completely oblivious to the profane echoes or the bore of the Sin Eater pressed against the small of her back. Stripped down to a skeletal frame, the Sin Eater was barely fourteen inches long. Holstered on his right forearm, it was attached with actuators that flipped it into his waiting hand when his wrist tendons flexed in the proscribed manner. The clip held twenty rounds of 9 mm ammo. There was no trigger guard, no wasted inch of design. It was one of the most murderously efficient blasters ever made.

With any other hand weapon, Grant wouldn't have gotten so close to the prisoner. Megaera had already proved she was faster and stronger than she looked, but in her condition it was a wonder she could still walk, much less grope through the darkened tunnel. If she showed an inclination toward violence, a slight tap of his forefinger on the Sin Eater's firing stud would send three bullets into her spine.

As they strode along, a disjointed sensation of unreality clawed at Grant's pragmatic mind. With every step he took, the droning hum became louder and the more afraid he became. He was angry—angry at himself, at Kane and Brigid for agreeing to the mission, and at the set of circumstances that began a few days ago and now had him stumbling through a tunnel beneath the surface of the Moon.

He tried to remind himself the circumstances had actually begun inestimable aeons ago, yet not only did that knowledge fail to calm his mounting fear, but it was also almost impossible for his mind to grasp. The concept slipped through the fingers of his mind like wisps of smoke, despite all of the tangible evidence he had seen over the past couple of years. To keep his mind from racing over the horizon into the abyss of terror, he laboriously reviewed everything he had learned, either firsthand or from others, about the Annunaki, the so-called Serpent Kings.

A century before the nukecaust of January 20, 2001, enlightened nineteenth-century minds found it fashionable to speculate that Earth's nearest alien neighbors would be found right next door, on the planet Mars.

A hundred years later it was discovered that alien neighbors were a lot closer than Victorian-era scientific theorists ever dreamed. They had lived on Earth for a very, very, *very* long time. So long a time, in fact, their descendants felt they had the prior claim.

Humankind's interaction with a nonhuman species had begun literally at the dawn of Earth's history. That relationship and communication had continued unbroken for thousands of years, cloaked by ritual, religion and mystical traditions. The interaction first began in what was later known as Mesopotamia when the Annunaki arrived.

Lakesh had told him, Brigid and Kane about the Annunaki, the Serpent Kings, the dragon lords of legend. At the time it had seemed like so much folklore, sheer speculation, despite the many and culturally diverse ancient histories that mentioned a reptilian race that had interacted with humanity since literally the dawn of time.

According to Lakesh, biblical verses dealing with the fashioning of the first humans were condensed renderings of much more detailed Sumerian texts, found inscribed on clay tablets on which the creation of humanity was credited to the Annunaki, which translated roughly as "Those Who from Heaven to Earth Came."

The Annunaki arrived on Earth nearly a half a million years ago from the planet Nibiru, a world in the solar system but one that orbited a fair distance away from the Sun, returning to the vicinity of Earth only once every thirty-six hundred years.

Tall and cold of eye and heart, the Annunaki were a highly developed reptilian race with a natural gift for organization. They viewed Earth as a vast treasure trove of natural resources, upon which their technology depended. As labor was their scarcest commodity, the Annunaki's chief scientist, Enki, set about redesigning the Earth's primitive inhabitants into models of maximized potential.

The Annunaki remolded the indigenous protohumans, grading them at rough intellectual levels and classifying them by physique, agility and dexterity. After much trial and error, a perfect model was attained, which served as the template for succeeding generations. But during the creation process myriad monstrosities were also birthed, which gave rise to the legends of the cyclops, the centaur, the giant.

The early generations of human slave labor were only a step above the existing hominoid species, but they were encouraged to breed so each successive descendant would be superior to its predecessors. The human brain improved and technical skills grew, along with cogent thoughts and the ability to deal with abstract concepts.

After thousands of years, the human slave race rebelled against the Annunaki, who had failed to notice the expansion of cognition on the part of their thralls. Although essentially a peaceful people, Enki's half brother, Enlil, arranged for a catastrophe to destroy their labor force, as Earth had become an unprofitable enterprise. The catastrophe was recorded in ancient texts, and even cultural memory, as the Flood.

As the waters slowly receded, the handful of human

survivors bred and multiplied. Over the ensuing centuries, nations and empires rose and fell. Then the Tuatha de Danaan arrived. Unlike the Annunaki, the human-appearing Tuatha de Danaan took humankind under their protection. They were reported to be an aristocratic race of scientists, warriors and poets, preferring their privacy and able to make themselves invisible, but still keeping touch with the human race.

Music was their principal technology; they used sound waves to lift and move massive objects and often employed it as a weapon. The essence of Danaan science stemmed from music—the controlled manipulation of sound waves—and this became recorded in legend as the "music of the spheres."

Eventually, a task force of Annunaki returned to reclaim their world and their slaves. By this time, they were few in number and used guile instead of force to achieve their objectives. They worked to turn humans against the Danaan, by filling them with jealousy and fear. Humankind became embroiled in the conflict between the two races, a conflagration that extended even to the outer planets of the solar system, and became immortalized and disguised in human legends as a war in heaven.

Finally, when it appeared that Earth was threatened with devastation, the war abated under terms. A pact was struck whereby the two races intermingled to create a new one, which was to serve as a bridge between the two. From this pact sprang the entities later known as the Grays or the Archons.

The feeble illumination shed from the panels inset into the rock walls grew dimmer and dimmer. Megaera was unaffected, but Grant paused long enough to remove a pair of dark-lensed glasses from a pouch on his belt and put them on. The electrochemical polymer of the lenses took advantage of all available light, providing him with a limited form of night vision. He carried a Nighthawk microlight but he was loath to use it, fearing the glow it produced would pinpoint his position to anyone coming down the dark passageway ahead.

The corridor Grant and Megaera navigated reminded him of passageways in an ancient tomb. There seemed to be nothing but shadows behind them, and ahead of them only murk. The almost impenetrable darkness was a complete counterpoint to the literally blinding light he had been subjected to when he, Brigid and Kane were forced to march across the Mare Frigoris, the Sea of Ice. The plain of vitrified pumice reflected sunlight at such an unremittingly high intensity, he had lost his sight for a little while. Now he would do anything to be back there. The irony made him smile, but only for a second.

The tunnel suddenly opened into a vast space, and he received the impression of a dome-roofed cavern, but it was in almost absolute darkness. Only a faint ray of light from above seeped into the place, scarcely affecting the treated lenses of his night-vision glasses so he could see more than a few feet. He pulled Megaera to a halt and took a slow, silent survey of their surroundings.

They stood on an elevated table of rock, not more than ten feet wide. He saw gloomy chasms and labyrinthine connecting caverns all around. Loose pebbles and gravel trembled slightly, even shimmied on the ground. He stared at them in disbelief for a long moment, trying to understand what caused the movement. He felt no vibrations underfoot that could be ascribed to tremors, and primitive fear clouded his mind.

Carefully, Grant stepped to the edge of the rock table and looked down into the impenetrable blackness. He kicked a pebble over the rim and waited for a sound indicating it had hit bottom. It never came, and he backed away, repressing a shudder. The fear he had been battling for the past few minutes now threatened to explode into a full-fledged panic attack, something he had never experienced before in a lifetime fraught with narrow escapes.

Between clenched teeth, he demanded, "Now what? Where the hell are we?"

Megaera looked around with her blind eyes, turning her head very slowly, putting out her hand as though she were feeling her way along an invisible wall, reaching out for a vanished doorway.

"I'm waiting," he demanded in a snarl. "Where do we go from here?"

The stump of Megaera's right arm lifted upward, a grotesque travesty of a gesture. In her addled mental state she had forgotten about the amputation. "That way."

Squinting, Grant saw a flight of stairs apparently chipped out of the pumice stone leading upward to a square aperture from which the dim light spilled. "What's up there?"

In a creaky, strained whisper, Megaera answered, "You tell me. You're the one with the eyes."

Grant growled a curse beneath his breath. "You finally decide you have a sense of humor and it has to be at a time like this."

The old priestess lapsed back into silence again. He started toward the foot of the steps. He halted and looked over his shoulder. He couldn't make out Megaera's maimed face in the gloom, and for that he was grateful. "There doesn't happen to be a pack of carnobots waiting up there, by any chance?"

"No." Her reply was ghostly. "They fear the Thunder of Enki, as all mortals do." She paused and added in a tone touched with malicious amusement, "As do you."

Grant didn't reply. He stepped over a fissure and bounded over another to the foot of the stairs, aided by the lower gravity. Two long upward steps brought him into a tiny chamber, almost a vestibule carved out of solid rock. The loose gravel underfoot trembled, as it did in the cavern below. A transparent port made of thick armaglass occupied almost one wall. He realized it was sunk deep into the regolith, the inner wall of a crater. He looked through it, at the stark rock formations and the bone-white pumice plain.

Cruel, jagged escarpments and buttresses looked like the calcified skeleton of a huge animal in the unrelenting brilliance of sunlight unsoftened by an atmosphere. Reflecting back the glittering light of the tapestry of stars, the broken surface of the Moon stood out in sharp relief.

Grant remembered that Philboyd referred to the tumbled, rocky wilderness of the great southwest crater region as the "Wild Lands." Somewhere on the other side of the crater lay the Great Chasm, a vast slash carved through the barren lunar plain. Wide and cut in clean like a surgical incision, it measured eight hundred miles long and nearly fifty miles wide. Looking above the rim of the crater, he sought to catch a glimpse of Earth, but saw only the vast gulfs of space stretching onward and onward, until the mind flinched from trying to measure the distance.

He lowered his gaze to the interior of the crater—and froze into immobility. There were times when a man was faced with a sight so awe-inspiring, so far from his field of experience, that he had no touchstone by which he could compare and understand it. Grant's centers of reason became numbed and his eyes saw, but did not communicate the vision to the brain, an autonomic fail-safe against madness.

He gazed down at a broad causeway of black stone, much eroded and cracked by the weight of aeons, stretching across the crater floor. Black, square structures loomed on both sides of the channel. Great blocks of basalt and granite had fallen from the buildings, and broken statues lay in the lunar dust. The city was a tomb of cyclopean ruins.

The architecture was disturbingly alien. Spiral fluted columns formed portices to the low, windowless buildings that reminded him of bunkers—or mausoleums.

Less than a quarter mile northward towered the citadel of the Serpent Kings, a titanic black bulk dominating the surrounding structures like a giant monolith among a scattering of child's building blocks. The tower rose arrogantly, the stonework tapering in close at the top. On its highest point glinted a reflective object, like a beacon—or captive star.

Grant stood and stared in silence. His face was empty of all expression, but sweat ran down his cheeks. He tried not to think at all. He feared if his mind started working again, his reason would crack.

A faint handclapping sound broke the chains of commingled awe and terror that had rooted him to the spot. Sluggishly, his mind awoke and he recognized the distant noise as that of an explosion. He also realized the humming drone hovering at the periphery of his awareness had ceased.

Grant inhaled a deep, surprised breath, palming sweat away from his forehead. The fear and awe had disappeared with the drone, leaving only a natural, rational apprehension in its wake. Glancing down, he noticed the pebbles no longer quivered and a dour smile creased his lips.

Although he wasn't much of a scientist, Grant was a weapons aficionado and after being on the receiving end of an infrasound wand, he had consulted the Cerberus database to learn more about the science of sonics. He had learned that properly pitched and focused, certain frequencies triggered instinctive fear reactions and impaired rational thought. Rather ashamedly he realized the shimmying gravel should have been the tip-off that sonic vibrations were the culprits.

Now that he was no longer engulfed by fear, he took a closer look at his surroundings. The tiny observation post was of relatively recent construction, comprised of shored up cross braces and I beams. He guessed it had been built by the colonists of the Manitius base. The fact the armaglass port was deeply inset into the regolith made him think of a duck blind. The apparent purpose of the post was to enable people to watch the citadel and the surrounding area in secret.

Most of the crater city, if it could be called that, looked as though it had been shattered by giant hands. Broken columns and masses of stone debris were scattered in wide patterns, indicative of an aerial bombardment. He recalled that remains of a giant geodesic dome had been found two centuries before, but he didn't see anything resembling it. As he started to turn away from the ob port, a flicker of movement commanded his attention.

With narrowed eyes he gazed across the crater floor

toward the citadel and for a long moment saw nothing. Then he saw the TAV, rocketing toward the citadel, holding a course so close to the ground the dust sprayed up in a backwash. The little orbit-to-ground transatmospheric vehicle looked identical to the one that had hunted him, Brigid and Kane across the Sea of Ice.

Then, to his surprise, another flying craft rose out of a depression in the citadel's courtyard. Even from that distance he could see the gun emplacements, the crude seams in the metal. It looked primitive in comparison to the TAV, like an early prototype. Its hull appeared to be made of dark, rivet-studded bronze. It looked to be considerably larger than the first vehicle, in length and beam.

The dark craft veered sharply toward the TAV. Ribbed wings of alloy unfolded on either side of the ship, lending it an ominous resemblance to a giant, netherworldly Manta ray. The small rocket tubes tipping the wings spit narrow tongues of blue flame and the vehicle banked.

From a gun turret spit shells, soaring across the crater toward the TAV. The smaller craft swung around in a wide turn. The winged ship looked crude, but it was better armed than the TAV. Grant counted the rate of fire, noting that once every half second a shell exploded from a gun emplacement. He presumed it was firing steel-and-tungsten-carbide pellets, like those in the handguns used by Philboyd and his group of disaffected scientists. According to him, they used dial-a-recoil gas systems to minimize the force with which the shooter would be moved backward.

A series of bright flashes suddenly ran in a ragged sequence on the TAV's port side. The ship rocked and a puff of escaped atmosphere or smoke surrounded its tail in a gray-white ring. Then it banked and arrowed away, climbing above the rim of the crater with the winged ship in pursuit. Both craft disappeared from view, leaving Grant to wonder what the hell he had just witnessed. Obviously, the TAV had intended to attack the citadel, but had been driven off—but he had no idea who was piloting what ship.

Still feeling ten times better than he had when he ascended the steps, Grant clambered down them, back into the cavern. He opened his mouth to call Megaera's name and closed it again. The old priestess was nowhere to be seen. Quickly, he took out his Nighthawk microlight and cast its amber 5,000-candlepower beam all around. The table of rock showed no footprints, no hint as to whether she had deliberately thrown herself into an abyss, accidentally fallen or entered one of the adjoining tunnels.

Grant stood for a long moment, teeth and fists clenched in baffled rage, and turned a complete circle. All the adjoining fissures looked like maws of giant mutie animals, jaws agape as they prepared to devour him if he was foolish enough to enter.

Straining his hearing, Grant tilted his head toward first one opening, then the other, striving to catch even the slightest sound that would give him a clue to Megaera's direction. After a moment, he gave up the exercise. With the deceptive acoustics in the place, he couldn't be sure from which fissure a sound emanated, even if there had been one.

Grant took a deep breath of resolve and strode to the far edge of the rock table, eyes darting back and forth between the two fissures nearest to him. He figured if an old deranged woman, half-crippled and completely blind could navigate one of the passageways, so could he. On impulse he chose the opening on his right, stepping over a wide crack in the cavern floor. The thread-thin beam of his Nighthawk didn't penetrate the deep dark more than ten feet ahead of him.

The passageway was extremely narrow, barely large enough to admit him and then only if he turned sideways. He shone his flashlight up and down. The path was like a seam between the unfinished wall and the foundation of a building.

Grant crabwalked along the gap, the beam from his microlight cutting through a gray mist of dust stirred up by his shuffling feet. Jagged edges of lunar rock caught at his chest. The passage curved steeply downward, following a fault in the bedrock. He assumed the path would eventually take him to a point on a level with the crater floor. The ground beneath Grant's feet suddenly fell away under the pressure of his 235 pounds.

Grant managed to keep from crying out when he dropped, thrashing, into darkness. He didn't fall far, nor was it as much as a fall as a rear-end slide. Dust and grit rose in nostril-clogging clouds as his body plowed a trench through the slope of loose, ancient dirt.

Skidding to a slow stop on the seat of his EVA suit, he shone the Nighthawk beam around. He had emerged through a triangular cleft between towering rock walls. Cautiously he rose, casting the light onto the floor, noting absently how the mineral deposits reflected back the amber beam in a dull glitter. He saw the footprints at the same time he heard the rustle of fabric behind him. He tried to roll aside, but a concussion exploded a bomb of stars inside his skull.

Chapter 4

Neither Kane nor Brigid overtly reacted to the voice. The echoes in the chamber made it almost impossible to pinpoint the speaker's location anyway, so they didn't waste time making fools of themselves by goggling around. They stood their ground amid the shards of shattered crystal and waited, their expressions composed. Both people figured that if whoever spoke meant to kill them he or she—the echoes made it difficult to identify a gender—would have done so without announcing it beforehand.

Due to her many years as an archivist in the Cobaltville Historical Division, Brigid had worked hard at perfecting a poker face. Since archivists were always watched, probably more than anyone else working in the other divisions, she had developed an outward persona of cool calm, unflappable and immutable.

Kane by nature wasn't so restrained, but due to all the missions he had shared with Brigid, he had absorbed some of her stoicism in the face of the unknown, if only by osmosis. Still, it required a great effort to keep his Sin Eater holstered to his forearm. He fought the almost automatic reflex to tense his wrist tendons and feel the solid slap of its butt into the palm of his hand. Without a word, he unslung his Copperhead from his shoulder and handed it to Brigid. The close-assault weapon was a stripped-down auto-blaster, gas operated, with a 700 round per minute rate of fire. The magazine held fifteen rounds of 4.85 mm steel-jacketed bullets. Two feet in length, the grip and trigger unit were placed in front of the breech allowing for one-handed use. An optical image intensifier scope was fitted on top, as well as a laser autotargeter.

Brigid didn't care much for guns, but she accepted the Copperhead almost gratefully. After waiting for what seemed like an appropriate amount of time, Kane inquired mildly, ''Is that all you've got to say?''

When no answer was forthcoming, Kane side-mouthed to Brigid, ''Maybe they lost interest in us.''

''I don't think so,'' she whispered back. ''More than likely they're watching us, studying us, to see what we'll do next.''

The voice came again, as if wafting down from a great height. ''Very perceptive.''

This time, neither Brigid nor Kane could maintain a disinterested facade. Both people skipped around, expecting to see someone standing right behind them. With a faint drone, the tiny electric motor within Kane's forearm holster propelled the Sin Eater into his hand. He raised it as he turned.

All they saw were the strange machines and the wreckage of the infrasound generator. Icy fingers tapped a ditty of dread along the buttons of Kane's spine. Conjecture and speculation whirled through his mind. He knew there was no way he and Brigid's whispered exchange could have been overheard unless the speaker was right at their shoulders—or, his inner voice of alarm told him, they were invisible.

Just to be on the safe side, he swiped the barrel of his pistol through the air on his left and launched a kick directly in front of him, at the point where he figured an invisible eavesdropper's groin would be located. Neither gun nor foot encountered any resistance.

Brigid eyed his actions with arched brows and then announced, "You must have excellent ears."

The response wasn't what either one of them expected. It was a laugh, a rising and falling titter with a hint of sob. The laugh was full of bitterness and even a touch of self-pity and underscored by a note of hysteria.

Kane groaned. He had heard the same kind of laugh in different places from different people over the past couple of years, and the common denominator was madness. Without bothering to lower his voice, he said with mock enthusiasm, "All *right!* We've got another fused-out asshole to deal with, Baptiste. My favorite."

"Fused out?" The hollow voice seemed to bounce from one wall to the other and slide along the shadow-shrouded ceiling. "Does that mean what I think it does?"

"It does," Kane confirmed loudly, eyes darting this

way and that. He was becoming frustrated by his inability to find the source of the voice. He detected an odd inflection to the words, a trace of an accent that touched a chord of recognition within him.

"If it means insane, then I won't presume to debate you. What else would you expect to find in an asylum but insanity?"

"Good point," Brigid commented dryly. "But are you a warder or an inmate?"

Her question elicited only another burst of wild laughter.

Kane said, "They're easily amused, whoever they are."

"Have you seen another visitor like us?" called Brigid.

The laughter climbed in volume as if the inquiry were the punchline to a fabulously funny joke. Then, the laughter cut off abruptly as if a plug had been pulled or the lid of a box slammed shut. Or, Kane's inner voice of alarm suggested, a padded cell door had been closed.

"Was that a yes, a no, or an 'I don't know what you're talking about' laugh?" Kane asked.

"I guess our amusement value wore off," Brigid said dourly.

"I can't imagine why. The Moon has been the Satellite of a Million Laughs since we got here."

Brigid frowned, combing nervous fingers through her tousled mane of hair. Kane knew her well enough to recognize the meaning of the absent gesture. Confidently he told her, "Don't worry about Grant. He's still alive."

She cast him a skeptical glance. "How can you possibly know that? We saw half of the Great Chasm cave in on him—"

"I don't know it," Kane broke in. "I feel it." He turned to face her, his pale eyes hard with certainty. "It's the same way my gut always told me you were alive when my head told me otherwise. The same way you and Grant knew I was alive in Area 51 and came after me."

Brigid met his steady gaze, drew in a long, slow breath through her nostrils and nodded curtly. "Understood."

She smiled up at him wanly. "You're taking all of this a lot better than I expected. You haven't started shooting or swearing or anything too crazy."

"The day is young, Baptiste."

Brigid nodded, gesturing to the items in the chamber. "But these things are not."

Kane grunted. "Industrious bunch, the Annunaki."

In a low voice, she intoned, "Dark Satanic mills. Appropriate in a way."

Kane was by now accustomed to her enigmatic remarks, but he was no less irked by them, particularly since they all seemed to center in on dead zones in his education. He always felt that he was playing straight man to one of her academic performances. Brigid Baptiste wasn't quite the ambulatory encyclopedia she appeared to be, since most of her seemingly limitless supply of knowledge was due to her eidetic memory, but her apparent familiarity with an astounding variety of topics never failed to impress and frequently irritate him. She retained just about everything she ever read, particularly during her years as an archivist. A vast amount of predark historical information had survived the nukecaust, particularly documents stored in underground vaults. Tons of it, in fact, everything from novels to encyclopedias, to magazines printed on coated stock that survived just about anything. Much more data was digitized, stored on computer diskettes, usually government documents.

Although her primary duty as an archivist was not to record predark history, but to revise, rewrite and often times completely disguise it, she learned early how to separate fiction from the truth, a cover story from a falsehood and scientific theory from fact.

"Why is it appropriate?" he asked, despite his first impulse to ignore her cryptic comment.

Quietly, she quoted, "'And did the Countenance Divine shine forth upon our clouded hills. And was Jerusalem builded here among these dark Satanic mills?'"

"Are you asking me or telling me?"

"Neither. It's a stanza from a poem by William Blake. I just think it sort of fits the situation, since we're here to find a devil. Or the devil."

Kane only nodded, swallowing his irritation, but conceding she had a point nevertheless. He took his Nighthawk microlight from his belt, affixed it to his left wrist and started off, thinking about devils, those spawned from hell and spawned from science.

Over the past two years, he, Brigid and Grant had contended with both, but never had they undertaken such a hazardous mission to such a bizarre place to reach an objective literally named DEVIL. A host of memories swirled through Kane's mind as he stalked through the gloom.

A mission a few months ago had brought he and his two friends to the primary Operation Chronos installation, a place they assumed had been uninhabited and forgotten since the nukecaust of two centuries before. Only much later did they find out the installation was inhabited by an old enemy, the brilliant but deranged dwarf, Sindri. He himself told them while he investigated the installation, he had discovered a special encoded program that was linked to, but separate from Chronos. It was code-named Parallax Points. Sindri was far more interested in the workings of the temporal dilator than the Parallax Points program, but his tamperings with the technology caused it to overload and reach critical mass, resulting in a violent meltdown of its energy core.

When the radiation in the installation ebbed to a nonlethal level, Kane, Grant and Brigid returned. No trace of Sindri was ever found, but none of them believed he had perished. It was more likely he used the facility's mat-trans unit to gate to his space station haven, *Parallax Red.*

In the weeks following the incident, Brigid and Lakesh made several visits to the Operation Chronos redoubt, salvaging what could be salvaged. Most of the machinery was damaged beyond any reasonable expectation of repair, but the data pertaining to the so-called parallax points was retrieved and put to use, including the protective garments Kane had named shadow suits.

At the same time, Lakesh built the second version of the interphaser, or to be technically precise, a quantum interphase matter-transmission inducer. The interphaser was Lakesh's latest creation, actually a newer version that evolved from the Totality Concept's Project Cerberus. Before the nukecaust, the objective of Project Cerberus was essentially devoted to converting matter to energy and transmitting the energy to a receiving unit and converting it back again to matter.

Although a working teleportation device had been more or less perfected in the latter years of the twentieth century with the development of the mat-trans gateway units, Lakesh had gone even beyond that accomplishment. Nearly two years before, he had constructed a small device on the same scientific principle as the mat-trans inducers, an interphaser designed to interact with naturally occurring quantum vortices. Theoretically, the interphaser opened dimensional rifts much like the gateways, but instead of the rifts being pathways through linear space, Lakesh had envisioned them as a method to travel through the gaps in normal space-time.

The interphaser had not functioned according to its design, and due to interference caused by Lord Strongbow's similar device, the so-called Singularity, its dilated temporal energy had sent Kane, Brigid, Domi and Grant on a short, disembodied trip into the past.

Although the interphaser had been lost, its memory disk had been retrieved, and using the data recorded on it, Lakesh had tried to duplicate the dilation effect by turning the Cerberus mat-trans unit into a time machine.

Such efforts were not new. Operation Chronos, a major subdivision of the Totality Concept, had been devoted to manipulating the nature of time, building on the breakthroughs of Project Cerberus. During development of the mat-trans gateways, the Cerberus researchers observed a number of side effects. On occasion, traversing the quantum pathways resulted in minor temporal anomalies, such as arriving at a destination three seconds before the jump initiator was actually engaged.

Lakesh found that time could not be measured or accurately perceived in the quantum stream. Hypothetically, constant jumpers might find themselves physically rejuvenated, with the toll of time erased if enough "backward time" was accumulated in their metabolisms. Conversely, jumpers might find themselves prematurely aged if the quantum stream pushed them farther into the future with each journey. From these temporal anomalies, Operation Chronos had been the starting point, using the gateway technology, to develop time travel.

Therefore, the interphaser was more than a miniaturized version of a gateway unit, even though it employed much of the same hardware and operating principles. The mat-trans gateways functioned by tapping into the quantum stream, the invisible pathways that crisscrossed outside of perceived physical space and terminating in wormholes. The interphaser interacted with the energy within a naturally occurring vortex and caused a temporary overlapping of two dimensions. The vortex then became an intersection point, a discontinuous quantum jump, beyond relativistic space-time.

According to Lakesh, evidence indicated there were many vortex nodes, centers of intense energy, located in the same proximity on each of the planets of the solar system, and those points correlated to vortex centers on Earth. The power points of the planet, places that naturally generated specific types of energy, possessed both positive and projective frequencies, and others were negative and receptive. He referred to the positive energy as *prana,* which was old Sanskrit term, meaning "the world soul."

Lakesh was sure some ancient peoples were aware of these symmetrical geoenergies and constructed monuments over the vortex points in order to manipulate them. He suspected the knowledge was suppressed over the centuries. Kane had no reason to doubt the suppression of such knowledge, even if he was skeptical of everything else.

The Parallax Points program was actually a map of all the vortex points on the planet. Decrypting the program was laborious and time-consuming, and each newly discovered set of coordinates was fed into the interphaser's targeting computer.

For the first time in two hundred years, the Cerberus redoubt reverted to its original purpose—not a sanctuary for exiles or the headquarters of a resistance against the tyranny of the barons, but a facility dedicated to unfathoming the eternal mysteries of space and time.

Kane, Grant and Brigid had endured weeks of hard training in the use of the interphaser on short hops, selecting vortex points near the redoubt—or at least, near in the sense that if they couldn't make the return trip through a quantum channel they could conceivably walk back to the installation. Only recently had they begun making jumps farther and farther afield from Cerberus. So far, the interphaser hadn't materialized them either in a lake or an ocean or underground, a possibility that Kane privately feared. He knew an analogical computer was built into the interphaser, and it automatically selected a vortex point above solid ground.

However, everyone was nonplussed when one set of parallax point coordinates led to a location not just above solid ground but off the planet itself, on the Moon. All of them knew the stories about predark space settlements, even of bases on the Moon, of course. Even Sindri had told about a how a small secret base had been established on the Moon in the Manitius Crater region. According to him, this site was chosen because of its proximity to artifacts that some scientists speculated were the shattered remains of an incredibly ancient city, once protected by massive geodesic domes.

A remote probe had been dispatched first, and it returned not just with evidence the Manitius Moon colony was still inhabited, but populated by Megaera, her Furies, a disaffected group of scientists and marauding packs of carnobots, all under the sway of Enki, a flesh-and-blood devil, and a machine known by the acronym of DEVIL.

They strode beneath an arch that bore the cup-and-spiral design, and Kane repressed a shiver. The sigil seemed like a cold and judgmental eye, a dragon's eye, watching him with detached amusement as they foolishly strolled into its lair.

The two people walked into a tremendous hall. Its vaulted roof was lost in thick shadows. A forest of black pillars soared all about them, supporting the unseen ceiling far above. Kane glanced down and came to a sudden halt, pulling Brigid to a stop. She started to speak, then followed his downward gaze.

The floor of the dark hall was a vast, circular mirror. Its silvery surface reflected back the beam of his microlight. Dimly, they could see their own reflections.

''What the hell is this thing for?'' he asked.

Brigid craned her neck, gazing upward. "Just a guess, but there might be a skylight in the ceiling. When the Sun is in the proper position, it strikes the mirror and provides heat and light. It might be a giant semiconductor solar cell."

Kane gazed at the mirror dubiously. "And what happens if the skylight opens while we're crossing it? Terminal sunburn?"

"If the Sun is the proper position, more than likely."

"Then let's go around the damn thing."

They circled the rim of the mirror, wending their way among the support columns, dust and other objects crunching beneath their feet. The beam of his Nighthawk gleamed dully from a reflective surface in the gap between a pair of pillars. Brigid saw it, too, and they walked over to it. Lying on the floor, half covered by a layer of moon dust, was a small shape both of them instantly recognized, but its familiarity did nothing to ease their tension.

Kane felt his throat constrict and the moisture in his mouth dry out. Brigid nudged it with a boot, breaking it free of its covering of lunar grit. She bent and picked it up, turning it over in her gloved hands.

It resembled nothing so much as a lopsided wedge made of a glassy, iridescent gold. The leading edge was strangely elongated, like the neck of a glass bottle that had been heated and stretched out. Where there should have been a set of double-banked strings, there were only empty frets.

"A Danaan harp," Brigid said. "On the Moon."

"I was under the distinct impression the Danaan had a base on Mars, not the Moon." Kane surprised himself by how calm his voice sounded.

"That was Sindri's conjecture," Brigid reminded him. "There's no reason the Tuatha de Danaan and the Annunaki couldn't have shared technology, particularly during the time of the pact. The infrasound generator is evidence of that."

Kane nodded slowly. "It might be evidence of something else. What if everything we ever heard about the Annunaki and the Danaan wasn't the whole truth? Like the legends about how both races retreated to 'realms invisible'?" He crooked the index fingers of his hands to indicate quotation marks.

Brigid's eyes narrowed. "You mean the Danaan and the Annunaki continued to make war on each other?"

"I mean the exact opposite. What if the pact went a lot further than a simple mixture of their genetic material to create Balam's people, the First Folk?"

Brigid didn't speak, digesting Kane's theory, so he continued, "Isn't it possible that both the Danaan and the Annunaki were so weakened by their war, they decided to hang together instead of hanging separately?"

"You're making a lot of assumptions based on very little."

Kane took a deep breath. "You never saw one of Megaera's Furies unmasked, did you?"

She shook her head.

"I found a dead one in Chicago. He was definitely a hybrid of some sort, but not like the barons or any we'd ever seen."

Quickly he described the man's features. Kane remembered how he had been much taller than the average hybrid and his eyes hadn't possessed the prominent supraorbital ridge arches, either. "Maybe he carried some Annunaki genetic material," he concluded, "or maybe it was Danaan. According to legend, the Danaan interbred with humanity in ancient times, just like the Annunaki did. And we know people are still alive with Danaan bloodlines."

She didn't respond to his oblique reference to Fand and the Priory of Awen. "An interesting theory, Kane. But the Furies serve Megaera and Megaera serves Enki. That's quite a turnaround from the age-old rivalry between the Danaan and the Annunaki. The Danaan were reputed to protectors of humanity. "

"That's the entire point I'm making. *Reputed* to be."

"The implications are—"

He cut her off with a sharp gesture. "I can figure those out myself, Baptiste. Let's get the hell out of here and find a place that's defensible."

Brigid nodded and fell into step beside him, tucking the harp beneath an arm. They hadn't gone far when they paused, hearing the echoes of a faraway cry, long with rising and falling inflections that were wordless yet sounded as though they might have come from a human throat.

"Laughing boy is back," Kane muttered.

The laughing call was repeated from a different direction and Brigid said grimly, "And this time he's brought company."

Chapter 5

Grant wasn't aware of losing consciousness completely. He had a vague recollection of falling and then a sensation of rough rock grinding into the side of his face. Then, almost immediately following the sensation, he was squinting away from bright light flickering into his eyes.

He twisted his head and saw a small bronze lamp glowing on a stool close to him. Absently, he noted the base was deeply inscribed with Sumerian cuneiform characters. A strangely shaped bulb, like a half-open tulip blossom, cast a stark yellow light.

By its illumination he realized he was sitting, his back to a wall. Although his thought processes moved sluggishly, like half-frozen mud, he tried to scoot closer to the lamp to examine it. Sickening pain exploded in his head and he sank back, grunting involuntarily. He realized his wrists and ankles were bound to pitons driven deep into the rock floor. Multiple strands of silver wire were drawn through eyebolts in all four pitons and expertly twisted and knotted around his extremities. He also saw he no longer wore the bulky EVA suit, but its removal hadn't made much of a positive contribution to his freedom of movement.

Grant heard a rustle of movement outside the pool of luminescence cast by the lamp, then a sympathetic female voice said, "I struck you too hard, I fear. But then, in the dark facing an armed stranger, one has to be careful. I hope you understand."

Grant looked around, trying to wince at the throbbing the movement triggered in his skull. In bland tone, he said, "Sure."

A new voice, in a gravelly male timbre with a touch of a British accent, demanded, "You feel like talking now, mate?"

"About what, for instance?"

"About who you are, where you're from and why you wear the skin of a Fury."

Grant glanced down at himself. He had almost forgotten about the black shadow suit. "This old thing? Just something I threw on."

"Perhaps you can give us an indication as to where you threw it on."

Grant wasn't certain who had addressed him this time, the male or female, but he saw no reason for dissembling. "I found it on a island in the Cific called Thunder Isle."

There was long period of silence. Grant sensed tension and disbelief, then both voices demanded in unison, "Earth?"

Grant snorted disdainfully. "You got a place called Thunder Isle on the Moon?"

The female said, "Please don't lie to us, my friend. It upsets us to be lied to."

Grant lifted his eyebrows in a mockery of ingenuous surprise, even though it hurt. "You don't say. What a coincidence—it upsets the hell out of me to be coldcocked, trussed up and interrogated by people I can't see."

There was nothing to warn him, no hint of movement, no sound preceding the foot darting out of the shadows and kicking him under the jaw with a force that drove his head back. If not for the wall behind him, the kick might have snapped his neck.

As it was, for a few moments he saw nothing, not even the wavering yellow glow of the brass lamp. When the hollow roar within the confines of his skull faded to a dull mutter, Grant kept his eyes closed, chin upon his chest. The first thing he heard was angry, snapping voices.

"Why did you do that?"

"We've got no time for his bullshit! Keel is missing, we've got the Furies hunting us all over the place and the patrol hasn't reported in—"

"And so you try to kill the one man who might be able to tell us something about all of that? You're an asshole, Cleve!"

"And you're a stupid, sentimental cow! You think playing nice with this bastard will get us anywhere?"

Grant slowly and carefully opened his eyes, a fraction at a time, hoping his heavy brows would hide the fact he was looking at them. A man and a woman wearing the same kind of zippered, one-piece coverall garment that the people in the Manitius base wore stood very close to his outstretched legs.

The man named Cleve was heavyset, his round face half-concealed by a matted salt-and-pepper beard. A strip of dirty cloth was tied around his broad forehead, and at first Grant thought it was strictly decorative until he saw the dark bloodstain encrusting half its length.

The woman appeared surprisingly young, slim and small waisted. Her long dark hair was a tangle of Medusa snarls. Protruding from makeshift holsters around their waists Grant saw the blocky butts of the tungsten-carbide pellet guns. The pistols held the general configuration of a revolver, but instead of a cylinder, small round ammo drums were fitted into the place where there were normally trigger guards. There were no real triggers, just curving switches inset into the grip.

The barrels were unusually long, nearly ten inches in length. The weapons were made of a lightweight alloy that resembled dulled chrome. A unit of energy inside the grip moved a piston, which propelled the explosive projectile. Grant knew the guns were deadly, having seen Eduardo destroy a carnobot with one a few hours before. At least, he assumed it was a few hours. Time had lost all meaning in the dark catacombs of the Moon, but he reviewed all he had learned about the place, before and after his arrival.

Before he, Kane and Brigid embarked on the lunar mission, Megaera's disjointed references to a "Devil on the Moon'' were fed into the Cerberus database, and it listed only one possible connection linking the Moon with the concept of a devil. In predark years, a number of different tests were conducted on the Manitius base, from the military application of particle-beam lasers to test flights of transatmospheric vehicles.

A terraforming project was also based there. There were only two general strategies for colonizing alien worlds—either alter humanity to fit the planet through pantropic science, as was done with the transadapts on Mars, or alter the planet to fit humanity. Mars was the first attempt at terraforming, but due to its rarefied atmosphere, that planet was abandoned and attention turned toward Venus.

Because that world was believed to be suffering from a runaway greenhouse effect, giving it an average surface temperature of around 470 degrees Celsius, the astrophysicists of the day suggested Venus could be terraformed by the introduction of a planetismal device—essentially a heavy-mass projectile. The plan was to detonate planetismal projectiles at geosynchronous points around Venus. Biocatalytic chemicals such as fluorocarbons, as well as photon radiation, would blanket the surface, ideally triggering a reaction to positively alter the planetary atmospheric conditions.

According to the info found in the database, only one such terraforming device was ever constructed, in geosynchronous parking orbit above the Manitius base. It was called a Deep Electromotive Valence Induration Lithospherimal process, or known by the acronym of DEVIL.

Brigid postulated that the DEVIL device could be a weapon of cataclysmic proportions. She theorized that the Annunaki practiced some form of terraforming on Earth hundreds of thousand of years ago, and quite possibly it was by use of that technology that they caused the Flood, the deluge of ancient legend. Judging by Megaera's tale, a society loosely based on the Sumerian civilization had taken root in the Manitius colony, but the only way to learn more was to conduct a hands-on investigation—and that meant undertaking the unprecedented step of activating an interphase point on the Moon.

Although they arrived safely, with Megaera in tow, she escaped them. Later the Cerberus team made contact with a group of astrophysicists who had been attached to the DEVIL project. Eduardo, Mariah, Philboyd and Neukirk explained how construction on the Manitius base began in the late 1970s, after the shuttlecraft program began in earnest. The Manitius site was chosen because the astronauts of the early Apollo missions reported a base had already existed in the crater. Chambers and tunnels had been dug into the regolith and extended for miles.

As Mariah described it, the objective of the Manitius base was twofold—to establish a self-sufficient colony and to provide a jumping-off point to ferry materials and personnel to build a space station on the

Moon's dark side. There were also agricultural and mining ventures. Construction of the base was an ongoing process, expanding it, improving it, modifying it. By the mid-1990s, there were over three hundred more or less permanent residents. Around that time, the DEVIL project was attached to the Manitius base.

To the dismay of Kane, Brigid and Grant, the scientists informed them of the true purpose of the DEVIL process—in its original incarnation, DEVIL involved the covert assembly in low Moon orbit of a planetismal projectile, but according to Mariah and Philboyd, the device mutated into not just a travesty of the original project, but into a genocidal monster.

Grant returned his attention to the coveralled woman whose voice quavered in both fear and fury. "That's the whole goddamn point! He's a *stranger!* We've never seen him before, so we've got find out who he is, not beat him to death!"

Cleve muttered something indistinct, then he made a short, sharp gesture toward Grant. "Your call, Nora."

The woman sighed and squatted between Grant's splayed legs. Her expression was sad, her brown eyes seeming to swim with tears. She held a clay cup of water to Grant's lips. "Stranger, can you hear me?"

Carefully, Grant lifted his head, his face showing nothing. "Very clearly, Nora."

The woman chuckled, but it sounded forced. "Good. Here, drink this."

Grant did as she suggested, wetting his parched

throat. As he gulped the cool water, Nora said, "My friend, I want you to be honest with me. It would be far better to tell us voluntarily who you are and where you're from than to make us force it out of you."

Grant grunted, as if he found Nora's veiled threat slightly ridiculous. "I don't have any reason to trust you. You've tied me up and booted me around, and that doesn't incline me toward cooperation."

"If we let you go," demanded Cleve, "will you talk?"

Grant tried to shrug, but it wasn't easy. "Why not?"

A tense silence stretched out among the three people. Nora broke it by declaring firmly, "All right."

She rose and backed away into the shadows. Grant heard metal objects clinking, then she returned with a pair of needle-nosed pliers. She handed her pistol to Cleve, who quickly unholstered his own and drew a double-barreled bead on Grant's head. Shifting from one to the other, he said harshly, "One wrong move and I'll blow your head off."

Grant chuckled briefly, mirthlessly. "You've got experience in this kind of thing, don't you?"

"A little," Nora replied bleakly. "Unfortunately."

Moving swiftly and methodically, Nora snipped the wire strands from the pitons and backed away, allowing Grant to unwind the bonds from his wrists and ankles. The man and woman watched him apprehensively as he did so. Grant slowly stood, silently enduring the pain of returning circulation. The gun barrels shifted with him, like a pair of dark eyes. He had no wish to find out if the shadow suit would turn away an explosive pellet. He desperately wished he was wearing his Magistrate body armor, even though in many ways the shadow suits were superior to the polycarbonate exoskeleton.

Although the black, skintight garments didn't appear as if they could offer protection from a mosquito bite, they were impervious to most wavelengths of radiation. The suits were climate controlled for environments with up to 150 degrees, and as cold as minus ten degrees Fahrenheit. Microfilaments controlled the internal temperature.

The manufacturing technique was known in predark days as electrospin, lacing electrically charged polymer particles to form a dense web of formfitting fibers. Composed of a weave of spider silk, Monocrys and Spectra fabrics, the garments were essentially a single crystal metallic microfiber with a very dense molecular structure. The outer Monocrys sheathing went opaque when exposed to radiation, and the Kevlar and Spectra layers provided protection against blunt trauma. The fibers were embedded with enzymes and other catalysts that broke down all toxic and infectious agents on contact. The spider silk allowed flexibility, but it traded protection from firearms for freedom of movement.

Grant felt the shadow suits were superior to the Magistrate armor, if for nothing other than their internal subsystems. Built around nanotechnologies, the microelectromechanical systems combined computers with tiny semiconductor chips. The nanotechnology reduced the size of the electronic components to one-millionth of a meter, roughly ten times the size of an atom. The inner layer was lined by carbon nanotubes only a nanometer wide, rolled-up sheets of graphite with a tensile strength greater than steel. The suits were almost impossible to tear, but a heavy-caliber bullet could penetrate them. Unlike the Mag body armor, the shadow suit wouldn't redistribute the kinetic shock.

Therefore, Grant took great care to move slowly and not agitate Cleve's trigger fingers. He took advantage of the silence to survey his surroundings, not that there was much to see.

He, Cleve and Nora were in a small room with rough-hewed rock walls and floor. A series of shelves were bracketed to the far wall, beside a door made of thick planks. It had no knob or handle, only a drop bar.

Both people continued to eye him anxiously as he arose. He towered over Cleve by nearly half a foot. He gingerly probed the swelling on the back of his head and examined his fingertips. They were dry, so Nora's blow hadn't broken the skin. He contemplated not giving them his name, but he was tired of being addressed as outlander and stranger. Curtly, he said, "My name is Grant. I'm from Earth. Philboyd, Neukirk, Mariah and Eduardo sent me here."

Nora and Cleve stared at him uncomprehendingly.

"Don't you know who I'm talking about?" he demanded impatiently.

Nora ducked her head in a jerky nod. "Yes, we do, but—"

"But what?"

Cleve said in a faint aspirated whisper, "We thought they were dead. Killed months ago in a raid."

"No, they're very much alive, though Eduardo had a rib broken by a carnobot. We saved his life, if that means anything to you."

Both the man and woman sagged visibly in relief. The barrels of the two pistols drooped a little. "It does," Cleve said. "But who is 'we'? How did you get here?"

Tersely, without elaboration, he told of their first encounter with Megaera and her Furies in Chicago. He related how Sindri apparently brought her there during his experiments with the Parallax Points program and how they had repeated his mistake. Although he alluded to Cerberus and the interphaser, he didn't go into detail or mention any names. Earlier, Neukirk had hinted that he at least was aware of Lakesh as the creator of the gateways, but nothing beyond that.

"Where's this interphaser thing?" Nora asked, a blend of skepticism and hope in her eyes and voice.

Grant started to gesture, then realized he had no idea in what direction he should point. "Back at the base, in Megaera's statuary collection."

Brigid had hidden the interphaser among the carbonized victims of the Oubolus, but he didn't tell Nora that.

Cleve pursed his lips in disappointment. "Hell of a long way from here."

"Now that you mention it," Grant replied, "just where is here?"

"Inside the regolith of the Plato Crater," Nora answered. "On the border between Mare Frigoris and Mare Imbrium. Does that help you?"

Grant shook his head. "Not really, no."

"There's a network of ancient tunnels and passageways in here."

"Dug by the Annunaki?"

"That's what we thought at first," Cleve said. "Now we're not so sure. What did Philboyd and the others tell you about the different factions here?"

Grant didn't immediately answer, replaying the confusing and fragmented backstory related by the four astrophysicists. According to them, after the nukecaust the scientific staff of the Manitius base tried to come to terms with the reality of being forever marooned, that they could not expect any rescue missions. They attempted to convince the other inhabitants of the Moon colony of the same thing, but were never quite successful.

But even before the nukecaust forever separated 330 human beings 238,866 miles from the world of their birth, Manitius base was divided into two castes—the support personnel, with the military among them, and the scientists.

Unsurprisingly, the scientists composed the elite of the new society, and for a few years following the nukecaust, the two groups dwelt in peace, practicing a form of democracy. But over a period of time, there were many disagreements, which finally boiled over into dissension. The military and support people reached the conclusion that since scientists had brought on the holocaust, they should have no part of the new lunar society.

Grant recalled how Philboyd laid the blame on one of their own fellow scientists, a woman named Seramis. In the years preceding the nukecaust, she served as the chief geologist and historian. It was she who had made the initial discoveries that a highly developed race had, in ages past, planted a colony on the Moon. She continued her work even after the nukecaust. She had already uncovered the clues indicating the existence of a hidden city.

Seramis and a group of followers performed excavations in the so-called Wild Lands and discovered secrets about the Moon that she never told anyone. She found tunnels and passages that led to the crypts of the Serpent Kings, the Annunaki. She plundered the tombs of their dead and stole much of their technology. Seramis claimed that a vast lost knowledge was hidden in those catacombs, that on the Moon there were secrets that were old when Sumeria was new, were ancient when the pyramids were built in Egypt. She became so obsessed that she lost herself completely in the ancient culture of the Annunaki.

Grant repeated what he remembered of the story. Cleve and Nora regarded him dispassionately for a long moment, without speaking.

"Well?" he demanded. "That's not true?"

Nora touched her lips with the tip of her tongue. "It is and it isn't. We found out there's a lot more to this than two factions."

"Who else is involved?" Grant asked.

Before she could answer, a fist began to hammer on the door with such force, the small room echoed like the inside of a drum. A deep male voice demanded, "Cleve—open up!"

"Shit," Nora groaned between clenched teeth. "It's Saladin!"

"Who?" Grant asked.

"The lieutenant of Mac."

"Mac?" repeated Grant. "Who the hell is Mac?"

Nora started to speak, then closed her mouth, fear glinting in her eyes.

"Open up!" the voice demanded again.

Cleve hastily lifted the locking bar, and the door burst open, allowing a man to enter. He was wearing the same kind of space suit Grant had seen on the patrol in the cavern. His helmet was tucked under one arm, revealing a black haired, dusky-skinned, hawk-nosed face. Grant guessed him to be of Middle Eastern descent. A three-piece plasma rifle was cradled in his right arm.

Cleve gestured toward Grant. "We have him safe for you, as you can see, Saladin."

Grant stiffened as he saw a number of space-suited men crowding into the doorway behind Saladin. The black-haired man turned his head slightly toward them and said in a mocking tone, "He has him safe for us, see?"

Returning his gaze to Cleve, he stated, "I suppose it was your loyalty that prompted you to spirit this man away from us and hide him here?"

A ripple of contemptuous laughter passed among the men. Saladin flicked his gaze up and down Grant's form. "So you're the one we've been chasing halfway through the Great Chasm for the past eight hours."

Grant stiffened in surprise at the length of time, but he said only, "If you're here to take me to Megaera, you're liable to find her in pretty bad shape."

Saladin's teeth flashed in a grin. "No shit." He turned his head and nodded. The line of men parted, and one of them pushed forward a ragged, scorched scarecrow. Megaera was still murmuring prayers, seemingly oblivious to her surroundings.

"We found her on the level above us, trying to get back to the citadel, " Saladin declared. His grin widened, and a guffaw lurked at the back of his throat. "Finding her almost makes it worth losing some of our men, though Mac probably won't think so."

He stared at Cleve. "This man was armed. Where is his weapon?"

Cleve pointed toward the shelves on the wall. "There."

Saladin stepped over to them, groped and brought

forth Grant's holstered Sin Eater. He held it up, examining it, gauging its weight and balance. "A real weapon," he said admiringly. "A man's weapon. It's been a long time since I've seen anything so beautiful."

Narrowing his eyes, Saladin stared first at Nora then at Cleve. "Why did you think you could get away with this betrayal?"

Nora's shoulders stiffened and she retorted angrily, "We're loyal to Mac. We were serving his interests."

Saladin smirked. "Naturally. Well, your loyalty shall be rewarded once we find this man's companions."

To Grant he said, "Come along. Don't give us any trouble."

Grant didn't immediately move, and Cleve prodded him forward with the barrel of a pellet pistol, toward the waiting men. "You heard Saladin. Go."

Grant took a half step forward, but before the men could grasp him, he turned and smashed his right fist into the belly of Cleve. He grated, "A little something on the account you owe me."

Grant hadn't put much of his weight or strength into the blow, but Cleve folded in the middle, clutching at his midsection, a gassy wail escaping his lips. Both of his pistols clattered to the floor. Grant made no move to pick them up, since he was covered by the plasma rifles.

Saladin laughed heartily. "Well done, outlander. Welcome to the brotherhood of blood. You've already spilled some. Let's see if you're as eager to shed it."

Chapter 6

Kane moved ahead, unconsciously assuming the point man's position. It was a habit he had acquired during his years as a Magistrate, and he saw no reason to abandon it. Both Brigid and Grant had the utmost faith in Kane's instincts, in what he referred to as his point man's sense.

During his Mag days, because of his uncanny ability to sniff danger in the offing, he was always chosen to act as the advance scout. When he walked point, Kane felt electrically alive, sharply tuned to every nuance of his surroundings and what he was doing. He knew how to move silently, to slip always from one shadow to another, to bring his feet down softly. He stopped from time to time to listen, but there was nothing to hear, only the barely detectable sounds of Brigid's respiration.

Then his point man's sixth sense howled an alarm. The skin between his shoulder blades seemed to tighten, and the short hairs at the back of his neck tingled. What he called his point man's sense was really a combined manifestation of the five he had trained to the epitome of keenness. Something—some small, almost inaudible sound—had reached his ears and triggered the mental alarm.

Kane heeled around. As he did so, he thought he glimpsed a shadowy shape vanish behind one of the pillars. "What?" Brigid demanded. Fear glinted in her eyes, but it wasn't evident in her voice.

He didn't answer. He sidled over to the pillar, leading with his Sin Eater. He saw nothing. "What is it?" Brigid asked again.

Kane started to turn toward her, when the faintest of rustles touched his hearing and he spun around again and caught a brief view, almost subliminal, of a figure flitting from sight into the murk. This time he knew his imagination wasn't populating the gloom with silent stalkers.

With blood-chilling suddenness, the sobbing, shivery laughter sounded loudly from close by. Brigid automatically drew near to Kane, and they stood shoulder to shoulder. He didn't need to put his thoughts into words. Several someones were around them, surrounding them and finding them a source of humor.

Despite the fact that his flesh crawled with apprehension, Kane doubted the people sliding through the shadows were Furies. Not only were they not particularly stealthy in their approach, but also they weren't prone to tease the intended victims of their Oubolus rods with fleeting glimpses. The Furies were single-minded to the point of being automatons.

He also was pretty certain they weren't being stalked by any of the Manitius base's group of scientists. They were relying on him, Brigid and Grant to end the threat of DEVIL, one way or the other. Kane didn't trust Philboyd, Eduardo, Mariah and Neukirk, but they had provided the only hard intelligence about the conditions on the Moon. Still, the backstory about how the deranged society was based very loosely on Sumeria wasn't convincing.

Philboyd claimed that in the years immediately following the nukecaust, one of their own, a woman named Seramis, found a great science center of the Annunaki. She and her crew spent months exploring and excavating it, returning to the Manitius base only for supplies. She would not answer questions. One day, she went out to the citadel and didn't come back.

Actually, she did return some months later, but now in the guise of Megaera, or at least the scientists assumed Seramis and Megaera were one in the same. All they really knew was that a woman calling herself Megaera invaded the Manitius base with a contingent of Furies. Those who resisted were killed, calcified by the Oubolus rods. The rest were pursued like deer, hunted down, judged and turned into stone by Megaera and her Furies. After a few months, the main DEVIL technical staff decided to enter cryostasis, both as a way to spare the base's resources and to hide.

When they awoke more than a century later, they found Megaera still in charge and the DEVIL system not only operational, but mutated. Kane recollected the vid image he had seen of the device, still in geostationary orbit above the Manitius base: it resembled nothing so much as a sphere-shaped mass made of rusting plates of metal. When Brigid pointed out that it looked like junk, Neukirk had replied, "It was supposed to. A bunch of space junk in parking orbit. That way, nobody would get suspicious."

A closer view of the device showed them long, sleek rocket assemblies inset between the plates of rusted metal. Mariah identified the various components as nuke drivers, stabilizers and calibration equipment.

It was then the astrophysicist revealed the true meaning of the DEVIL acronym—Deep Entropic Valence Induration Lithospherimal. She explained that essentially DEVIL was built as an encapsulated, speeded-up personification of the second law of thermodynamics—the law of increasing entropy.

Mariah explained how all transfers of energy in the physical universe were controlled by the laws of thermodynamics. The first law stated that mass/energy cannot be created or destroyed. The second law added that the disorganization or entropy of the universe increases with every energy transfer. Some energy is always degraded to useless heat dissipation.

As usual, Brigid Baptiste made the connection before either Kane or Grant. She referred to the beginning of the universe, the Big Bang, as releasing a jolt of antientropy, resulting in increased complexity of mass. After the Big Bang, expansion of mass began to slow and reverse itself. When the mass caught up with the slowing expansion, the law of entropy applied.

Therefore, theoretically, entropy would cause the dimming of stars for lack of fuel. They would become black dwarfs, neutron stars or black holes. Multiple collisions between neutron stars could form supermassive black holes whose gravity would suck in everything, until there was no matter, no radiation, nothing. Entropy at its maximum was nonexistence. But the holes decayed faster than they shrank. Their lifetime was only about a second. The phenomenon depended not just on density but on total mass, so there was not a singularity at the center.

However, the DEVIL process had circumvented that phenomena, so once it was detonated, it could conceivably cause the Sun itself to age billions of years in a second due to a set of chain reactions Eduardo called "transliteration."

However, the astrophysicists took no responsibility for the mind-staggering destructive capabilities of the device. They blamed it on Enki, allegedly the last of the Serpent Kings.

So, whoever the stalkers in the shadows were, Kane knew it wasn't the scientists. They were terrified of control of the DEVIL process falling into the hands of Megaera, so they wouldn't be interfering with Kane's and Brigid's efforts to keep that from happening.

Regardless of the true identities of their pursuers, they apparently possessed intimate knowledge of the great hall, and knew precisely the location of all hiding places, which put Kane and Brigid at a grave disadvantage. But so far no weapons had been unleashed against them.

Kane came to a swift decision. He turned to take Brigid by the forearm and led her onto the mirrored floor, but she had already reached the same conclusion. Both people sprinted out of the murk among the support pillars. They heard rustling footfalls all around, and their legs pumped harder and faster. Hooting, laughing calls echoed back and forth.

They ran flat-out, but still couldn't lose their pursuers. Figures flitted on both sides of them, lithe and quick, seeking to draw ahead and cut them off. Kane had restrained the impulse to use his blaster before, but with a growled "Fuck this," he triggered a stuttering burst to his left. Orange smears of flame strobed against the gloom and ricochets keened. He heard no cries of pain or even fear, only a fresh burst of the mad laughter.

"I'm sure this has occurred to you," panted Brigid, "but what if they want us to go out onto the mirror so we can be fried like bugs under a magnifying glass?"

"At least we'd have some light and see who was frying us," he retorted breathlessly.

They reached the glassine floor, and their thickly treaded boot soles squeaked and squealed on the slick surface. They continued to run until they made it to what Kane estimated was the center of the huge mirror. They came to a halt, breathing hard, grimacing at the taste of the astringent air on their tongues.

Sweeping the barrel of his Sin Eater in left-to-right arcs, Kane looked for targets all around. He didn't find any, but he wasn't overly relieved. However, he was more or less satisfied with their position, since he could easily establish a 360-degree clear field of fire.

Hoarsely, Brigid said, "Look down."

Kane didn't take his eyes away from the forest of pillars encircling the mirror. "I know what the inside of my nostrils look like."

"The floor is clean."

"So?"

"So, everything else in here is covered with dust. But not the mirror. Does that suggest anything?"

He shrugged. "That the janitorial staff should be commended?"

"No." Brigid's tone was tight with anxiety, not irritation. "If it's a giant solar cell like I said—"

A prolonged rumbling vibration suddenly caused the floor to shiver beneath their boots. At the same time, they heard a rhythmic, mechanical throb. The mirror trembled violently underfoot, as if it were placed over the epicenter of a tremor.

"That's the same sound we heard earlier, back in the chasm," Brigid blurted. "The angle of this thing can be changed to catch the different positions of the Sun—"

Kane didn't wait for her say anything more, not that she seemed inclined to go on. Machinery clanked loudly, switches clicked, gears groaned and chain pulleys rattled. The two peopled whirled and began running toward the far side of the mirror. With a shuddering screech, the floor suddenly dipped down, turning its flat surface into an incline. At the same time, pivots began rotating the mirror in a slow counterclockwise circle.

Brigid's and Kane's feet slid out from under them and they fell onto their backsides. As they tried to rise, the floor tilted downward even more, and the traction of their heels and hands couldn't overcome gravity.

A pitch-black crescent yawned before and below them. Kane and Brigid slid toward it. They dug in their heels, placed the flats of their hands against the mirror but they couldn't brake themselves. From the dark opening wafted the clanking, clattering roar of a great machine. Their helmets rolled and bounced into the aperture, and they heard the clang of metal against metal and the shattering of glass.

Suddenly, the pitch of the floor changed, tilting up again, throwing them into backward somersaults. The rear of Kane's head struck the mirrored surface with a painful impact, the corner of a molar nipping into his tongue. The spin of the floor increased in speed, sending them rolling like logs. Still, by supporting herself with hands, knees and toes, Brigid managed to achieve a crouching posture. She shouted something, but her voice was drowned by the mechanical cacophony.

Lips drawn back from his teeth in a silent snarl,

tasting blood, Kane fought his way to his hands and knees, extending his Sin Eater at the end of his arm, finger depressing the firing stud. He didn't have a target, but at the moment he didn't give much of a damn. He intended to keep the trigger pressed and spray everything around the floor with 9 mm hollowpoints.

He managed to only squeeze off a triburst before the floor jounced up again, causing him to fall on his face. He released the trigger, fearing that Brigid would be caught by a stray shot. He got to his knees, but they slipped out from under him and he skidded on his left side into Brigid's legs. Crying out wordlessly in either anger or pain, she went down like a bowling pin. The mirror began wobbling up and down, like a gargantuan coin that had just been flipped. The two people rolled and wallowed like a pair of drunken ice skaters on a frozen pond.

The voice that had addressed them earlier spoke again. "We can keep this up all day, outlanders...or until I weary of the game and dump both of you into the workings, where you'll be mulched up like so much tree bark. What's it to be?"

Kane shouted, "What do you want us to do?"

"Take off that blaster and throw it over here, just to show me your good sense."

"Over where?" Kane demanded, voice thick with humiliated fury. He was completely disoriented as to the direction of the voice.

A dimly seen man-shape suddenly materialized at the rim of the mirrored floor. "Over here."

Kane struggled to unbuckle the straps and tabs of the Sin Eater's power holster. The rising-and-falling motion awoke nausea in his stomach. He wrenched off the holster his forearm and hurled it in a looping overhand. He heard it land with a thump rather than a clatter, so he knew he had cleared the glassine surface of the mirror.

"Much obliged," called the figure.

Almost immediately the giant mirror stopped its tilting, and with a prolonged pneumatic whoosh, the rotation ceased. Brigid and Kane immediately climbed to their feet. She had managed to retain the harp, tucked securely under an arm. The figure at the far edge of the floor approached them, walking with a steady, swift and almost danceresque grace. Both people had seen similar gaits before. Behind the figure, lurking in the shadows, other shapes shifted restlessly.

As the figure drew closer, his features grew more distinct and they saw it was a man. Kane's glare of rage turned into a wide-eyed stare of astonishment. The man was tall, about Kane's height, but he was so exceptionally lean he appeared taller. Absently, Kane noted that his torso seemed strangely elongated, but perfectly in proportion with his slender arms and legs.

His limbs were encased in a black, skintight covering like the shadow suits Kane and Brigid wore beneath their EVAs. An assortment of brightly colored cloth hung from his almost skeletal frame, giving him a scarecrowlike aspect. A long scarlet scrap was wound around his long neck and tossed carelessly over a shoulder, like a scarf, the frayed end dragging on the floor.

A yellow rag around his hips served as either a sash or a belt, and another length of bright green fabric was knotted around his left thigh for no apparent purpose, unless it was supposed to be decorative.

The man's face was long and bony, his chin a jutting V under the smaller V of his pursed lips. His long, narrow nose looked delicate, with tiny nostrils. His eyes were abnormally large, back-slanted, but without the epicanthic folds of the Asian. Kane couldn't tell their color, only that they were dark, depth on depth of darkness, but a magnetic fire seemed to burn within them. His smooth complexion held the blue-white hue of skim milk, marred by a curve of scar tissue along his right cheek.

The man's unnaturally long fingers bore many sigils and talismanic rings. One was a loop of iron, embossed with a cup-and-spiral glyph. Another glittered with a hexagonal red stone. Each ring was fashioned from a different substance—crystal, metal, gems and even what looked like polished, lacquered wood.

A mane of iron-gray hair grew down from a point on his forehead and high, flat temples. It was brushed back behind his ears, to fall in loose, artless tumbles about his shoulders. Kane looked at his ears and a length of slimy rope seemed to knot in his belly. The man's ears were positioned very low on his jawline, and though they lay close to the sides of his head and weren't large, he saw how they tapered to upswept points.

Now he knew how the man had overheard his and Brigid's whispered exchange, and he also knew his theory was correct. But being proved right was a cold comfort under the circumstances.

The tall man said cheerfully, "Ah, you've found my harp. I wondered where I'd misplaced it."

Kane didn't speak, but Brigid husked out in a voice muted by awe, "Tuatha de Danaan."

At her words, the man jerked to a sudden halt, as if shocked. He cocked his head at her curiously. He uttered the peculiarly melodious yet sobbing laugh and made an abrupt, intricate gesture with his left hand near his heart. "I bid thee felicitations and grant thee respect, otherbrothers. My name is Maccan. But you can call me Mac."

Chapter 7

Lakesh didn't enjoy acting as a tour guide. It evoked too many uncomfortable and embarrassing memories of his years laboring for the Totality Concept, when he was obliged to squire bureaucrats, high-ranking military officers and members of oversight committees around his facilities, both in Dulce, New Mexico, and back when the Cerberus installation was known as Redoubt Bravo.

Lakesh would strain to be charming and funny and diplomatic as he explained his work in the most basic layman's terms, but half the time his audience either didn't understand or didn't care to make even the most perfunctory effort to comprehend the methodology. The military representatives were only interested in the military applications of the Cerberus mat-trans network, and the oversight committee members cared only how much money was being spent to develop machines that seemed inspired by old science-fiction movies.

The bean counters were the hardest to impress, inasmuch as Project Cerberus and all of the Totality Concept researches were financed by black funds funneled away from other government projects, so their fixation on dollars and cents always seemed rather anally retentive.

Project Cerberus, like all the other Totality Concept divisions, was classified above top secret. A few high government officials knew it existed, as did members of the Joint Chiefs of Staff. The secrecy was believed to be more than important; it was considered to be almost a religion.

Developing a safe means for the transmission of matter was damnably expensive. Not even Lakesh could argue about that. Nor could he dispute the military's interests in it, either, but the mat-trans had less destructive applications, as well. Given wide use, the units could eliminate inefficient transportation systems and be used for space exploration and colonizing planets without the time- and money-consuming efforts to build spaceships.

However, matter transmission was found to be absolutely impossible to achieve by the employment of Einsteinian physics. Only quantum physics, coupled with quantum mechanics, had made it work beyond a couple of prototypes that transported steel balls only a few feet across a room. But even those crude early models couldn't have functioned at all without the basic components that predated the Totality Concept.

As the project's overseer, Lakesh experienced the epiphany and made that crucial breakthrough. Armed with this knowledge, under Lakesh's guidance the quantum interphase mat-transducers opened a rift in the hyperdimensional quantum stream, reduced organic and inorganic material to digital information and transmitted it along hyperdimensional pathways on a carrier wave.

In 1989, Lakesh himself had been the first successful long-distance matter transfer of a human subject, traveling a hundred yards from a prototype gateway chamber to a receiving booth. That initial success was replicated many times, and with the replication came the modifications and improvements of the quantum interphase mat-trans inducers, reaching the point where they were manufactured in modular form.

Sky Dog, of course, didn't know anything about the history of Project Cerberus. Therefore, he didn't react either like a soldier or a bookkeeper. But like them, when he entered the redoubt's central control complex, it was obvious the shaman had difficulty grasping the technological wonders arrayed before him.

The overhead lights in the long, vault-walled room automatically dimmed at sunset and came back on to full brightness at dawn. They were bright now, causing Sky Dog to squint at the consoles that ran the length of the walls. Indicator lights flickered, red, green and amber, circuits hummed, needles twitched and monitor screens displayed changing columns of numbers. He looked dispassionately at the computer terminals, glanced disinterestedly at the sheaves of paper scattered about the workstations and appeared to pay no attention to the status lights and blinking icons showing on various screens.

The shaman surveyed the spacious room slowly as

if committing everything to memory. He ignored the hunched form of Auerbach at the enviro-ops station, and the burly, red-haired man returned the favor. Lakesh didn't bother with introductions. Auerbach was, in many ways, directly but inadvertently responsible for the alliance struck by Sky Dog's people and the Cerberus personnel—not that he had acted the formal role of ambassador. He had been first an interloper, then a captive.

Sky Dog turned his head toward the enclosed main-frame computer system, but didn't ask any questions, so Lakesh didn't bother informing him that the redoubt's control complex contained five dedicated and eight shared subprocessors, all linked in a mainframe system. The advanced model used experimental error-correcting microchips of miniature size, which even reacted to quantum fluctuations. The biochip technology that was employed contained protein molecules sandwiched between microscopic glass-and-metal circuits.

The shaman glanced up at the huge Mercator relief map of the world spanning the far wall. Spots of light glowed in almost every continent, and thin glowing lines networked across the countries, like a web spun by a radioactive spider. For the first time, interest showed in his black eyes. "What is that?"

"That's a map of the world," Lakesh answered, "a current map, showing most of the geophysical changes since the holocaust."

"What do those lines and lights represent?"

"Kane told you about the gateways, didn't he?"

Sky Dog nodded. "Little rooms that take you to other little rooms, sometimes all the way across the world."

"That's one way of putting it," Lakesh replied dryly. He pointed to the map. "The lines show all the locations of all functioning gateway units indexed in the Cerberus mat-trans network. If any of the units were in use, the light representing its location would blink."

"Ah." Sky Dog turned back around, gazing across the complex toward the open door of the ready room. "May I see your little room?"

"Certainly."

Lakesh led the tall Amerindian through the operations center and into the adjacent room. He gestured to the free-standing, eight-foot-tall jump platform. "There you are…the quantum interphase mat-trans inducer. Commonly called a gateway unit."

The six-sided chamber was enclosed by slabs of brown tinted armaglass. All of the official Cerberus gateway units in mat-trans network were color coded so authorized jumpers could tell at a glance into which redoubt they had materialized.

Despite the fact it seemed an inefficient method of differentiating one installation from another, only personnel holding color-coded security clearances were allowed to make use of the system. Inasmuch as their use was restricted to a select few units, it was fairly easy for them to memorize which color designated what redoubt.

Armaglass was manufactured in the last decades of the twentieth century from a special compound that combined the properties of steel and glass. It was used as walls in the jump chambers to confine quantum energy overspills.

Lakesh usually felt a small flush of pride whenever he looked at this particular unit, since it was the first fully debugged matter-transfer inducer built after the prototypes. It served as the template for all subsequent units.

Sky Dog approached the unit warily, circling the elevated platform and eyeing his distorted reflection in the armaglass walls. "How does it work?"

"Kane didn't explain it to you?"

The corners of Sky Dog's mouth twitched as if he were trying to repress a grin. "He tried, but he never got very far. He'd either stop on his own or because my people would start laughing."

Lakesh didn't try to repress his own grin. He was a little comforted that Kane hadn't managed to convince the Amerindians that it was possible to travel instantaneously through invisible pathways. He had often wondered just what Kane talked about when he visited Sky Dog's people.

Most of the people in the redoubt—with the exception of Domi—were ville bred and they were accustomed to an artificial environment. Rarely did any of them stray more than ten yards from the edge of the plateau.

Kane, however, would frequently complain of suffering from redoubt-fever and borrow one of the vehicles to drive down the treacherous mountain road to the foothills to Sky Dog's permanent encampment.

No one asked what he did down there among the Amerindians, where he was known and admired as Unktomi Shunkaha. It was a name the band of Sioux and Cheyenne had bestowed upon him, first conceived as something of an insult. It became synonymous with cunning and courage after he orchestrated the Indian's victory over a Magistrate assault force.

After remaining with the band for a few days, Kane would show back up at the redoubt, oftentimes dirty and disheveled, but always relaxed. Lakesh and others wondered if Kane had a willing harem of Indian maidens who always looked forward to a visit from Unktomi Shunkaha, but everyone knew better than to inquire about it.

"Well," Lakesh said hesitantly, hoping he didn't sound patronizing, "I don't blame them for laughing. It's very difficult to describe. It sounds like magic, not science."

Sky Dog tentatively tapped an armaglass slab. "Is this how Unktomi Shunkaha and his friends got to the Moon?"

Lakesh shook his head. "Similar operating principle, but a different device."

Sky Dog turned to face him, his expression inscrutable. "And the woman I brought here…she is similar to a human being, but a different device, too?"

Lakesh was startled into chuckling. "Actually, you're not too far wrong. But she is definitely human. Just different."

"So I gathered." The man's grim slash of a mouth tightened. "I respect Unktomi Shunkaha as I respect no other, his *wasicun* blood notwithstanding. But I find it hard to believe he would lie with such a creature as her. They're called hybrids, unholy mixtures of human and not-human. You make war on them, do you not?"

Lakesh inwardly flinched from Sky Dog's unexpected display of revulsion. He groped for something noncommittal to say and finally murmured, "On those like her, yes. But as Kane is not like all white men, neither are all hybrids the same."

Sky Dog grunted. "Still, white men are human—their blood is the same as mine. Whatever our other differences, our roots are the same. When my people black their faces and make war on them, there is honor in it. We kill them and take their hair because they've done something to threaten or offend us. The very fact of the hybrids' existence is threatening and offensive. I assumed you waged war on them to exterminate them, to purge their seed from the Earth."

Lakesh felt a flush of both shame and anger warming the back of his neck. "Genocide is not our aim. If possible, we want to preserve both sides, reach an accord where we can live in peace with one another. As we here have done with your people.''

Sky Dog chuckled scornfully. ''And the way you do that is to lie with their women, to make more mixtures, hybrids of hybrids? That is not a warrior's path to victory.''

''Firstly,'' Lakesh said, an edge to his voice, ''we have no idea who the father of Quavell's child is, whether one of her own, Kane or someone else entirely. Secondarily, the path to victory is not always a straight route. You of all people should know that.''

Sky Dog lifted a challenging eyebrow. ''Will your medical expert be able to find out who has fathered the creature's child?''

Lakesh shrugged. ''I don't know. Is it really that important to you?''

Sky Dog didn't respond for such a long time, Lakesh wondered if he had heard the question. At length, the shaman answered in a low, grating voice, ''That would depend, Lakesh.''

''On what?''

''On how important it is to *you*.''

THE TREATMENT ROOM of the infirmary was deserted, all the beds empty. From the adjoining laboratory came the clink of metal. Lakesh detected a stinging whiff of chemicals, the tart smell of sterilizing fluids as he crossed the room. Sky Dog had decided to walk around the plateau and check on his horses, so Lakesh went to consult with Reba DeFore.

DeFore was removing a glass tube containing a ruby-red fluid from the centrifuge when Lakesh strode into the laboratory. She almost dropped the tube when she caught sight of Lakesh out of the corner of her eye. Swiftly, biting back a curse, she returned the tube to the clamp on the centrifuge.

Casting an angry glance over her shoulder, she said, "I liked it better when you shuffled. Made it harder for you to sneak up on someone."

Lakesh smiled, but due to the fresh memory of Sky Dog's words it was forced, perfunctory. "I never sneak. I might creep and skulk, but sneaking is not in my repertoire."

"But shuffling might be again," DeFore muttered, and then removed the tube from the centrifuge. She stepped farther down the black ceramic-topped trestle table.

Lakesh didn't respond to her oblique reference about his physical condition. Both of them had talked the matter to death for the past few months. Even after five years, he and DeFore still disagreed on a wide variety of matters. She had accused him of being overly demanding and high-handed, and sometimes he was sure she outright distrusted him, particularly after supplying Balam with the destination lock codes of the redoubt's gateway. Quite possibly she thought he was lying about the means of restored youth.

He couldn't blame her about that, not really. She didn't even pretend to understand how it had happened. The process Lakesh described flew so thoroughly in the face of all her medical training—as limited as it was—he might as well have attributed the cause to an angelic intervention.

All DeFore really knew was that a few months ago she watched Mohandas Lakesh Singh step into the gateway chamber as a hunched-over spindly old man who appeared to be fighting the grave for every hour he remained on the planet.

A day later, the gateway chamber activated, and when the door opened, Kane, Brigid Baptiste, Grant and Domi emerged. A well-built stranger wearing the white bodysuit of Cerberus duty personnel followed them. Lakesh still remembered how DeFore gaped in stunned amazement at the man's thick, glossy, black hair, his unlined olive complexion and toothy, excited grin. She recognized only the blue eyes and the long, aquiline nose as belonging to the Lakesh she had known these past five years.

She was very dubious about the story of Sam. Lakesh retained vivid memories of how Sam had laid his little hand against his midriff, and how a tingling warmth seemed to seep from it. The warmth swiftly became searing heat, like liquid fire, rippling through his veins and arteries. His heartbeat picked up in tempo, seeming to spread the heat through the rest of his body, a pulsing web of energy suffusing every separate cell and organ.

He was aflame with a searing pain, the same kind of agony a person felt when circulation was suddenly restored to a numb limb. His entire metabolism seemed to awaken to furious life from a long slumber, as if it had been jump-started by a powerful battery.

He still remembered with awe that after the sensation of heat faded, he realized two things more or less simultaneously—he wasn't wearing his glasses but he could see his hand perfectly. And by that perfect vision, he saw the flesh of that hand was smooth, the prominent veins having sunk back into firm flesh. The liver spots faded away even as he watched.

Later, Sam claimed he had increased Lakesh's production of two antioxidant enzymes, catalase and superoxide dismutase, and boosted his alkyglycerol level to the point where the aging process was for all intents and purposes reversed. For the first few weeks following Sam's treatment, his hair continued to darken and more and more of his wrinkles disappeared. But then the entire process reached a certain point and came to a halt. Lakesh estimated he had returned to a physical state approximating his midforties.

Lakesh didn't try to convince DeFore or anyone else his condition was permanent. He claimed he had no idea how long his vitality would last. Whether it would vanish overnight like the fabulous One Horse Shay and leave him a doddering old scarecrow again, or whether he would simply begin to age normally from that point onward, he couldn't be certain. However, he told her he wasn't about to waste the gift of youth, as transitory as it might be. DeFore didn't know who One Horse Shay had been or what was so fabulous about him, but she did notice Lakesh surreptitiously eyeing her bosom in a way he had never done before.

Lakesh stood quietly, hands clasped behind his back as DeFore busied herself with the micropipette assembly. She inserted a fluted end through the cap of the test tube and carefully worked it until the glass tip touched the red liquid. He admired the brisk, deft efficiency of the woman's movements and he silently thanked whatever form of providence had delivered DeFore into the Cerberus redoubt.

A stocky, buxom woman in her early thirties, DeFore always wore her ash-blond hair pulled back from her face, intricately braided at the back of her head. Its color contrasted starkly with the deep bronze of her skin and her dark brown eyes. She always looked good in the one-piece white jumpsuit most Cerberus Redoubt personnel wore as duty uniforms.

Reba DeFore was one of the few exiles who acted as a specialist. The ten people who lived in the Cerberus redoubt, regardless of their skills, acted in the capacity of support personnel. They worked rotating shifts, eight hours a day, seven days a week. For the most part, their work was the routine maintenance and monitoring of the installation's environmental systems, the satellite data feed, the security network.

However, everyone was given at least a superficial understanding of all the redoubt's systems, so they could pinch-hit in times of emergency. Fortunately, such a time had never arrived, but still and all, the installation was woefully understaffed. Their small numbers were a source of constant worry to Lakesh, particularly since he could no longer practice his secret recruitment program, so he felt it was important that everyone have a working knowledge of the redoubt's inner workings. DeFore had instructed two of the staff, Banks and Auerbach, in medicine, in case she was ever incapacitated or there was a medical crisis.

Grant and Kane were exempt from this cross-training, inasmuch as they served as the enforcement arm of Cerberus and undertook far and away the lion's share of the risks. On their downtime between missions they made sure all the ordnance in the armory was in good condition and occasionally tuned up the vehicles in the depot.

Brigid Baptiste, due to her eidetic memory, was the most multifaceted member of the redoubt's permanent staff, since she could step into any vacancy and perform the required tasks in an exemplary manner. However, her gifts were a two-edged sword, inasmuch as that same set of skills made her an indispensable addition to away missions.

Lakesh cleared his throat. "Is that a blood sample from our...?"

He paused to grope for a term, but DeFore quickly supplied one. "My patient. Actually, this a sample of the fetus's blood."

DeFore turned on the vacuum pump, and Lakesh watched as a tiny clot of liquid scarlet inched its way up through the pipette to a slide waiting on the analyzer's feeder tray. She closed it and her fingers clattered over the attached keyboard as she instructed the machine about which data to obtain and analyze.

"But you performed a physical examination of Quavell?"

Still inputting, DeFore answered distractedly. "Only as much as she allowed. Like she said, she's in perfect health, or appears to be. But I don't have much of a frame of reference for hybrids, you know. I've never seen one before, remember."

"And her child?"

"The fetal heartbeat was 160 beats per minute, which is normal." Lakesh watched as DeFore initiated the karyotype charting and the statistical analysis of the recombinant mitochrondrial DNA. The computer hummed purposefully.

"How far along is Quavell?" Lakesh asked.

DeFore turned toward him, resting an ample hip against the trestle table. "That's hard to tell, since she didn't permit an in utero examination. I don't know about the enlargement of the womb. I was able to take blood and urine samples. From those I'd guess she's about to enter her third trimester."

"What about the sex of the child?"

DeFore shook her head. "She wouldn't allow a sonogram, either. Told me it was unnecessary."

A rueful smile creased her full lips. "You've brought me some of the strangest patients over the past couple of years—a mind-controlled Mongolian warrior, a Martian transadapt...not to mention the time I took an EEG of Kane and got back three graphs—''

''This time I didn't bring you a patient,'' Lakesh broke in. ''She came on her own. What about paternity?''

''What about it?''

Choosing his words with care, Lakesh said, ''From her blood sample would you be able to identify the father of her child?''

DeFore frowned. ''Only if I had another blood sample available to compare it to and make a match.'' A perplexed look lined her face. ''Do you have someone in mind?''

Before he could answer, the computer chimed and printed out a long strip of paper. DeFore ripped it along the perforation and began to study the sequence of black squiggles imprinted along its length. After a moment, she glanced uneasily over at Lakesh.

He stepped closer, recognizing the symbols on the paper strip as DNA strands. ''Is there a problem?''

She shook her head. ''I don't know. I don't know what it is. It's—''

Her words trailed off and she narrowed her eyes. She began speaking again. ''Normally a gene sequence on a strand of DNA acts like a fingerprint for a given ethnic group. This specimen defies every pattern I'm familiar with…and those the computer is programmed to recognize.''

She used one of her fingernails to trace the sequence

and even to Lakesh's unpracticed eye, it appeared somehow fragmented.

With a sinking sensation in his belly, he asked, "Does that indicate a birth defect of some kind?"

"I don't know what it indicates. I need to do a full range of tests and analysis and that'll take time…and it'll require Quavell's complete cooperation."

Folding the printout, DeFore gazed directly into his face. "And frankly, I don't know if keeping her here for that period of time is such a sound strategy."

A little gruffly, Lakesh retorted, "She's an exceptionally useful font of information about the current state of the baronies and how they're reacting under the reign of the imperator."

"That information conduit works both ways. For example, how did a hybrid know how to find us?"

Lakesh shrugged. "Presumably she learned of our location from either Domi or Kane during their captivity in Area 51."

"'Presumably,'" she repeated with a slight sarcastic emphasis on the word. "And presumably if she knows, so do other hybrids. And if other hybrids know, so do the barons."

Lakesh scowled at her tone. "Supposition. Both Domi and Kane described Quavell as the de facto leader of a fifth column within Area 51, an antibaron brigade, so to speak."

"That's what they were told. Maybe that's what they believe. But I don't think the rest of us here can afford the same luxury."

Lakesh angled a challenging eyebrow at her. "Just what are you implying? That she's a spy, a Trojan horse, setting the stage for an invasion force to come battering at our door?"

"It's happened before," DeFore snapped. "Except the last time, they didn't need to batter at our door, since you opened it for the imperator and his mother. What was her name again, Erica something or another?"

"Erica van Sloan," Lakesh muttered absently.

Flatly, DeFore declared, "I think there might be a connection between Quavell, Sam and Erica something or another."

Lakesh uttered a dismissive, derisive sound. "That's quite the stretch."

DeFore's eyes turned cold. "You're the one who always claims there are no such things as coincidences, remember?"

"Synchronicity isn't the same thing as a conspiracy," Lakesh countered stiffly.

DeFore turned her back on him. "They aren't mutually exclusive, either, Lakesh."

Swallowing a sigh, Lakesh said wearily, "If it makes you feel better, I have every intention of thoroughly questioning Quavell. Do you know where she is?"

DeFore waved a negligent hand. "Domi has taken her under her wing. She was with her in here during the examination. You might want to try the cafeteria, since Quavell said she was hungry."

Lakesh nodded, realized DeFore wasn't looking at him, and annoyed, he turned sharply to leave the laboratory. A sudden pain stabbed through his right knee. The pain was brief, but it was familiar and he fought to prevent a cry from escaping his lips. Arthritis pains had become more and more frequent as of late, particularly when he made swift moves. He had come to accept that Sam's magical laying on of hands definitely had its limits, but the prospect of aging thirty years in thirty days didn't appeal to him.

As Lakesh walked swiftly through the infirmary and out into the corridor, he felt a cold dread spreading through him. The concept that Sam and Quavell were somehow in league seemed ridiculous on the face of it, but he couldn't afford to discard the possibility out of hand.

Although they had Quavell to provide valuable and perhaps even critical intelligence about the baronies, he couldn't shake the suspicion that she had them, too—perhaps right where she wanted them.

Chapter 8

The tunnel became little more than a curving ledge, with a rock wall on one side and yawning, impenetrable blackness on the other. It led upward, and the seven people inched their way along it, flattening themselves against the wall.

Finally, the ledge stopped slanting upward, widened and leveled out. They made their way through a short passageway. Grant noted how the composition of the tunnel walls and floor suddenly changed when they entered it. Both walls bore deep, horizontal grooves, and the stone floor was a series of concrete slabs. Having seen similar grooves in the walls at the Manitius base, he recalled how Brigid had opined they were marks caused by tunneling lasers.

The passageway opened into a bowl-shaped cave. Illuminated by the weird blue glow of the light panels, the cavern spread out before them in a fantastic and eerie panorama. Gigantic stalactites hung from the arched roof like stone spearheads. The cavern's floor rose to meet them in glassy ridges formed by alternate heating and cooling.

Grant didn't question Saladin or the other men about their destination. They didn't speak to him or bother to bind him. At first he thought it was due to inexperience on their part, then grudgingly realized they simply didn't think he was worth the effort. There was no place for him to go, unarmed and without an EVA suit. As it was, he found himself wheezing, laboring to fill his lungs with the rarefied air. No one else seemed to be experiencing any respiratory difficulties, so he knew if he tried to make a break for it, his captors would probably just wait until the exertion caused him to pass out and then retrieve him.

Saladin put Megaera in his charge and he marched along with a hand on her bony shoulder, guiding her away from collisions with boulders and preventing her falling into fissures in the floor. Grant found himself feeling sorry for her. Old, half-crippled and blind, she reminded him of Dregs he had encountered during his Mag years.

Saladin led the group through the rocky labyrinth, never pausing or hesitating to collect his bearings. Here and there amid the stone forest, pits of fire glowed and occasionally he saw a jet of yellow flame that burst up from a volcanic pocket burning far below. They were relics of the Moon's dead youth and responsible for the thin oxygen.

Saladin surefootedly wended his way through a maze of stalagmites. Many of them had been exposed to extreme heat in the dim past and were vitrified. Ghostly glows from the fire pits painted their glassine surfaces with flickering rainbow colors. Grant saw stacks of pipes and signs of excavation. Apparently, the original colonists had attempted to harness the thermal energies for heat and power.

The group of people followed Saladin through the mineral maze to the edge of a twenty-foot-wide drainage channel cutting through the floor. Through it flowed a sluggish stream of dark, algae-filmed water. That exuded the same open-cesspit stench as the peat bog he had crawled through. The atmosphere around it was thick, clammy and fetid. Grant noted how the current flowed into a wide-mouthed pipe protruding from the cavern wall. A limestone arch spanned the stream, and they trooped onto it. The incline wasn't steep, but the natural bridge was so narrow the little party had to walk along it single file. Grant and Megaera brought up the rear.

As they navigated it, Saladin suddenly came to a halt at the midway point, gesturing sharply behind him. His men immediately stopped. No one questioned him or even appeared to breathe. They stood stock-still, as if frozen. Grant, towering nearly a full head over everyone else, peered at the far side of the bridge. He saw only blue-lit shadows, and he shifted his feet impatiently. Then he glimpsed a blur of movement, a pair of vague gray outlines.

His skin prickled and he unconsciously held his breath as the shapes slunk closer. The dark gray, streamlined figures of carnobots scuttled close to the bank of the channel. The machines were roughly triangular in configuration. A smooth front rose to an almost comically tiny head, set at the apex of the triangle. The back was a long slope that tapered to the ground. Their four legs moved swiftly beneath them, positioned almost as kickstands might be beneath motorcycles.

Two tiny red eyes gleamed above a square snout and a mouth full of needle-tipped, alloyed teeth. The carnobots paused for a moment, their heads rising at the ends of segmented metal necks, turning this way and that, as if trying to catch a scent. Grant tensed, then realized their odor sensors were probably overwhelmed by the stink of the stream. Their photoreceptors detected movement and body heat, and with everyone wearing thermal-baffling outfits and standing still, the robots couldn't react to either signature.

The carnobots lowered their heads and moved on. Grant recalled how Philboyd claimed the deadly mechanisms had been manufactured back before the holocaust and field-tested on the Moon. Sometime during his and his companions' long period in stasis, their programming was altered.

Saladin waited until the carnobots were out of sight before moving forward again. He strode to the end of the arch and walked forward. Beyond the foot of the bridge the cavern floor rose in a wall. In it was hacked a shallow flight of steps leading to a metal-sheathed door set between a square frame of dark iron.

Saladin quickly bounded up the steps to the door. Grant couldn't tell how he opened it, since he saw no handle or knob, but slowly the portal began to swing inward, hinges squeaking. There seemed to be nothing beyond but dark. Then lights began to glow. The opening of the doors activated a lighting system. In swift succession, overhead neon tubes flickered to life and cast a steady yellow illumination.

Saladin and his men stepped over the threshold. A long, hexagonal shaft yawned away before them, the sharply angled walls glassy and gray. It was so long, the nether end was lost in the distance. Guiding Megaera with one hand, Grant walked into the passageway, his expression not registering his surge of astonishment. Inlaid in the walls behind glass panels stretched maddeningly intricate ribbons and patterns of circuitry. Tiny lights flashed and blinked intermittently, but synchronously. The air was fresh and without the cesspit taint.

Saladin and his men took long-legged, purposeful strides. Grant followed, but he didn't try to catch up. He studied the network of circuitry as he passed, trying to reason out its purpose. The glass panes threw back his distorted reflection, transforming his dark, mustached face into an elongated smear.

The passageway became a catwalk, stretching across a huge chamber, like a cavern made of steel. The walls, ceiling and floor of the chamber formed one continuous surface, making a huge, hollow ellipse measuring at least a hundred feet on the longer diameter. Grant glanced over the handrail, slowed his pace, then came to a stop, pulling Megaera to a halt.

Resting far below in a hangar were six winged aircraft, identical to the one he had glimpsed earlier, driving off the TAV. He saw now the resemblance to Earth's Manta rays was more than superficial, particularly with the ribbed, curving wings at full extension. The vehicles had fifteen-yard-long fuselages, twenty-yard wingspans with five-yard tails, tipped by spade-shaped rudders.

Although they appeared to be made of a burnished bronze alloy, Grant doubted that was the actual composition. Covering almost the entire surface were intricate geometric designs, deeply inscribed into the metal itself. There were interlocking swirling glyphs, the cup-and-spiral symbols he had seen before and even the elaborate Sumerian cuneiform markings. The cockpits were almost invisible, little more than elongated symmetrical oval humps in the exact center of the sleek topside fuselages.

Now he could see that features of the craft he had at first thought crude were only different—alien. He recalled the Aurora stealth plane he had shot down months before in New Mexico and recognized a similarity in configuration and design. He knew it wasn't a coincidence—just as he knew that the Manta ships had served as the template for both the Aurora and the TAVs.

One of Saladin's men looked over his shoulder and gestured sharply with the barrel of his plasma rifle, an unmistakable order for Grant to come along. Reluctantly, Grant stopped his visual examination of the aircraft and joined the others, guiding Megaera ahead of him.

The catwalk led into a circular chamber, the walls curving gracefully up to form a domed, transparent ceiling. A billion stars glittered frostily above it. Waist-high instrument panels encircled the rim of the dome, all of them blinking, clicking or both.

The chamber was full of people, at least a dozen men and women, some wearing zippered coveralls, others clad in an assortment of olive-green military fatigues and others in EVA suits. All of them wielded just as varied an assortment of weapons, from old AK-47s to bolt-action rifles with scopes and almost everything else in between.

Grant felt the tension in the air, as palpable as static electricity before a lightning storm. He had participated in enough councils of war to recognize one without having to be told what was going on.

The people milled about, clustering around someone or something in the center of the chamber. The few who noted his and Megaera's entrance did so by eyeing them briefly with a mixture of hostility and curiosity, then turning away. Grant and the old woman halted at the outer fringe of the ring of people. He wondered if he should draw attention to himself by demanding answers to the multitude of questions swirling through his mind, or if he should continue to be silent and unobtrusive, waiting for a chance to escape.

Before he could make up his mind, Saladin's sharp voice snapped, ''Outlander—get your ass up here.''

Leaving Megaera, Grant shouldered his way

through the throng, not allowing the surge of anger he felt at Saladin's autocratic tone to show on his face. Later he would express his displeasure.

When he reached the center of the chamber, he came to a sudden halt, his breath seizing momentarily in his lungs. Kane and Brigid Baptiste stood in the center of the ring of people. Like him, they had been stripped of their EVA suits. A smile of relief crossed Brigid's face, and she murmured something that sounded like "Thank God."

Kane, on other hand, seemed engrossed in conversation with someone and casually glanced his way, acknowledging his presence with a short nod. "Oh, there you are."

Grant opened his mouth to voice a loud and profane rebuke—he closed his mouth almost instantly when he saw the man with the pointed ears.

The man looked him up and down with eyes that might have been cut from azure crystals and drawled, "My name is Maccan. I'm told your name is Grant. Well, Grant, allow me to welcome you to the DEVIL's playground."

NEITHER KANE NOR BRIGID blamed Grant for simply standing and staring at Maccan. Although his expression was as immobile as if it had been carved from teak, Kane knew the big man was struck dumb with astonishment. He understood his reaction completely.

It was one thing to discuss the concept of an alien race that had once inhabited the solar system, even to see and touch their artifacts, but to come face-to-face with the living, breathing reality was more than startling—it was shocking, mind numbing, probably as close to madness as Grant was ever likely to get.

Brigid stepped close to him, moving slowly so as not to attract unwelcome attention from either Maccan or the armed people. Soothingly, she said, "He's one of the Tuatha de Danaan…I think. He looks strange, but he's closer to humanity in appearance than Balam, and you got used to him."

Maccan's mobile mouth twisted as if he tasted something exceptionally sour. "Balam," he echoed broodily. Instantly, his crystal blue eyes darkened, as if India ink had been poured into pools of clear water. "I remember him…he led the attack on our colony on Lahmu."

Kane caught Brigid's eye and mouthed, "Lahmu?"

"Mars," she mouthed back.

Kane nodded once in understanding. During the briefing before the phase transit to the Moon, Brigid had mentioned the possibility that the Tuatha de Danaan and the Annunaki may have been age-old rivals, competing with each other for the natural resources of the different planets in the solar system. After the pact, the Danaan established at least an outpost on Mars and were driven from it in the relatively recent past.

He recollected how upon their first encounter with Sindri, he told them that beginning in the 1860s and going to the 1870s, astronomers on Earth reported monstrous explosions occurring on Mars—visible even with the primitive telescopes of the day. The phenomenon ended abruptly in 1872. Sindri theorized the astronomers were witnessing aerial bombardments and missile attacks.

Grant visibly pulled himself together, giving Kane the impression of a man waking from a bad dream, but not finding his waking reality any more pleasant. Taking a very long, very deep breath, he gazed directly at Maccan and demanded, "Are we prisoners or what?"

"At this point," interjected Saladin, "you're what."

Kane surreptitiously studied the dark man. He was obviously hard-bitten, but he exuded the quality of a military man.

Brigid said mildly, "I don't believe we've had the pleasure. Maccan told us your name, but little beyond that."

His black eyes fixed on her intently. "That's because there's very little to tell. My people and I are in his service."

"In his service for what?" Kane ventured.

Maccan turned toward him, his eyes slowly changing color, lightening to a pewter gray. The effect was chilling, and Kane felt a quiver of xenophobia the likes of which he hadn't experienced since the first day he had met Balam.

"You have a rather intrusive tongue, Kane." Maccan's tone held no particular emotion. "You remind me of a human warrior who meddled in the affairs of the Danaan, on Ogyia. I found his arrogance intolerable."

Kane didn't respond, remembering that Ogyia was an ancient synonym for Ireland. He had met several people there who claimed Danaan ancestry. One of whom, Fand, believed him to be the reincarnation of the great Celtic warlord Cuchulainn. A diminutive of Cuchulainn was Ka'in, but this didn't seem to be the appropriate time to point out the connection to Maccan.

Maccan's steady gaze didn't falter, but the color of his eyes continued to lighten. Kane hoped that meant he was calming down. "Your life, and those of your companions, is mine. And to keep it you need to know when to listen and when to ask questions."

Maccan raised his voice. "Bring the old witch-bitch forward."

The people shifted position, murmuring, then Megaera was rudely thrust into the center of the room. Kane and Brigid winced when they saw her. Maccan, however, uttered his peculiar sobbing laugh.

"Whatever happened to you, my lady?" he asked, mimicking a courtly bow even though she could not see it. His gesture elicited a ripple of appreciative laughter from the onlookers.

Grant didn't expect her to reply, but she did with a surprising degree of dignity. "I bear my wounds proudly, demon. They were incurred in service to my god."

Maccan stepped closer to her, thrusting his lower

lip out petulantly. "Now, you see I don't understand that. I *never* understood it. Why would you worship that ancient bag of scales as a god, but vilify me as a demon? I mean, your kind invaded our tombs, revived us both at the same time, stole my instruments and devices, yet you decided I was a demon and he was god."

He turned toward the assembled people, gesturing grandly as if beseeching them to make clear a murky point. "Is there *anyone* on this thrice-damned rock who resembles a demon?"

He received more laughter from the people, but Megaera seemed serenely unaware of it. She spoke, but her words were unintelligible. Maccan waved everyone to silence. "What did you say?"

"Your kind arrived later. You deceived humanity on Earth, just as you deceived us here. You gave us weapons, but they destroyed only our faith in you, not our enemies." Megaera's voice was calm and steady. "You promised us power, but you have no power."

Maccan nodded in agreement. "I have nothing. The day of my kind has passed. Neither I nor your god have anything to offer you. All here is dead, worn-out, corroded, crumbled, useless. But Enki wishes the end of everything."

"An ending that will be a new beginning," Megaera retorted.

Maccan laughed sibilantly. It was not the sobbing titter they had heard before, but more like noxious gas leaking from a faulty valve. "I know your motives are pure. The mysteries of humankind's origins must be preserved, and you believe you are the guardians of those mysteries. But that makes you and your followers no less fools. Thrice, four times fools.

"You violated the most fundamental element of a priesthood, Megaera—you began to believe in your own lies. You managed the religion and reaped the benefits, you made the rules and played the game according to them. But you forgot you are only mortal. You can be killed and tortured and mutilated, just like you have done to all the sinners."

Megaera murmured, "I served my god."

"You served only a delusion created by a crazed ancestor of yours, Megaera." Maccan's tone became low and smooth, almost sympathetic. "And do you think Enki is unaware of this? He knows, just as I do. He only used you to achieve his own ends."

"His own ends that will result in a new beginning," Megaera shot back smugly. "That is what you fear."

Maccan stroked his chin musingly. "Perhaps you are right. I do not want a new beginning for either Enki or myself. We've had our time, our reign, our worshipers. But the life of humankind is not the life of either the Annunaki or the Danaan, nor is human death our death.

"We ceded our power of life and death to the First Folk, the spawn of our combined seed. But Los, Urizen, Lam—all of them squandered that inheritance."

Kane repressed a shiver. Despite Maccan's contemplative tone, his eyes were changing again, red glints swimming in them, slowly filling the gray irises.

Maccan paused to sigh heavily. "As you have squandered your life in service to Enki."

Megaera drew herself up regally. "My life has had purpose. We have levied judgment on the sinners of two worlds. None of my ancestors, those who carried my name and title, can boast of that."

Maccan smiled thinly. "If such a small accomplishment gives you comfort now, as you stand on the brink of death, then I shall not attempt to disaccommodate you of it."

He turned to Saladin. "Have you a knife? Preferably one that has been sharpened in the last century?"

Saladin bent, unzipped the seal of his boot and withdrew a long combat knife. Grant recognized it as his own. He had dropped it in the chasm, but he didn't think Saladin or Maccan would appreciate his raising an issue of ownership.

Saladin presented it to him hilt first. Maccan examined the fourteen-inch-long, tungsten-steel knife, thumbing the blued, double-edged blade. "Exquisite manufacture."

He stepped very close to Megaera and murmured, "Your term of service to your god is over. However, you may be able to provide a small boon to your demon."

Maccan planted the heel of his free hand against Megaera's chin and slowly forced her head back, until her blind eyes gazed up at the domed roof arching overhead. Then he pressed the point of the blade against her throat.

Uttering a wordless cry of horror and anger, Brigid lunged forward, reaching for Maccan. Saladin grabbed her by the left arm and Brigid's swift, left-legged snap kick caught him in the midsection, driving the air from his lungs. As he bent in the middle, Brigid shifted her balance and delivered a roundhouse kick from the right. The weighted sole of her boot caught the man in the temple, slamming him dazed to the floor. Her movements were so quick, so practiced and economical, both Kane and Grant were taken completely by surprise.

Brigid continued her forward rush, but without even looking at her, Maccan shot out his left arm, and his hand closed around her throat. Kane and Grant made attempts at lunges of their own, but strong arms restrained them and the barrels of a variety of weapons were trained on them.

They could only watch in helpless frustration as Brigid tried to pry Maccan's inhumanly long fingers from her neck. Maccan's grip tightened, ropy muscles rippling along his arm. He swung her up and off her feet as if she weighed no more than a straw-filled dummy. He held her suspended there while Brigid clutched at his wrist and gagged for air, feet kicking for the floor.

"Do not presume bearing the name of one of my own kind makes me predisposed to look on you with favor." Maccan's voice was a low, threatening growl.

His eyes gleamed like drops of fresh blood. "Your life is mine. If I give it back to you, it's because you can be of service to me, not because of my merciful nature."

He opened his hand and Brigid fell to the floor, crouching there on her hands and knees, taking in great, shuddery gasps of air. She clutched at her throat, face contorted in pain. Kane gazed at her, trying to tamp down the seething rage building in him. He lifted his eyes toward Maccan, and the rage boiled over into hatred. The men holding him felt him tense and they clamped down tighter, immobilizing him. The bore of a steel pellet pistol pressed against the side of his head, and he forced himself to relax in his captor's grips.

Survival first, he reminded himself grimly, then revenge.

After Brigid had begun breathing more or less normally again, she was dragged to her feet, her arms wrenched behind her in hammerlocks. Maccan watched, his mouth twisting in a smirk, then he returned his attention to Megaera and swiftly slashed her throat open from ear to ear. The old woman made no outcry or effort to struggle.

Maccan didn't even try to avoid the blood that gushed forth. He was drenched in the liquid vermilion, but he thrust the tip of the knife into the incision he had made in Megaera's throat and separated two of the cervical vertebrae. Then he sawed vigorously at the flesh, tendon and muscle that held the old woman's head to her body. He clutched a handful of her hair and, when her body fell limply to the floor, he held her head in one hand. He raised it high for all to see.

The people in the room roared and howled in approval, shaking their weapons over their heads, stamping their feet, splashing blood in speckled patterns in all directions. Maccan stepped over to Brigid and dangled Megaera's head before her. "You will take this back to the citadel. To any you meet, you will say, 'Maccan gives you a last gift and a final message. It is time to pay the devil his due.'"

Brigid made no reply, but her eyes flashed with emerald sparks of loathing.

Kane glanced over at Grant and mouthed, "Time to go."

Grant nodded.

Chapter 9

Lakesh was in the mood for a briefing, but he didn't go to the officially designated briefing theater on the third level. Big and blue walled, it was equipped with ten rows of theater-type chairs facing a raised speaking dais and a rear-projection screen. It was built to accommodate the majority of the installation's personnel, back before the nukecaust, when military and scientific advisers visited.

Now, because the briefings rarely involved more than a handful of people, they were almost always convened in the more intimate dining hall. When Lakesh entered the cafeteria, he saw Domi seated at a table near the serving station. Quavell stood nearby, examining the food in the trays.

Farrell and Bry, two more Cerberus personnel, sat on the far side of the room dawdling over their breakfast, and they nodded to him as he came in. Farrell was a rangy, middle-aged man who affected a shaved head, a goatee and a gold-hoop earring after watching an old predark vid called *Hell's Angels on Wheels*.

Bry, who served as Lakesh's technical lieutenant, had short, curly copper hair and was a round-shouldered man of small stature. His expression was always one of consternation, no matter his true mood. Both men were studies in physical contrasts, but they now they shared a similar manner—they surreptitiously eyed Quavell with a mixture of suspicion and fascination.

On his way to the coffeemaker, Lakesh asked them quietly, "Has Domi introduced you to our guest?"

Bry nodded. Farrell simply said, "Yeah," and let the matter rest. The two men showed no inclination to continue the conversation, so Lakesh poured himself a cup of coffee and joined Domi at her table. One of the few advantages of being an exile in Cerberus was unrestricted access to genuine coffee, not the bitter synthetic gruel that had become the common, subpar substitute since skydark, the generation-long nuclear winter. Literally tons of freeze-dried packets of the real article were cached in the redoubt's storage areas. There was enough coffee to last the exiles several lifetimes.

While Quavell daintily sampled the food at the serving station, Lakesh turned to Domi and inquired, "Has she found anything to her liking?"

Domi nodded. "Oatmeal and ice cream."

Lakesh felt his eyebrows crawl toward his hairline. "Never heard of that combination."

"She needs food that's easily digestible to her simplified intestinal tract."

Lakesh nodded, assuming Domi was only repeating what Quavell had said. He blew on his coffee to cool it and sipped slowly, using the process to give himself time to properly phrase the multitude of questions he intended to ask.

Domi didn't wait for him. In a voice barely above a whisper she said, "I know what you want to ask. I'm pretty sure the answer is yes."

Lakesh smiled ruefully. "Pretty sure? She didn't tell you?"

She shook her bone-white head. "No need."

"Then how do you know?"

Domi shrugged. "Her eyes. They change whenever his name is mentioned. A man wouldn't know, but another woman can tell."

Lakesh frowned. "Are you sure we're talking about the same thing?"

Domi returned his frown. "What did you want to know about?"

"First and foremost, how she managed to get out of Area 51 without being pursued and apprehended."

Quavell returned to the table, bearing a tray laden with a plate of oatmeal that had two scoops of ice cream swimming in it. As she placed the tray on the table, Lakesh rose and pulled the chair out for her. Quavell acknowledged the gallantry with a gracious nod. Lakesh found himself studying the way her swollen belly was adequately covered and supported by the fabric of her one-piece garment. Absently, he guessed the material was a synthetic polymer with a high degree of elasticity, so one size would indeed fit all. When he caught himself thinking about her clothes rather than the more important issues, he sat back down and swallowed a mouthful of coffee to wash down his own frivolity of thought.

Quavell said matter-of-factly, "This is not the type of food I'm accustomed to, but it as close an approximation to the microorganisms I normally ingest as I'm likely to find."

"Microorganisms?" Domi echoed, sounding a little disgusted.

"They consist primarily of single-cell proteins. They have very little taste."

Lakesh didn't know how to reply to her statement so he said inanely, "That's a shame."

Quavell regarded him curiously with her huge blue eyes, then spooned up ice cream and oatmeal and swallowed it. "You have many questions for me, Mohandas Lakesh Singh."

"That I do, madam."

Quavell's eyes flicked swiftly sideways toward Farrell and Bry, who were straining to overhear the conversation but trying not to be too obvious about it. Lakesh cleared his throat and made an elaborate show of peeling back the cuff of his sleeve to consult his wrist chron. Loudly he announced, "It's 0720. Shift change began some time ago. I'm sure Auerbach would prefer to be relieved from his post...unless you made a prior agreement with him about extending his shift while you two loitered in here."

Farrell and Bry didn't reply, but they rose stiffly from the table and strode out without a backward glance. They left their cups, plates, wadded-up napkins and food-encrusted eating utensils on the table. It was a breach of protocol, but Lakesh didn't call them back. It was a small enough protest against authority to overlook. However, it wasn't as if he were the primary authority figure in the redoubt. The mini-coup d'état staged by Kane, Brigid and Grant nearly a year before had seen to that.

Lakesh hadn't been totally unseated from his position of authority, but he was now answerable to a more democratic process. At first he bitterly resented what he construed as the usurping of his power by ingrates, but over the past few months he had felt the burden of responsibility ease from his shoulders. Now he felt almost grateful. Almost, but not quite, because he had been coerced into sharing his command.

Almost every exile in the redoubt had arrived as a convicted criminal—after Lakesh had set them up, framing them for crimes against their respective villes. He admitted it was a cruel, heartless plan with a barely acceptable risk factor, but it was the only way to spirit them out of their villes, turn them against the barons and make them feel indebted to him.

This bit of explosive and potentially fatal knowledge had not been shared with the exiles. Grant's grim prediction of what the others might do to him if they learned of it still echoed in his memory: ''I think they'd lynch you.''

When Bry and Farrell were gone and definitely out of earshot, Lakesh said firmly, ''I do indeed have questions, madam.'' He employed that particular form of address rather than "young lady" because at her age, despite her appearance, he would have felt rather foolish. "They have gone unanswered for some months now, and it's past time they were resolved."

Quavell nodded, and a ghost of a smile played over the high planes of her face. Not for the first time Lakesh was struck by the delicate, almost elfin beauty of the hybrid race. All in all, they were a beautiful folk, almost too perfect to be real. Their builds were small, slender and gracile. All of their faces had sharp planes, with finely complexioned skin stretched tight over prominent shelves of cheekbones. The craniums were very high and smooth, the ears small and set low on the head. Their back-slanting eyes were large, shadowed by sweeping supraorbital ridges.

Only hair, eye color and slight variations in height differentiated them. Even their expressions were markedly similar—a vast pride, a diffident superiority, authority and even ruthlessness. They were the avatars of the new humans who would inherit the Earth. Or so they believed.

But just like the caste system in place in the villes, the hybrids observed a similar one. If the first phase of human evolution produced a package of adaptations for a particular and distinct way of life, the second phase was an effort to control that way of life by controlling the environment. The focus switched to a cultural evolution from a physical evolution.

The hybrids, at least by way their way of thinking, represented the final phase of human evolution. They created wholesale, planned alterations in living organisms and were empowered to control not only their environment but also the evolution of other species. And at the pinnacle of that evolutionary achievement were the barons, as high above ordinary hybrids bred as servants, like Quavell, as the hybrids were above mere humans.

What made the barons so superior had nothing to do with their physical attributes. The brains of the barons could absorb and process information with exceptional speed, and their cognitive abilities were little short of supernatural.

Almost from the moment the barons emerged from the incubation chambers, they possessed IQs so far beyond the range of standard tests as to render them meaningless. They mastered language in a matter of weeks, speaking in whole sentences. All of Nature's design flaws in the human brain were corrected, modified and improved, specifically the hypothalamus, which regulated the complex biochemical systems of the body.

They could control all autonomic functions of their brains and bodies, even to the manufacture and release of chemicals and hormones. They could speed or slow their heartbeats, increase and decrease the amount of adrenaline in their bloodstreams.

They possessed complete control over that mysterious portion of the brain known as the limbic system, a portion that predark scientists had always known possessed great reserves of electromagnetic power and strength.

Although they were bred for brilliance, all barons had emotional limitations placed upon their enormous intellects. They were captives of their shared Archon hive-mind heritage, captives of a remorseless mind-set that didn't carry with it the simple comprehension of the importance to humans of individual liberty.

Smug in their hybrid arrogance, the baronial oligarchy didn't understand the primal beast buried inside the human psyche, the beast that always gave humans a fair chance of winning in the deadly game of survival of the fittest. Visceral emotions didn't play a large part in the psychologies of the so-called new humans. Even their bursts of passion were of the most rudimentary kind, so complex human emotions like loyalty, self-sacrifice and anger were complete mysteries to them.

Quavell said, "Domi has informed me that neither she nor Kane ever provided you with the entire story of their captivity in the Area 51 installation. I gather Kane was too ashamed to relate the details, and Domi respected his reticence."

Lakesh nodded. "That pretty much encapsulates it, yes."

Quavell propped her elbows on the edge of the table and steepled her fingers beneath her chin. Quietly, she intoned, "When Baron Cobalt captured Kane there, he exacted what he considered a due and just revenge for his part in the destruction of the Dulce installation.''

Lakesh didn't respond. Despite her neutral tone, he detected a hint of anger when she referred to the incident. Her anger was understandable, since the destruction of the installation was a flashpoint, a major cornerstone in the covert war against the baronial oligarchy, an unintentional victory with wide-ranging repercussions.

Not even Lakesh could argue that the hybrid race was as intellectually superior to humankind as the Cro-Magnon was to the Neanderthal, but they paid a heavy price for their superior abilities. Physically, they were fragile, their autoimmune systems at the mercy of infections and diseases that had little effect on the primitive humans they ruled. Nor could they reproduce by intercourse. The nine barons were the products of in vitro fertilization, as were all their offspring.

Therefore the barons were forced to live insulated, isolated existences, cloaking themselves in theatrical trappings that not only added to their semidivine mystique, but also protected them from contamination—both psychological and physical.

Once a year, the oligarchy traveled to an installation beneath the Archuleta Mesa in Dulce, New Mexicom for medical treatments. They visited the installation to receive fresh transfusions of blood and a regimen of biochemical genetic therapy designed to strengthen their autoimmune systems, which granted them another year of life and power.

Grant, Kane, Brigid Baptiste and Domi had inadvertently destroyed the critical medical facility beneath the mesa in New Mexico by simple dint of shooting down an aircraft. The impact of the crash breached the magnetic-field container of the two-tiered fusion generator—or at least that was Brigid's theory. Whatever happened, no one, not even the hybrids who survived, could argue with the cataclysmic aftermath. The result had been akin to unleashing the energy of the Sun inside a root cellar. Although much of the kinetic force and heat were channeled upward and out through the hangar doors, a scorching, smashing wave of destruction swept through the installation. If not for the series of vanadium blast-shield bulkheads, the entire mesa could have come tumbling down.

Lakesh sighed heavily. "So Baron Cobalt tortured him? I feared as much."

"I suppose in some ways what was done to Kane could be construed as torture." Quavell's lips twitched as if she were trying to repress a smile. "The baron determined that inasmuch as Kane was responsible for the crisis, then he would contribute to its alleviation."

Lakesh quirked an eyebrow in puzzlement. "I don't understand."

Quavell took a deep breath. "I will be blunt, employing your own vernacular. Kane was pressed into stud service."

Lakesh's hand, holding his cup midway from the table to his mouth, froze. He stared incredulously at the blank beauty of Quavell's face, then slammed the cup down so quickly hot coffee sloshed out of it onto his hand. He didn't feel the pain. His loud, demanding "What?" was a reedy rasp.

Murmuring in irritation, Domi used napkins to sop up the spreading puddle of coffee. She said, "Don't look so upset, Lakesh. He didn't do it willingly."

"Indeed not." Quavell's placid expression had not altered.

Lakesh dried his hand with a napkin, shaking his head. "It's not Kane's willingness or lack thereof I find difficult to accept. The hybrids don't procreate—at least not in a conventional fashion. I mean—"

He paused, trying to get his racing thoughts in some kind of order. All he could think of to say was, "How?"

Crisply, Quavell said, "A man of your years should know how."

Lakesh slitted his eyes, trying to control his sudden surge of anger. "Very droll," he replied sourly. "You know damn good and well what I mean."

Quavell bowed her head at the rebuke. "I do. I apologize. Humor is still a new concept for me. Shall I explain?"

"Yes," Lakesh bit out, his tone brooking no debate. "You shall."

In a cool, clinical voice, Quavell began to talk. Lakesh knew the back story, but he allowed Quavell to tell it in the hopes that some new information would come forth. After the destruction of the mesa installation, the barons held an emergency council that dealt with only one topic—the survival of their people. Baron Cobalt, whom Lakesh had once served as a high adviser, put forth a proposal that would not only save the hybrids, but also elevate him to a new position of power.

The barons really didn't have much of a choice. After the destruction of the New Mexico medical facilities, they were left without access to the ectogenesis techniques of fetal development outside the womb, so it wasn't simply the baronial oligarchy in danger of extinction, but the entire hybrid race.

Baron Cobalt presented his fellow barons with a way to stave off extinction by occupying Area 51, but only if he was elevated to a position of the highest authority.

Area 51 was the predark unclassified code name for a training area on Nellis Air Force base, also known as Groom Lake, or "Dreamland." Contained in the dry lake bed was a vast installation, extending deep into the desert floor. Only a few of the buildings were aboveground. Area 51 was more than just a military installation; it served as an international base operated by a consortium from many countries. Baron Cobalt proposed that its operation be overseen by a consortium of barons, which in turn would be overseen by him.

Since Area 51's history was intertwined with rumors of alien involvement, Baron Cobalt had used its medical facilities as a substitute for those destroyed in

New Mexico. No one could be sure if the aliens referred to by the predark conspiracy theorists were the Archons, but more than likely they were, inasmuch as the equipment that still existed was already designed to be compatible with the hybrid metabolisms.

In any event, Baron Cobalt reactivated the installation, turning it into a processing and treatment center, and transferred the surviving human and hybrid personnel from the Dulce facility.

Still the medical treatments that addressed the congenital autoimmune system deficiencies of the hybrids were not enough to insure the continued survival of the race. The necessary equipment and raw material to implement procreation had yet to be installed. Baron Cobalt unilaterally decided that the conventional means of conception was the only option to keep the hybrid race alive.

When Baron Cobalt dangled the medical treatments before his fellow barons like a carrot on a stick, rather than share them freely, war was the inevitable result—particularly after Sam, supported by none other than Balam, hijacked not only Cobalt's plan but also the title of imperator.

Kane and Domi were unaware of the appearance of Sam and the return of Balam when they penetrated the Area 51 facility and were captured. Domi was found by a little group of insurgents led by Quavell, while Kane was sentenced by Baron Cobalt to what amounted to stud service.

According to Quavell, during Kane's two weeks of

captivity, he was fed a steady diet of protein laced with a stimulant of the catecholamine group. It affected the renal blood supply, increasing cardiac output without increasing the need for cardiac oxygen consumption.

Combined with the food loaded with protein to speed sperm production, the stimulant provided Kane with hours of high energy. Since he was forced to achieve erection and ejaculation six times a day every two days, his energy and sperm count had to be preternaturally high, even higher than was normal for him.

Although Quavell didn't mention it, Lakesh knew the main reason Kane was chosen to impregnate the female hybrids was simply due to the fact male hybrids were incapable of engaging in conventional acts of procreation, at least physically. Their organs of reproduction were so underdeveloped as to be vestigial.

Kane wasn't the first human male to be pressed into service. There had been other men before him, but they had performed unsatisfactorily due to their terror of the hybrids. At first the females selected for the process donned wigs and wore cosmetics in order to appear more human to the trapped sperm donors. The men had to be strapped down and, even after the application of an aphrodisiac gel, had difficulty maintaining an erection.

Quavell confided to Kane that not every hybrid agreed with the baronial policy toward humanity, and helped him and Domi escape.

Lakesh stared at her skeptically. "And no one in Area 51 suspected your complicity in their escape?"

Quavell shook her head. "Why should they? When the combined forces of Barons Sharpe and Snakefish attacked, it was assumed Kane and Domi escaped during the chaos. And there was chaos."

"Take my word for it," Domi interjected.

"How were you able to effect your own escape?" he demanded. "How did you know where to find us?"

"Is that really important to you, Lakesh?"

"It's not only important to me," he countered tersely, "but I know such a subject will be very important to Kane, upon his return."

"If that is so, when he returns, I shall tell him." Her voice carried a note of finality, an unspoken declaration the discussion on that particular topic was closed.

"How many are like you?" he asked. "I mean, how many females did Kane impregnate?"

"As far as I know, I am the only one."

"Then it seems to me," he said, striving to sound casual, "that you would be watched constantly, pampered even."

Quavell fixed him with a calm, steady stare, but Lakesh felt his nape hairs tingling. "Perhaps I was. But with the advent of the imperator and the fall of Cobaltville, everything is different. The child I carry may very well be a symbol that the old ways are dying, but that does not mean everyone wants the old ways to perish. The barons would continue to use humans as they used Kane, but as enslaved breeding stock.''

''And the progeny born of these unions?''

''Genetic material, to be processed and used to keep the oligarchy alive. That is all.''

''That doesn't seem to fit with the imperator's agenda,'' Lakesh said. ''Sam is fixated on unification, just as Balam's folk and the barons are, but with a different objective. His stated intent is to end the tyranny of the barons and unify both hybrid and human and build a new Earth. If indeed female hybrids can conceive offspring by human males, then a continued division between the so-called old and new human is pretty much without merit.''

Quavell sighed. ''In the coming months, the entire structure of the baronies will change. Everything you know, everything you think you know, will be obsolete.''

''Curious,'' Lakesh said, not bothering to soften the hard edge of sarcasm in his voice. ''I was told the same thing by Sam.''

''The imperator is being groomed for the role of conqueror.'' Quavell's tone was flat, confident.

''That may be so,'' Lakesh pointed out, ''but he's only a child.''

''He's also not human. Nor is he one of my people. Already he has made considerable inroads into toppling the old order and enfranchising his forces.''

''But not all the barons support him.''

''True,'' Quavell conceded with a nod, ''but those

who do not will not undertake resistance against him, either. Even if all the baronies united against the imperator, it would require months to prepare any kind of military campaign and they must do so in secret, else they would not have access to the medical facility in Dreamland.

"Also, they would have to subdue the civil unrest that has been growing in their villes, and secretly supply their forces and integrate the infrastructure necessary for a full-scale war—all without revealing these actions to the imperator."

"You seem to know a great deal," Lakesh observed. "Although much of it sounds like speculation, drawn from inference."

"Perhaps." Quavell cocked her head at him at a quizzical angle. "However, in my estimation, you are in no position to discount what I have told you and what I have yet to tell you."

Lakesh's lips compressed in a tight line. "And in my estimation, you're in no position to set down conditions. We here in Cerberus have a decision to make about you, Quavell. I haven't made up my mind whether to have Sky Dog take you back to the foothills and let you fend for yourself, or keep you here as a prisoner. At this juncture, the choice is mine to make."

"I can be a valuable resource," Quavell stated, "presupposing your inborn prejudices toward my kind does not blind you to that."

Lakesh gritted his teeth. He found it harder and

harder to leash his anger. He didn't know if his loss of self-control was due to his rejuvenating hormone levels or whether he had simply had a surfeit of hybrid arrogance, hybrid diffidence.

In a voice pitched so low it was almost a growl, Lakesh said, "You're a good one to talk about prejudices, Quavell. Doesn't your kind refer to my kind as 'apelings' and 'ape-kin'?"

Without waiting for her to reply, he snapped, "Your kind is an evolutionary dead end. The new human depends solely on the apeling for survival. You're parasites, living off our essences."

Quavell sat silently, eyes locked on Lakesh's, not objecting to the charges he leveled. At length she said, "I will not presume to debate you. My folk are not the ultimate in evolution, either physically or mentally. Indeed, on the scale of our forebears, those you call the Archons, our collective intellects might be far below average."

Lakesh blinked in surprise at Quavell's serenely spoken admission of fallibility. "Yes," she went on, "we were indoctrinated to believe that the old humans had reached the limit of their development and it was time for a younger, more vital race to occupy Earth. I and a few others no longer subscribe to that belief.

"The restrictions placed on your race were artificial—therefore, we had no way to know your true potential, just as you had no way to explore it. Humanity was forced to live down to its lowest impulses.

And though force can subdue and even destroy, it cannot aid development.''

Quavell touched her belly, then her heart and her high forehead. ''Here, here and here lies the true path for both of our peoples to learn our potentials, Mohandas Lakesh Singh. Old and new human alike must cease seeking power and devote themselves to the development and fulfillment of life.''

Lakesh stared at her, shaken and impressed by the sound of conviction in her quietly spoken declaration. Domi smiled, first at Quavell, then at Lakesh. ''Well,'' she announced, ''I've made my choice.''

Not removing his gaze from Quavell, Lakesh nodded slowly. ''So have I.''

He pushed back his chair, rose and extended a hand toward her. ''Let's find you some permanent quarters.''

Chapter 10

To the surprise but not necessarily the relief of Grant, Brigid and Kane, Maccan ordered them released. The crimson tint had faded from his eyes, but he still dangled Megaera's severed head before his face. Pursing his lips, he blew it an impish kiss, then wheeled around toward the door.

"Come with me," he commanded. "'Tis time to separate the sheep from the rams, the wheat from the chaff and the truly mad from the merely deluded."

He stood beside the doorway as his people trooped through it. Fixing his huge eyes on Brigid, he said, "I'll be sending an escort to fetch you very soon, woman. Then you may deliver my gift."

Underhanded, he tossed Megaera's head toward Brigid. She made no effort to catch it. Instead, she swiftly sidestepped and the head thumped to the floor, where it rolled to the bulkhead like an awkward ball. Maccan uttered his sob of a laugh, then swept through the door, his long scarf flapping like a ragged cloak. The heavy metal portal slid shut behind him with the unmistakable clack of lock solenoids catching and holding.

For a long moment, none of the three people spoke.

Then Kane gently nudged Megaera's head with a foot and remarked conversationally, "The legends don't say much about the Tuatha de Danaan being such slobs."

"Don't," Brigid snapped, turning her back and staring up through the transparent domed ceiling.

"I don't see Megaera's death as worth mourning," Kane said. "She tried to kill you, kill all of us at one time or another."

Grant folded his arms over his broad chest and muttered, "She was fused-out, Kane. Driven crazy by living up here, then snatched to Earth by Sindri and sent back again. She may have deserved to die, but not like this."

Kane regarded him with puzzled eyes. "You, too? Since when did you become so softhearted?"

Grant whirled on him, lips peeled back from his teeth in a silent snarl. "Shut up. Shut the fuck up. I killed at least four men over the past few hours, and I still don't know why."

Kane glared at him, choking down a profane comeback. He realized Grant looked haggard, his eyes netted with red, the lines on either side of his nose etched deep. All of them were bone weary, exhausted, having gone without food and water for at least a day. All of their tempers were short.

Kane moved across the circular room, avoiding the pool of Megaera's blood, and made a show of examining a glass-covered instrument panel. The display surfaces glowed with words and icons. Although he wasn't familiar with the technical terminology, at least the language was English. He started to press one of the underlit icons, then thought better of it. "This place is of human manufacture," he said. "Maybe part of the DEVIL control systems, if Maccan's bad pun had a basis in reality."

"Maccan," echoed Grant in a guttural growl. He strode over to Brigid. "Nobody said anything about the Danaan being up here. It was Enki we were worried about."

Brigid's eyes flashed with momentary anger at the accusatory note in Grant's statement. "I have to admit finding a Danaan on the Moon is the last thing I expected. I was prepared for Annunaki since we saw Enlil's body and the image captured by the vid probe. I was convinced of their reality. But I always assumed the Tuatha de Danaan were long, long gone."

"Most of them probably are," put in Kane, sitting on the edge of a console. "Let's compare war stories. Maybe we can come up with a why and figure out what the hell is going on here."

Curtly, Grant related all that had befallen him since the cave-in at the cavern. When he mentioned Cleve and Nora, both Brigid and Kane raised their eyebrows, but didn't ask any questions.

Kane and Brigid took turns relating their travails in the citadel. When they finished, Grant blew out a disgusted breath. "None of this makes any damn sense at all. We've been chased around like rats in a maze since we got here, and we still don't know who is what and what is who.''

"Yeah," agreed Kane gloomily. "Philboyd and his group didn't say anything about a Tuatha de Danaan presence here. Maybe they weren't aware of it. We've been barking up the wrong red herring.''

Brigid cast him a glance of exasperation. "We've been barking up—oh, never mind. Mix all the metaphors you want.''

Kane gave her a narrow-eyed stare. "What?''

"What about this Maccan asshole?'' Grant demanded. "If he's one of the Danaan, why did Megaera call him a demon? Aren't they supposed to be the good guys?''

Brigid frowned. "I don't know what gave you that idea.''

Kane pushed himself to his feet. "You did," he declared, a hint of angry challenge in his voice. "You told us all about how the Danaan came to Earth and settled in Ireland and protected humanity from the nasty, conniving Annunaki.''

"All I did," she shot back impatiently, "was to repeat what I was told. I learned the history from the Speaking Stone of Cascorach. Since it was a Danaan artifact, it stands to reason it would be programmed with their own personal slant on their past. Obviously, it would be favorable.''

Kane dry-scrubbed his hair in angry frustration. "Yeah, but since then, you've studied all the legends and the myths about both races, the snake faces and the pointy ears.''

She nodded. "Legends and myths. Those are the key words. Not facts.''

"Did you ever come across anything about Maccan?'' asked Grant.

"As a matter of fact,'' Brigid replied, "I did.''

When she added nothing more, Kane demanded, "Well?''

She shrugged. "Legends, like I said.''

"Even fairy tales would be better than what we're working with now,'' retorted Kane. "Which is precisely nothing.''

Absently, Brigid combed her fingers through her tangled hair. "I suppose we may be able to correlate some of the lore with what we've seen so far and come up with a provisional hypothesis.''

"Go to it, then,'' Grant rumbled. "It's not like we've got anything better to do at the moment.''

Brigid nodded and leaned against a console. "The myth that gave a unified basis to the lore of the Tuatha de Danaan was that of a primordial conflict between a divine race and a demonic race, in Gaelic called the Fomhoire or the Formorians.''

The name struck a chord of recognition within Kane, but he decided not say anything.

"The Formorians had divided Ireland into five provinces, which all converged on Balor's Hill.'' Brigid looked toward Kane. "Who knows who he is.''

"Evil-eye.'' Kane didn't elaborate on how he knew

or how he had fought a half-blind, maimed giant of a man who might have been a reincarnation of the legendary Formorian chieftain.

Brigid continued, "They practiced strange magical rites in their hill forts and continued to hold the country in a tyrannical grip until the coming of the Tuatha de Danaan.

"The Danaan are described as arriving on Ireland from the sky. The four cities that they originated were Findias, Gorias, Murias and Falias. The Danaan were skilled in poetry and magic. With them they brought four great treasures, Nuada's sword, Lugh's terrible spear, the Dagda's cauldron and the Stone of Fal, the Lia Fail or Stone of Destiny."

"We know all that stuff," Grant broke in impatiently. "Strongbow had stolen all of those artifacts and kept them in a vault in New London's Ministry of Defense."

Brigid acted as if she hadn't heard. "The Tuatha de Danaan met the armies of the Formorians on the Plain of the Sea near Leinster. They bargained for peace and the division of Ireland, but their offer was refused. On summer solstice, the armies of the two factions met near the pass of Benlevi. For four days, groups of single combatants fought. The Danaan chief, Nuada, lost his hand in battle, but the Formorian king, Bochaid, was killed and Prince Bress took his place. In a peace gesture, the Danaan offered the surviving Formorians one-fifth of the Ireland, and they chose Connaught."

Kane and Grant exchanged weary glances but neither man decided to break into Brigid's dissertation. If focusing on ancient history kept her mind from dwelling on the brutal murder she had witnessed, then it was all to the good.

"Diancecht, physician of the Danaan, made Nuada a marvelous silver hand," Brigid continued. "It could move like a real one, so it's apparent the Danaan had expertise in prosthetics. In an attempt for permanent peace with the Formorians, the Danaan asked Prince Bress to become the king of both peoples and thus unite them. Bress agreed and married Brigit, the daughter of the Dagda, the high Danaan ruler. At the same time, Cian, son of Diancecht married Ethniu, daughter of the Formorian general, Balor.

"Bress promised to abdicate if his rule ever displeased the Danaan, but he soon began to tax them into poverty. His people began to victimize and enslave the Celtic tribes, and so the Danaan insisted Bress abdicate his position. He did so, but he also declared war. The Danaan were victorious, driving the surviving Formorians into the sea."

"And where does Maccan enter into this mix of arranged marriages, crawfishing on promises and war?" Kane demanded.

"I'm getting to that," replied Brigid. "Maccan was a chieftain among the Tuatha de Danaan. He resided at the tumulus of Newgrange. An alternative appellation for him was Aonghus, which means 'true vigor' or 'young son.' Maccan corresponds to the Welsh mythical figure Mabon and to the British Celtic Maponos, who was identified in inscriptions with the Greek god Apollo.'' She gave Kane a meaningful glance. ''He was associated with a golden harp that made irresistibly sweet music, which turned enemies into allies.''

Kane nodded in understanding. ''Go on.''

''He came to possess Newgrange by tricking his father, the king of the Danaan. Maccan was the symbol of youth that denied the process of aging. He was present at the second battle of Moytirra where the Firbolgs were defeated.''

''And so,'' Grant ventured, ''after that, he decided to move to the Moon?''

Brigid glowered at him. ''I'm telling you all of this as a way to put the legends into some sort of historical order. It's as much for me as for you and Kane.''

''Thanks,'' Kane said dryly. ''But we've known for some time the Danaan were supposed to be an aristocratic race of scientists, warriors and poets, preferring their privacy and able to make themselves invisible—but keeping in touch with the human race.''

He paused, then added musingly, ''But none of the legends ever say where they came from. Or where they went.''

''That's true,'' Brigid admitted. ''But internal evidence indicates the Danaan were a very old race even when they established a colony on Earth, at least twenty thousand years ago, maybe even more. Everything about them is both simple and complex. The myths show the Danaan frequently interbred with other races for diplomatic reasons, so they were well versed in the politics of compromise.''

"Which makes them seem human, at any rate," grunted Grant.

"Yes," Brigid agreed. "But they're not. None of the old myth cycles ever say they were human. An atmosphere of magic and mystery was deliberately fostered by the Danaan so the indigenous Celts wouldn't become overly familiar with them. In post-medieval literature the Danaan are represented as having both salutary and demonic groups among them.

"They were thus suitable as powerful beings to be introduced into a variety of literary narratives. As well as being a vestige of the idea of a divine people, the Danaan were also a version of the ancient concept of quasi-human communities living beside the human one. And as such they became the source of fairy lore.''

Kane snorted. "If Maccan is the average representative, they're anything but fairies.''

Brigid acknowledged his comment with a wry smile. "They—or entities very much like the Danaan—showed up in the UFO lore of the twentieth century. Researchers referred to them the Nordics, primarily because both men and women wore their fair hair long. They were often seen working side-by-side with the so-called Grays, who we now know were Balam's people. The First Folk, Maccan called them.''

"The First Folk," Kane repeated grimly. "The off-spring of Annunaki and Danaan. The Archons."

All of the Cerberus exiles had believed the oligarchy of barons was under the sway of the Archon Directorate, a nonhuman race that allegedly influenced human affairs through political chaos, staged wars, famines, plagues and natural disasters. The nuclear apocalypse of 2001 was all part of the Archon Directorate's strategy. With the destruction of social structures and severe depopulation, the Archons established the nine barons and distributed predark technology among them to consolidate their power over Earth and its disenfranchised, spiritually beaten human inhabitants.

But over the past couple of years, all of the Cerberus exiles had learned that the elaborate back story was all a ruse, bits of truth mixed in with outrageous fiction. The Archon Directorate did not exist except as a vast cover story, created in the twentieth century and grown larger with each succeeding generation. The only so-called Archon on Earth was Balam, the last of an extinct race that had once shared the planet with humankind.

After three years of imprisonment in the Cerberus redoubt, Balam finally revealed the truth behind the Directorate and the hybridization program initiated centuries before. Even more shocking was Balam's assertion that he and his ancient folk were of human stock, not alien but alienated.

Though they still didn't know how much to believe,

none of the Cerberus personnel any longer subscribed to the fatalistic belief that the human race had had its day and only extinction lay ahead. Balam had indicated that was not true, only another control mechanism.

Nevertheless, the barons, the half-human hybrids spawned from Balam's DNA, still ruled. Lakesh had learned that the DNA of Balam's folk was infinitely adaptable, malleable, its segments able to achieve a near seamless sequencing pattern with whatever biological material was spliced to it. In some ways, it acted like a virus, overwriting other genetic codes, picking and choosing the best human qualities to enhance. Their DNA could be tinkered with to create endless variations, adjusted and fine-tuned.

Strongbow had led them all to believe that Annunaki DNA possessed the same qualities, so it was possible some people on the Moon were mixtures of human and Tuatha de Danaan.

"None of this is really new information," Kane said darkly. "The Danaan, the Annunaki, the Archons, all fighting for possession of Earth at one time or another, while we stupid humans run around trying not to get squashed. Then comes the nuke and the barons, the bastard grandchildren of the snake faces and the pointy ears walk away with the entire prize."

Kane knew he was oversimplifying, but he didn't care, and neither did Brigid or Grant. And now it appeared as if there were exiles thousands and thousands of miles from their home worlds—not just the human colonists, but the Danaan and the Annunaki, forever separated from realms unknown and perhaps even unimaginable.

Kane grappled with a surge of reason-corroding fear. It was not fear of death that suddenly oppressed him; it was a soul-deep dread they would fail in their mission. Since he no longer had a clear picture of the mission objective, he began to doubt his skills were up to the challenge.

A series of mechanical clicks from the door commanded all of their attention. Reflexively, they moved to the center of the room, standing shoulder to shoulder. With a pneumatic hiss, the thick metal portal slid aside.

"Must be your escort," Kane side-mouthed to Brigid.

Three people hesitantly entered the observation chamber. Grant recognized all three of them, although only one was familiar to Brigid and Kane. Nora, Cleve and Philboyd looked around the circular room in bewilderment.

Brigid said quietly, "To quote our host, 'Welcome to the devil's playground.'"

Chapter 11

Philboyd's eyes blinked rapidly, like the wings of a butterfly in the throes of heatstroke. In fitful jerks, he turned his head, gaping at the transparent dome, the lighted display boards and then at the puddle of Megaera's blood on the floor. When his eyes fixed on her severed head they widened, narrowed, then closed altogether.

The door rumbled shut, and the lock solenoids caught loudly. Philboyd jumped, bleating wordlessly in fear. Trying to avoid tramping through the blood, he nearly collided with Grant, who put out his hands and steadied him.

Philboyd was a tall man, a little over six feet, long limbed and lanky of build. He wore a faded green, zippered coverall. Blond-white hair was swept back from a receding hairline. He wore black-rimmed eyeglasses. The right lenses showed a spiderweb pattern of cracks. His cheeks appeared to be pitted with the sort of scars associated with chronic teenage acne.

Staring at Grant, then at Kane and Brigid, Philboyd husked out, "You're alive. All of you are alive. I didn't expect it."

"Yeah," Grant agreed. "We're alive and so are

you. And we didn't expect you and so we want to know why you're here. We left you at the mining complex."

Philboyd swallowed hard, his Adam's apple rising and falling. He wiped at the sheen of sweat on his face and winced when his fingers encountered a purple welt on his forehead. "That's where those soldiers—Saladin and his bunch—found me. They must have backtracked the heat emissions of my flitter-gig and—"

He broke off and exclaimed, "My flitter-gig! Where is it?"

"It's on the far side of the Sea of Ice," Kane said. "And it's very broken. Sorry."

Philboyd began blinking again, this time in an obvious effort to hold back tears. The flitter-gig was the astrophysicist's pet name for one of the three of the TAVs out of the fleet of ten that had once been part of the Manitius colony's stock. Finding it in a salvage yard, he had repaired and customized it, referring to it as a classic, one of the secret prototypes made back in the 1990s. Grant, Kane and Brigid had used it to fly to the Great Chasm, but it had crash-landed on the edge of the Mare Frigoris.

Addressing the other two people, Brigid said, "I presume you know each other. My name is Baptiste. This is Kane. You've met Grant. You must be Nora and Cleve."

Nora nodded, raking her hair out of her eyes.

Cleve grunted. "Yeah, we know each other. Philboyd was our department supervisor on the project, back in the old days when we still pulled pay.''

His lips twisted beneath his whiskers in a poor attempt at a smirk of superiority. ''But we didn't need Phil old boy when we put the DEVIL control nexus back online.''

Philboyd spun, eyes gleaming with a wild, incredulous light. He started to say something to Cleve, then shouldered Brigid aside so he could lean over the display consoles. In a strangulated voice, he said, ''Oh, my dear God…PDM energy valving system shows green…EM spectrum handoff nominal…power level on standby.''

He wheeled back around, his shoulders shaking, his mouth working. Spittle flecked his lips. ''You dumb stupid fucks…you've done it! God in heaven—why?''

The last word came out as a screech of anguish and fury. He hurled himself across the room at Cleve. The two men clutched at each other and exchanged a clumsy flurry of blows. They reeled back and forth, gasping out curses. Nora shrank back against the door, crying out both their names.

Kane and Grant exchanged weary, disgusted glances and stepped forward to separate the two combatants. Grant secured Philboyd in a full nelson and jerked him backward while Kane twisted Cleve's right arm up behind his back and applied pressure to the shoulder socket, forcing the swearing man to his knees.

''That's enough!'' shouted Grant.

Philboyd struggled in Grant's arms. "You don't understand! He's put the means of global annihilation into the hands of a lunatic!"

"And which lunatic is that?" Brigid demanded angrily. "Enki, who we've yet to see, or Maccan who enjoys decapitating old women?"

"Enki, of course!" sputtered Philboyd.

"Maccan, who the hell else?" Cleve managed to grunt.

Kane groaned. "Oh, for God's sake."

He suddenly relinquished his grip on Cleve, and the man almost collapsed face first to the deck. Kane kicked him in the rump and barked, "Get up."

He moved to Nora and grabbed her roughly by the forearm, dragging her into the center of the room. Kane swept his cold eyes over Cleve, Philboyd and Nora. In a low, dangerous tone, heavy with menace, he said, "Somebody better start talking. And when they do, they damn fucking well better make sense or they'll wish Maccan and Enki were in here instead of me."

Grant released Philboyd, who rolled his shoulders and rubbed the back of his neck. He eyed Kane reproachfully. "I told you everything I know."

Brigid bit out, "Not exactly. You claimed that after the rebellion led by the first Megaera, all the scientists were killed. Only you, Mariah, Eduardo and Neukirk were left. They captured you and put you into cryostasis."

Grant's eyebrows met at the bridge of his nose.

"That's right. You said you four were the main DEVIL project team. Megaera needed you—or she figured she would need you at some future date, so you were put into cold storage."

Kane nodded toward Nora and Cleve. "You didn't mention these two."

"That's because I thought they were dead," Philboyd replied defensively. "Besides, they weren't the main DEVIL team. They were part of an ancillary group, utility infielders."

Kane didn't understand the reference, but he didn't say so. "You claimed you and your team were revived a little over a year ago. The DEVIL platform's positioning system had malfunctioned and Megaera expected you to fix it."

Philboyd nodded. "That's right. But instead, we downloaded all the secondary analogs from our mainframes, and changed all the access codes, targeting and trajectory programs, recognition signals and launch commands. All the primary codes were rewritten, and any attempts to delete the new program resulted in an immediate lockout. Like I said, we modified one of the base's life hutch habitats to triangulate and control the DEVIL platform's orbital position. Megaera didn't know there was a main data core."

"You didn't let us know, either," snapped Brigid.

"I didn't think it was important. We controlled the platform from the habitat station. I didn't think this complex was even active any longer."

He shifted his gaze to Nora and Cleve and his face

contorted in anger. "But you managed to undo everything we've done."

"It's not like we had any goddamn choice!" Cleve bellowed. "Maybe if you'd bothered searching for us—"

"What the hell are you talking about?" Grant demanded.

Nora said matter-of-factly, "Another thing he neglected to mention is how four of us volunteered to go out and secure the DEVIL nexus, to make sure the modified life hutch station would be the only means of controlling and communicating with the platform."

"I didn't mention it because you never came back!" brayed Philboyd. "That was over eight months ago!"

"Four of you?" Kane inquired.

"Humphries was killed shortly after we arrived here," Nora answered. "An accident—he fell into one of the thermal vents in the cavern. Dave Janiesch went missing only a day or two ago. We don't know what happened to him."

Grant thought back to the man who saved him from the carnobot in the Blue Gallery, but he decided to keep the incident to himself.

Cleve nodded toward Philboyd. "We thought the DEVIL team was dead, too. We left Manitius base in the middle of a Fury raid. Our plan was to make our way overland, figuring Megaera wouldn't think we'd take such a risk. Right as we entered the air lock, we saw the Furies and carnobots."

Fixing an accusatory stare on Philboyd's face, he added grimly, "Through the porthole I saw Eduardo go down, his face torn to pieces. You can't blame us for thinking you were dead and not coming back or even trying to get a message to you."

Philboyd's shoulders sagged in resignation. "I suppose not. He was seriously injured and carries a gruesome scar, but he's still alive."

Cleve sighed. "That's something. Well, this entire set of circumstances has been the cock-up of cock-ups, hasn't it? Like a very, very long and very unfunny Benny Hill skit."

Neither Kane, Brigid nor Grant recognized the name of Benny Hill, but they assumed it was an enigmatic reference to a person alive before the nukecaust. But at the mention of his name, some of the angry tension between the three physicists ebbed a bit, and they even tried smiling feebly at one another.

"If it means anything," Philboyd said, "I'm glad you two made it."

"We managed to make the trek overland safely enough," Nora said. "But when we entered the citadel we were captured by Saladin and his boys."

"And who the hell is he?" asked Grant.

Philboyd said, "I figure him to be one of the descendants of the Manitius military personnel."

Nora nodded. "But he's not part of Megaera's group of fanatics. He and his group have apparently occupied the citadel and this area for a long, long time. They guarded it from the Furies."

"Why?" Kane demanded.

Cleve touched his bandaged head and winced. "Megaera's sect believed the DEVIL process was created by Annunaki science, and therefore it belonged to Enki to do with as he willed. Since human scientists took it off-line, they felt human scientists had the responsibility to reactivate it."

"And Saladin didn't agree?" inquired Brigid.

"He didn't care one way or another," Cleve answered. "He had a vague awareness of it, a general idea of its function, as did everyone born in the colony. It wasn't until Maccan showed up and decided he wanted it for himself that Saladin made it his personal crusade."

"Showed up?" echoed Kane. "Explain."

"I wish I could," Nora said. "But showed up isn't really applicable. Resurrected would be the correct term."

"Goddammit!" Grant spit in angry frustration. "Is the citadel property of the Annunaki or the Tuatha de Danaan?"

Cleve favored him with a bleak stare. "You want a quick, easy answer, but we don't have one. All we have is speculation."

"Oh, good," Kane commented with icy sarcasm. "We always enjoy risking our asses on speculation. How did you know?"

Cleve ignored the remark. Nora toyed with her tangled hair nervously, winding locks around her fingers. "Apparently, there is a lot of history between the Annunaki and the Danaan. There was a terrible war between them—"

"Yeah, we know all about it," Grant interrupted harshly. "Move on from there."

"After they came to terms," Nora stated, "they established outposts on the planets in the solar system. For some reason, the Annunaki couldn't return to their home world…Nibiru, I believe it's called. I think, but I can't be sure, that these outposts already existed. Which planet belonged to what race, I have no idea.

"At any rate, part of the pact between the Danaan and the Annunaki was an agreement that Man should stay on the planet of his birth. Both races feared that humanity would take its internecine squabbles to the stars."

Kane snorted disdainfully. "They're good ones to talk."

A smile tugged at the corners of Nora's mouth. "A custodial race, who they called the First Folk, was put in charge of Earth. A watch post of sorts was established here, on the Moon. It was Annunaki territory, their royal cemetery, a necropolis. I think Enki volunteered to act as its caretaker."

Brigid, Kane and Grant retained vivid recollections of passing through a mausoleum of mummified Annunaki remains in the Great Chasm, so they knew that part of Nora's story was true.

"The citadel was enclosed by a dome," the woman went on, "but it was destroyed centuries and centuries ago."

"By whom?" Brigid asked.

"Dissenters. The First Folk were the result of mingled genetic material between Danaan, Annunaki and
superior humans. They were created as a bridge between the two races and to act as their ears and eyes
on Earth...the watchdogs of Man."

"The First Folk were the dissenters?" Kane's tone
was full of disbelief. "They destroyed the protective
dome? Why?"

Nora shook her head. "The First Folk were charged
by their forebears to restrict human development, but
as the centuries wore on, they felt it was blasphemous
to do so. After all, they carried the genes of homo
sapiens, as well. They felt it was a crime to curtail
Man's wisdom, to hide new sciences from him, to
direct him away from new inventions, particularly
those that would enrich the planet as a whole."

Images, fragments of memories wheeled through
Kane's mind. He remembered the history lesson
Balam had telepathically imparted to him over a year
before, regarding the First Folk's civilization. Balam
referred to them as the root race, and he showed Kane
how they had established many settlements all over
Earth, spreading out from the primary center deep in
the heart of Asia.

The people were cast in the mold of humanity, but
they were not human as Kane defined the term. They
were dome-skulled slender creatures, very tall and
graceful. Their tranquil eyes were big and opalescent,
their flesh tones a pale blue.

They were a branch on the mysterious tree of evolution, yet the twigs of humanity sprouted from their bough. They were a bridge, not only between two races, but flowing within them, mixed with the blood of their nonhuman forebears was the blood of humanity.

The First Folk were mortal, though exceptionally long-lived. Like the humanity to which they were genetically connected, they loved and experienced joy and sadness. Their cities were centers of learning, and the citizens did not suffer from want. They knew no enemies; they had no need to fight for survival. As the end result of a fight for survival between their ancestors, the beings had been born to live on the world of humans and guide them away from the path of war, which had nearly destroyed Earth.

Their duty was to keep the ancient secrets of their ancestors alive, yet not propagate the same errors as their forebears, especially in their dealings with Man, to whom they were inextricably bound.

Humanity was still struggling to overcome a global cataclysm, the Deluge brought about by Enlil, striving again for civilization. The graceful folk in the cities, the outposts, did what they could to help them rebuild. They insinuated themselves into schools, into political circles, prompting and assisting men into making the right decisions.

They sought out humans of vision, humans with superior traits. They mingled their blood with them, initiated them into their secrets and advised them. On many continents, new centers of learning arose, empires and dynasties spread out carrying the seeds of civilization.

"At some point," Nora continued, "a leader of the Folk—Lam, I think I heard him called—sought to convince the Annunaki and Danaan representatives to allow humanity to grow and evolve without strictures. Instead, they threatened to destroy humanity again, as Enlil had done millennia before.

"The First Folk knew their forebears had too many weapons in their arsenals, stolen and adapted from other worlds they had visited and exploited, to be able to defend Earth against them. They didn't have the resources to fight an all-out war, but now that they had aroused their forebears suspicions, they had to take action."

Nora paused, frowning. "I'm not clear on this, but apparently the First Folk resorted to subterfuge. They employed something, an energy called 'protplanic force.' It destroyed the dome over the citadel here and pretty much demolished the settlement. Enki took refuge in some sort of suspended-animation canister, a stasis unit. There was retaliation, a blow-back effect, a reverse reaction the First Folk hadn't foreseen. It nearly destroyed the Earth—and certainly decimated their civilization."

Kane sensed Brigid looking at him, her eyebrows raised questioningly. He glanced her way and nodded in confirmation. "That ties in with what Balam told—showed—me."

"I thought as much," she replied. "But now we know how the cataclysms happened."

Kane recalled Balam's psionic images, about how the magnetic poles of the Earth shifted and the great glaciers and ice centers at the poles withdrew toward new positions. Vast portions of the ocean floor rose, while equally vast landmasses sank beneath the waves. The configuration of the Earth altered.

Convulsions shook mountains, the nights blazed with flame-spouting volcanoes. Earthquakes shook the walls and towers of the First Folk's cities. Their proud, thousand-year-old civilization crashed into ruins within a day. Many of the Folk died quickly, others lingered in a state of near-death for years. The vast knowledge of their ancestors, the technical achievements bequeathed to them, became their only means of survival.

They had no choice but to change themselves with the world, to alter their physiologies. Using ancient techniques, the race transformed itself in order to survive. Muscle tissue became less dense, motor reflexes sharpened, optic capacities broadened. A new range of abilities developed, allowing them to live on a planet whose magnetic fields had changed, whose weather was drastically unpredictable.

Their need for sustenance veered away from the near depleted resources of their environment. They found new means of nourishment other than the ingestion of bulk matter. The proud, unified race of teachers and artisans degenerated, scattered, and became a lost tribe skulking in the wilderness. The survivors had no choice but to spread out from the cities.

A few of them stayed, trying to adapt, the land changing them before they changed the land. Their physical appearance altered further as they retreated. The changes wrought were subtle, gradual. In adapting themselves to the changing conditions of the planet, they who had been graceful neogods became small, furtive shadow dwellers.

Only a handful of the folk remained among the lichen-covered stone walls of their once proud city. The new generations born to them were distortions of what they had been. The weak died before they could produce offspring, and the infant mortality rate was frightful for a thousand years. They did not leave the ruins to find out how humanity had fared in the aftermath of the catastrophes.

Humankind adapted much faster to the postcatastrophic world, and new generations began to explore, to conquer. They conquered with a vengeance and ruthlessness and spilled oceans of blood. In their explorations, they found their way into the city—men in leather harnesses, helmets of bronze, bearing bows, spears and swords.

They brought war to the stunted survivors of the catastrophes, viewing them not as their progenitors had, as mentors or semidivine oracles, but as things—neither man, beast nor demon, but imbued with characteristics superior and inferior to all three.

The men pursued the small folk through the vast

ruins of their city, slaughtering and butchering, until they had no choice but to fight back. The farther they had retreated from the world, the greater had grown their powers in other ways. The humans fled in blind panic, but the folk knew others would inevitably return.

Savage humanity had not been defeated, only beaten back. They knew they could not hope to defeat humankind, but they determined to control them. If nothing else, they still possessed the monumental pride of their race and devotion to the continuity of their people. To accomplish that, they knew they had to retreat even further.

Lam, the last of the First Folk, rallied his people, becoming a spiritual leader, a general and a mentor. He knew his folk could not stay hidden forever, nor did they care to do so. The human race could not be influenced without interaction.

Under Lam's guidance, he and some of his people ascended again into the world of men, to influence the Phoenicians, the Romans, the Sumerians, the Egyptians, the Aztecs. Lam was known throughout human historical epochs, but by names such as Osiris, Quetzacoatal, Nyarlthotep, Tsong Kaba and many others.

In the centuries following the catastrophe, Lam and his people continued to interact and influence human affairs, from the economic to the spiritual. They allowed things to happen they could have stopped, or nudged events in another direction.

Quietly, Kane said, "It explains a lot, fills in some

blanks. It's one reason why Balam's people didn't simply leave the Earth when things went to shit. They caused the cataclysms when they tried to defend us.''

Nora's eyes flicked from Kane to Brigid to Grant. ''You seem to know a lot about all of this.''

''Not as much as we thought,'' replied Brigid. ''But, yes, we know the bare bones of the story.''

''So you know that the descendants of the First Folk still secretly watched over humankind?'' Cleve asked.

''Up until a minute ago,'' answered Grant, ''we wouldn't have called it watching.''

''Anyway,'' Nora declared, ''at the dawn of Earth's industrial revolution, the descendants were afraid of more reprisals from their forebears. They embarked on a series of raids against the Annunaki and Danaan outposts on the solar planets. I got the impression they were pretty successful, since I overheard Maccan bitching about it.''

''He said something about an attack on Mars,'' Brigid ventured. ''If it's the same incident we know about, it only happened in the relatively recent past…about four hundred years ago.''

''You call that relatively recent?'' Cleve asked dourly.

Nora gave him a level stare. ''When you're dealing with life spans that can be measured in thousands of years, maybe even tens of thousands of years, four centuries are probably last week to Enki and Maccan.''

Kane made a short, sharp gesture of impatience.

"It's irrelevant how long either one of them have been around. I can understand Enki being here. But Maccan—he's a wild card."

Nora sighed and shrugged helplessly. "I wish I could tell you more about him. All we've been able to figure out—and that's from some of his rants I overheard—is that Maccan is an exile from his own people. It's either self-imposed, or he was banished for some kind of transgression."

"Just how many factions are here on the Moon?" Grant wanted to know. "We've got the Furies, who worship the Annunaki as gods, and we've got Saladin and his group, who serve Maccan…who has a grudge against Enki. And both factions are engaged in a tug-of-war over the DEVIL process."

"And the rest of us are caught between the DEVIL and the deep blue sea," Cleve murmured. He chuckled, but nobody else did.

"Let's assume that either Maccan or Enki wants to detonate the DEVIL platform," said Kane.

"That's a given," Philboyd commented.

"In which case," continued Kane, "there's got to be a rhyme and a reason. A detonation date."

Brigid stepped over to the control consoles, her eyes flitting back and forth across the lighted display panels. "Maybe this can tell us something."

Philboyd joined her. "Could be. Let me try to recall some of the more recent data, access the log—"

Even as he spoke, Brigid's fingers pressed a pair of glowing icons. The overhead dome suddenly darkened, as if a huge blanket had been dropped over it from the outside. The chamber became eerily illuminated by the lighted displays, casting everyone's features into multicolored shadows.

"At least we know how to turn out the lights when we leave," Kane remarked.

To his annoyed surprise, Nora shushed him into silence. She stared upward at the arched ceiling, her mouth slightly open. "Something's happening."

Kane followed her gaze. Lights and geometric shapes appeared to swim across the underside of the dome, sliding, joining and coalescing into definite forms. Words flashed by, then symbols. Spheres moved across the dome in an intricate pattern, a dance that was too complicated to follow at first. Red, blue, green and even striped orbs glided back and forth.

"It's a map of our solar system," Brigid murmured. "A plot of orbital trajectories. See, there's Earth…Mars…Mercury…Jupiter."

Kane counted the representatives of the planets. "I thought there were only nine planets. We've got one extra."

"Nibiru," declared Brigid. "Watch how it's tracking on the far side of the Sun, almost in extra-solar space."

All of them watched in silence as the small sphere inched its way around the yellow-orange disk of Sol, arced across the path of Mercury, then took up position near Jupiter.

"Now we know," Brigid announced flatly.

"Know what?" Grant demanded.

She pointed to the holographic representations floating over their heads. "Nibiru, the home planet of the
Annunaki, returns to our part of space every thirty-six
hundred years. It's here now, right outside the gravity
well of Jupiter."

She turned, gazing steadily at Grant and Kane. "To
commemorate its return, either Enki or Maccan intends to use the DEVIL process to destroy it—and
quite possibly the rest of the solar system."

Brigid glanced down at a display screen and said
grimly, "We're at T-minus ten hours."

Grant stared at the images on the ceiling with knitted brows, casting his eyes into shadow. Then he dry-
washed his face with his hands. "Why does this shit
always happen to us?"

Chapter 12

For a very long moment following Brigid Baptiste's announcement and Grant's profane rhetorical question, no one spoke or moved. They continued to stare unblinkingly at the holographic representation of the solar system glowing overhead.

Then Cleve waved his hands in furious denial. "Whoa, hold on, whoa! We're getting a little ahead of ourselves, aren't we?"

Philboyd speared him with a frosty glare. "How so?"

Cleve gestured to the images on the ceiling and then to the numbers scrolling across one of the glass-covered monitor screens. "We don't know if the process even works, all right? It's strictly theoretical. We never did more than run computer simulations, back when some of us thought it was only a terra-forming device."

"I'm pretty sure it'll work," Brigid said darkly. "To a moral certainty."

"Are you a physicist?" Cleve challenged.

"No," she snapped. "But I—we've—had experiences with both Annunaki and Danaan artifacts. The similarity between the two always puzzled me, but I wrote it off to the fact that the First Folk's descendants borrowed from both races.''

"What kind of artifacts?'' Nora wanted to know.

"Some technological, some biological. But one thing we learned is that it all shared a basic template. I'm certain the DEVIL design is derived from the same source as most of the other Totality Concept tech.''

Nora's eyes widened in shock. "You know about that?'' Her voice quavered with dread. "Even we only heard scraps about the researches. It was classified as above top secret.''

"That was over two hundred years ago,'' Kane pointed out dryly. "I think all the security clearances have expired by now.''

Brigid said crisply, "DEVIL was constructed according to design specs and along scientific principles that the Danaan and the Annunaki mastered before the rise of Sumeria. By applying quantum mechanics, they understood and knew how to manipulate the four forces of the universe that came into existence as the result of an explosion of intense energy—the big bang. The entire soup of particles, wavicles and atoms interacted in a destructive and constructive but balanced reaction.''

Philboyd rubbed his jaw contemplatively. "Yeah. The uneven distribution of mass triggered instability in the matrix, gravity condensing and compressing until the first stars ignited. It's been a process of solar evolution ever since. If the DEVIL platform is detonated in the vicinity of celestial bodies, in theory the radiation it releases will upset the balance.''

''Enough of this shit!'' Grant half shouted.

Philboyd looked at him with an expression of hurt surprise. ''I'm trying to explain how when the mass and energy contents of the universe catch up with its slowing expansion, the law of entropy will apply to the universe as a whole, as it now applies to its separate parts—''

Grant clapped a hand over the man's mouth, turning the rest of his sentence into a muffled mumble. Gazing directly into Philboyd's eyes, he said, ''If it's a bomb like you make it out to be, then it has to have an effect radius. You told us the thing is equipped with nuke drivers, rocket engines, right? Why can't you set those off and push it out into deep space?''

He removed his hand from Philboyd's mouth. The physicist cleared his throat and replied sullenly, ''Two reasons. Even if we could do that, ten hours just isn't enough time for the platform to reach a point of dead space. It would still be within the solar system with matter for it to react with.''

''And the second reason?'' grated Kane.

Philboyd shook his head. ''Like I told you before, the DEVIL process releases a wave, a tsunami of what amounts to antienergy. But unlike a tidal wave, it doesn't wash away what it comes in contact with. It's like a sponge. When it strikes anything, whether it's the Moon or the Sun, it'll suck up a billion years' worth of potential energy—robbing this part of the universe of a billion years of existence.''

"Why in the bloody pink Jesus hell would either Maccan or Enki want to do that?'' Cleve demanded raggedly. "They'd die, too!''

"Maybe that's the whole point,'' Kane ventured.

Nora eyed him dubiously. "A suicide pact or something? Hell of a big-time way to off yourself.''

"The Annunaki and the Tuatha de Danaan have made pacts before,'' Kane countered. "And both Enki and Maccan have lived big-time lives. Think about it—they might be the last of their kind, the sole survivors of two mighty races, two star-spanning empires now completely alone in the universe. Both of their reigns passed a long, long time ago. Now they feel they've lived long enough. They have no reason to go on. The race they created to carry forward their legacy turned on them, so they can't even take satisfaction in their accomplishments.''

"'How sharper than a serpent's tooth,''' Brigid quoted softly, "'it is to have a thankless child.'''

Kane threw her a crooked half smile, but there was no humor in it. "Ironic, isn't it? Balam's folk turn on their parents to defend us and we turn on them.''

"Who's Balam?'' Philboyd asked suspiciously.

"Never mind,'' Grant told him gruffly.

To Kane he said, "If either Maccan or Enki want to die, if both of them want to die, there are a lot easier ways to do it than this.''

Kane nodded. "They want to do more than die.

They want to take Nibiru with them, too. Wipe out the last vestige of their civilization, expunge it from the galaxy.''

Brigid said, ''It could be that after all these centuries of being worshiped as gods, they're trapped in a millennia-old pattern. Maybe they ended up thinking they're gods, too. And gods don't just fade away quietly. They require a Ragnarok, a heaven-shaking Armageddon to mark their passing.''

Cleve made a scoffing sound. ''What are you doing—psychoanalyzing them? You're wasting your time.''

''We can't afford not to try to understand their motivations, even if they are deranged,'' Nora said sharply.

Taking a deep breath, Brigid replied, ''Their motives are definitely deranged, but they're fairly simple. Maccan, Enki or both intends to make this part of the solar system a blood sacrifice of truly monstrous proportions.''

Kane said grimly, ''Like the gods they believe they are, Enki and Maccan want to be sent to their graves with sacrifices.''

''WELL, NOW THAT WE KNOW what the fused-out bastards are up to, shouldn't we start thinking about a way to stop them?'' Grant asked.

''Stop them how?'' Cleve's voice was hushed with fatalistic acceptance. ''The countdown to detonation is already encoded, transmitted by tight-beam telemetry from here to the platform. There's nothing we can do."

Brigid studied the consoles. "Is there a way to access the original construction specs of the DEVIL platform?"

Nora reached over and ran her fingers over the keys. Overhead, the representation of the solar system flashed and faded. It was almost instantly replaced by a jumble of cylinders, ellipses, squares, octagons and bevel-edged rectangles. The geometric shapes bent and coiled like snakes, flowed together, merged and finally shaped themselves into a three-dimensional schematic.

On the ceiling glowed the cutaway outline of a two-tiered octagon connected by a double array of slender cylinders. It roughly resembled a barbell, with one weighted end twice the breadth of the other. All the pieces of hardware were labeled, with arrow-tipped lines pointing to them.

Grant folded his arms over his broad chest and examined the diagram with a critical eye. "This is how it really looks inside all that junk you covered it up with?"

"Yes," Philboyd answered. "Like I said, the outer shell was built around it only for protective coloration, to make it look like construction discards in parking orbit."

"It's not as big as I thought it would be," Kane observed, narrowing his eyes. "About fifty yards long by a hundred at its widest point. Why is one part larger than the other?''

''The biggest section houses the particle accelerator,'' Nora explained.

''Is that what powers it?'' Grant inquired.

''No,'' Cleve answered. ''A fusion reactor does.''

''Show us,'' requested Brigid.

Nora touched another button and the image expanded, the larger of the tiers magnifying to show a pair of cubes projecting from the underside. One of the cubes slowly rotated.

Brigid said in satisfaction, ''An Archon generator. I figured as much. It's the same type you have on Manitius base.''

''Archon?'' repeated Cleve. ''I never heard of that company.''

''I've heard of them,'' Phiboyd interjected. ''And they're not a company. From what I recall, they were the reporting agency of the DEVIL project. The Archon something or other.''

''Directive,'' Brigid said. ''The Archon Directive.''

Philboyd regarded her curiously. ''Who are they? Code name for some division of the Totality Concept?''

''You might say that,'' she replied absently. Pointing up to the cubes, she stated, ''The generator provides power for the particle accelerator, right?''

''Right,'' Nora said.

''So the process itself is actuated by the particle accelerator?''

"Right," Nora said again. "Wavicles are produced, which then open up a rift in the quantum field—what used to be called the space-time continuum—and allow neutrinos to pour into the accelerator, which tips the balance and begins the reaction."

"How large is this rift?" Kane asked.

Philbody lifted a shoulder in a shrug. "About medium-sized on the quantum scale. Big enough for electrons. There's no way to plug it, if that's what you're thinking."

Grant growled deep in his throat. "This is all so much mumbo jumbo, but with a coat of technobabble slapped on it to make it sound reasonable."

"Actually," Cleve said gloomily, "that's what a lot of the DEVIL technicians thought."

"I don't understand what possible function this damn thing could serve," groused Grant. "It's nothing but a doomsday machine."

"Actually," said Philboyd very tentatively, as if he expected Grant to gag him again, "the DEVIL process was intended for an essential use. If it was positioned into the orbital path of a neutron star, it could kick its collapse into overdrive, increasing its mass to the maximum possible density for matter in this universe. It would drop out, so to speak, leaving an empty black hole in space, a singularity.

"Then, hypothetically at least, you'd have a kind of interstellar motorway junction, a wormhole with spaceships using it to travel from one end of the galaxy to the other."

"Hypothetically," Grant mimicked bitterly, turning away from him.

"If we can take out the generator," Kane declared, "then it'll deactivate the particle accelerator and keep the process from engaging." He arched an eyebrow toward the physicists. "Agree, disagree, don't know?"

"I suppose it would." Philboyd sounded uncertain. "But you'd have to breach the outer shielding and then the internal magnetic field that contains the combustion chamber."

"It can be done," Brigid said confidently. "We'll get a mini-nuclear explosion, but everyone down here should be safe enough."

Brigid, Grant and Kane had seen generators of that type before in various and unlikely places around the world. Lakesh had put forth the initial speculation they were fusion reactors, the energy output held in a delicately balanced magnetic matrix. When the matrix was breached, an explosion of apocalyptic proportions resulted, which was what caused the destruction of the Dulce installation.

"So even if the generator blows up, it won't initiate the process?" Kane pressed. "We'll get a big-ass fireball, but we won't have jump-started the entropic process?"

Philboyd nodded, but his expression was doubtful. "I don't know. It sounds reasonable, but this is completely off-the-wall, total speculation on an unprecedented event."

"The particle accelerator is the key component," Nora said. "But how do you figure to knock anything out? I mean, the platform is way up there and we're way down here."

Grant surveyed the three scientists with intent eyes. "I plan to get way up there from way down here. Earlier today I saw a TAV make a run on the citadel. It was chased off by one of the craft in there." He nodded toward the door and the hangar beyond. "I'm assuming one of Maccan's boys flew that ship. Who piloted the other one?"

"Furies, probably," Cleve answered. "Ever since Maccan occupied this part of the citadel acreage, they make flyovers."

"And Furies are the ones who made us crash your flitter-gig, Philboyd," Grant commented. "Does anybody know if Maccan's crates are aerospace planes like the TAVs? They look pretty old to me."

"I would imagine they'd have the same capabilities as the TAV," Philboyd said. "I got a look at them when they brought me in—in my estimation, they're the prototype for the TAV."

Grant nodded approvingly. "I had the same impression. Good."

Face and voice expressing alarm, Nora exclaimed, "You don't really think you can steal a flyer and shoot down the DEVIL platform!"

"I sure as hell intend to try...but not shoot it down. My target will be the generator."

"What makes you so certain you can pilot one of

those old ships?'' demanded Philboyd. "I mean, you told me back at the mine you could fly choppers, but—''

"If those Manta ships are the prototypes for the TAVs,'' Grant broke in, "then they ought to be fairly simple to jockey.''

"Grant,'' Brigid murmured, worry shining in her eyes, "that's an awfully chancy 'ought to be' to risk your life on.''

He nodded in acceptance of her opinion. "I really don't see that we have many options available to us. We do nothing, and in ten hours we age a billion years inside of a second, or I try to keep that from happening. Or die trying, anyway.''

Kane's teeth flashed in the semigloom of the chamber. "I don't know about the rest of you, but I'm excited about this plan.''

"Don't be,'' Philboyd said warningly. "The platform has a self-defense system. It can generate and launch plasmoids of varying size, range and power.''

"How about explaining what a plasmoid is for the technologically challenged in the class?'' inquired Kane. "What kind of power are we talking about?''

"Electrical, magnetic, mechanical and thermal. Especially thermal. If you take a quantity of gas and heat it to a point where the atomic particles begin to disassociate and the substance ionizes…'' Philboyd's words trailed off, and he shrugged as if he had already explained everything.

"Heat it to what kind of temperature?" Brigid asked impatiently. "How hot?"

"Oh, ten thousand degrees or so—plasmoids can be as cool as seven thousand degrees, but there's really no upper limit short of mass-energy conversion, which only happens inside stars. So to answer your question…ten thousand degrees Celsius."

"Celsius?" echoed Grant.

"Centigrade. The ionized gas is probably released with a spin on it, what we called 'body English.'"

"Who is 'we'?" Kane demanded.

Sounding peeved, Philboyd retorted, "Those of us born before the nukecaust. Anyway, a moving electrical charge generates a magnetic field that's temporarily self-sustaining. Surface turbulence tends to prevent the heat escaping and its own field holds it together, until something stops its motion."

"Something?" Brigid asked. "Like a population center?"

"Any kind of something. Then the plasmoid releases whatever volume of superheated electrically charged gas makes it up. If it was the size of a pinhead, it wouldn't last very long and probably wouldn't even burn a hole in cloth."

Grant scowled. "What's the range of this thing?"

"That depends on the speed of its launch."

"So its destructive capability depends on speed and size?"

Philboyd shook his head. "Not necessarily the size. A larger plasmoid wouldn't be powerful. Its destructive capacity is governed by the amount of energy stored within it—temperature, electrical charge, turbulence. All those factors are more important than size.'' He flicked his eyes up and down Grant's frame. ''We predarkers learned that size isn't everything.''

''What about speed?'' Brigid asked.

''Plasmoids usually have a peak velocity in the neighborhood of five hundred feet per second.''

''That's not really very fast,'' Kane pointed out. ''The muzzle velocity of our handblasters is considerably higher.''

Philboyd smirked. ''It's still a little too fast to outrun or to duck.''

Grant grunted. ''I guess I'll find out the hard way the speed of the Manta ships.''

Kane smiled wryly. ''You wouldn't have it any other way.'' His smile vanished as he addressed everyone. ''In a few minutes, Maccan or Saladin will troop in here to take Baptiste out to deliver the message to Enki. All of us need to be alert, to watch for our chance to make a break for it and cover for Grant.''

Cleve suddenly seemed to have trouble speaking and swallowing. ''Some of us might be killed. All of us might be killed.''

''At least you won't be dying of old age,'' Kane replied matter-of-factly. ''But that will happen in about in ten hours, anyway. If I'm going out, I'd prefer to do so while I can still make a fairly passable corpse.''

Nobody laughed, but Kane hadn't really expected them to.

Chapter 13

If there was one thing Erica van Sloan missed about the chaotic, anarchic twentieth century, it was cigarettes.

The nuclear holocaust had pretty much completed what government legislation had begun in regards to tobacco, since it was no longer cultivated as a crop. What now sprang from the irradiated soil of the old Carolinas would probably have a far more deleterious effect than all the secondhand smoke in history.

Hardly anyone but outlanders used tobacco in any form any longer. There were mild drugs available that were much safer, less offensive to others and just as sedative. Smoking was certainly forbidden in all the Administrative Monoliths and the residential Enclaves of the baronies.

Sloan knew some enterprising souls grew hidden fields of it somewhere, but she seriously doubted they were anywhere within walking distance of the Xian province of China.

A cigarette, preferably mentholated, would make waiting for an audience with the imperator much easier to bear. She was in an agony of nervous impatience, but she did her best to appear composed before the imperial guards patrolling the perimeter of the pyramid.

She watched them through the dark lenses of her sunglasses and wondered briefly if they were watching her through the tinted, full-face visors of their helmets.

They wore high black boots, ebony leggings and tailored tunics. Emblazoned on the left sleeve was a familiar symbol—a red, thick-walled pyramid partially bisected by three elongated but reversed triangles. Small disks topped each triangle, lending them a resemblance to round-hilted daggers. The guards cradled wicked-looking SIG-AMT submachine guns in their arms. They seemed to pay more attention to the weapons than to her, and for a moment she felt an irrational surge of jealousy.

Erica van Sloan was tall and beautiful, with a flawless complexion the hue of fine honey. Her long, straight hair, swept back from a high forehead and pronounced widow's peak, tumbled artlessly about her shoulders. It was so black as to be blue when the light caught it—except for the wide strip of gray running like a bleached-out ribbon through the left side of her tresses.

The large, feline-slanted eyes above high, regal cheekbones swam with glints of violet. The mark of an aristocrat showed in her delicate features, with the arch of brows and her thin-bridged nose.

A graceful, swanlike neck led to a slender body

encased all in black—high-heeled black boots, jodh-
purs of a shiny black fabric, with an ebony satin tunic
tailored to conform to the thrust of her full breasts.
Her left sleeve bore the same insignia as the guards.
Once it had served as the unifying emblem of the Archon Directorate, as well as Overproject Excalibur, the
Totality Concept's division devoted to genetic engineering. Now it was the insignia of the imperator.

At the sound of churning vanes in the distance,
Sloan lifted her gaze, watching the Deathbird flying
over the grass-covered ridges and hills. Painted a
matte, nonreflective black, the helicopter's sleek,
streamlined contours were interrupted by only the two
ventral stub wings. Each wing carried a pod of sixteen
57 mm missiles. The pair of T700-701 turboshaft engines was equipped with noise baffles so only the
sound of the steel blades slicing through the air was
audible.

The Deathbirds were modified AH-64 Apache attack gunships, and most of the the fleet had been reen-
gineered and retrofitted dozens of times. The foreport
of the black chopper was tinted a smoky hue, so the
pilot and the gunner were nearly invisible.

Sloan had often wondered where Sam had found
the machines, whether he had looted a ville of its fleet
or found another source, but she never put the question to him, just as she had never asked too many
penetrating questions about his choice of headquarters.

After all, China was very, very far away from the network of villes and the governing body of barons.

The brow of a grassy hill overlooked a thickly wooded valley roughly a mile across. A river flowed through the valley, the foaming blue waters cascading down a gentle fall to the west. Dominating the entire valley was the vast, pyramidal structure that shouldered the blue sky.

It was composed of countless fitted blocks of stone, the top quarried perfectly flat. Bright sunlight played along the white facade of the monstrous monolith. Standing at its base, Sloan could see only a small portion of its staggering proportions.

Before the nukecaust, the existence of the Great Pyramid of China was repeatedly denied by the Communist government. Archaeologists believed it to have been part of the tomb of Emperor Shih Hunag Ti. Sam had told her the immense structure had originally been painted black on the north side, blue-gray on the east, red on the south and white on the west. The apex was painted yellow. The significance of the colors apparently had to do with the Taoist system of the five phases of existence.

Sam claimed the pyramid was thought to have been built during the Hsia dynasty, which reigned from 2205 to 1767 BCE. Though very little was known about the Hsias, history was considered to have begun with the Chou dynasty of 1122 BCE. The emperors produced by the Hsia dynasty were allegedly the first authentic rulers of China following the semimythical Five Monarchs.

Sloan didn't know how much to believe, but she never had reason to doubt Sam's words before—until yesterday. Almost unconsciously she touched the strip of gray in her hair. She knew it was foolish to allow what amounted to vanity to upset her so intensely. She also didn't like feeling suspicious of Sam. After what he had done for her, for the entire inefficient ville network, and what he planned for the entire world, the emotion made her feel ashamed.

She looked again at the bucolic majesty of the Xian valley. The mountains, the hills, the river all reminded her of the pleasures she had enjoyed and taken for granted as a young woman. Then there had been plenty of forests and beaches and pretty little places where she drank wine and flirted and seduced or allowed herself to be seduced.

Until a few months before, Sloan had convinced herself all those experiences were in the dead past. There was no room for the small pleasures in the nuke-scarred shockscape at the dawn of the twenty-third century. Like rest the of humanity, she taken the permanence of the Earth for granted. Then, on January 20, 2001, mountains walked, plains became inland seas, earthquakes and tidal waves resculpted coastal regions and billions died. For the following generations, nothing was permanent—especially dreams of love, security and a future.

Sloan was one of the lucky ones, or so she had been told. Like many other scientists and military officers attached to the Totality Concept, she sat out the nuclear exchange and the skydark in the Anthill complex, the most ambitious Continuity of Government installation ever built. The prolonged nuclear winter changed ideas about a new world order. Even if the personnel managed to outlast the big freeze, the skydark, they would still sicken and die, either from radiation sickness or simply old age. So they embarked on a radical and daring plan.

Over a period of years, everyone living in the Anthill was turned into a cyborg, a hybridization of human and machine. Since the main difficulty in constructing interfaces between mechanical-electric and organic systems was the wiring, Sloan oversaw the implantation of SQUIDs directly into the brain. The superconducting quantum interface devices, one-hundredth of a micron across, facilitated the subject's control over his or her new prostheses.

Of course, the transformations didn't solve all of the Anthill's survival issues. Compensation for the natural aging process of organs and tissues had to be taken into account. The Anthill personnel needed a supply of fresh organs, preferably those of young people, but obviously the supply was severely limited. So a solution was sought—cryogenics, or a variation thereof.

Inspired by the method of keeping organic materials

fresh by pumping a hermetically sealed vault full of dry nitrogen gas and lowering the temperature to below freezing, the internal temperatures inside the installation were lowered just enough to preserve the tissues, but not low enough to damage the organs.

Other scientific disciplines were blended. The interior of the entire facility was permeated with low-level electrostatic fields of the kind hospitals experimented with to maintain the sterility of operating rooms. The form of cryogenesis employed at the installation wasn't the standard freezing process relying on immersing a subject in liquid nitrogen and the removal of blood and organs.

It utilized a technology that employed a stasis screen tied in with the electrostatic sterilizing fields, which for all intents and purposes turned the Anthill complex into an encapsulated deep-storage vault. This process created a form of active suspended animation, almost as if the personnel were enclosed by an impenetrable bubble of space and time, slowing to a crawl all metabolic processes. The people achieved a form of immortality, but one completely dependent on technology.

However, even those measures were temporary. Sloan volunteered to enter a stasis canister for a period of time, to be resurrected at some future date when the sun shone again and the world was secure.

When Sloan awakened, more than 122 years had passed. During her long slumber, the Anthill instal-

lation suffered near-catastrophic damage and a number of stasis units malfunctioned. Her canister was one
of those.

Due to that malfunction, her SQUIDs interface had
inflicted neurological damage on her body. She was
resurrected as a cripple, her long, shapely legs little
more than withered, atrophied sticks.

Sam had not only restored her youth, but he had
also put life back on her legs again. He also gave her
purpose beyond acting as adviser to the baronial oligarchy. She dedicated her life to building a new, pro-
ductive society on the framework of the ville system.
Since cybernetic principles were applied to manage-
ment and organizational theory, she always had much
to offer in the way of streamlining ville government.
Just as everything that occurred in the universe could
be analyzed into cause-and-effect chains, the chains
themselves could be used to build organizational models.

Now, months after the overthrow of Baron Cobalt,
a new model was being constructed and Sloan was
using Cobaltville as the template. She threw herself
into the task with an obsessive fixation that surprised
even her. Her devotion sprang mainly from a sense of
liberation. For more than thirty years following her
revival from stasis, Sloan had spent almost every minute of it in artificial environments.

Confined to a wheelchair, she rarely ventured out-
doors and had lived for three decades without know-

ing the varied tang of natural air, without seeing or smelling the sea or taking walks in the rain or the snow. She had been separated from everything she took for granted in her old life and hadn't realized how much she loved it until it was taken from her.

Then Sam, her precious son, a mixture of her in vitro genetic material spliced with that of Enlil's, had given it back—or at least returned the promise of it.

Erica's sexual energy had also been enhanced since Sam restored her youth. She often wondered if Lakesh experienced a similar phenomenon. She had toyed with the possibility that Sam had stimulated her metabolism in such a way that her endorphin level was unnaturally high, but she never thought to ask him about it. It wasn't seemly for a mother to ask her son a question of that nature.

But now she intended to demand answers. Sloan had been preparing to engage in a ménage à trois with two of the Baronial Guardsmen in Cobaltville when, preening naked before a mirror, she saw the strip of gray in her hair. All erotic, sensual inclinations had been subsumed by a sudden flood of wild panic—a vision of how she had looked only a few months before crowded into the forefront of her mind. She knew she would rather die than become a gnarled, withered, paralyzed and withered old crone again.

Sloan had wasted little time in reaching the secret gateway unit on Level A of the Admin Monolith and keying in the destination lock codes for the mat-trans chamber in the Xian pyramid. But since materializing within it, she had done nothing but wait, informed that the imperator was otherwise engaged. She loitered outside, which at least gave her time to regain control of her emotions. She was no longer stricken with terror. She told herself over and over again that Sam would not allow her to age, that he would once more lay his hands on her and spread his youth-giving bioenergy through her body.

A voice from behind her commanded her attention. "Imperial Mother? The lord imperator will see you now."

Sloan turned, seeing a small Asian man in a black uniform at the square-cut doorway. "Shall I escort the imperial mother to the Chamber of the Heart?"

"No," she snapped. "Nor shall you or anyone here disturb me or my son there."

The man nodded deferentially and stepped aside as Sloan strode into the pyramid. She stalked purposefully down the passageway, taking long-legged strides, her boot heels clacking in a steady rhythm against the stone floor. She went through an open doorway and into the Hall of Memory, as Sam called it. As far as she was concerned it was museum, a central clearinghouse of several ancient cultures.

A tall, round sandstone pillar bearing ornate carvings of birds and animal heads was bracketed by two large sculptures, one a feathered jaguar and the other a serpent with wings. Silken tapestries depicting Asian ideographs hung from the walls. There were other tapestries, all bearing twisting geometric designs.

Suspended from the ceiling by thin steel wires was a huge gold disk in the form of the Re-Horakhte falcon. The upcurving wings were inlaid with colored glass. The sun disk atop the beaked head was a cabochon-cut carnelian.

Ceramic effigy jars and elegantly crafted vessels depicting animal-headed gods and goddesses from the Egyptian pantheon were stacked in neat pyramids. Arrayed on a long shelf on the opposite wall were a dozen small statuettes representing laborers in the Land of the Dead. Against the right wall was a granite twelve-foot-tall replica of the seated figure of Ramses III. It towered over a cluster of dark basalt blocks inscribed with deep rune markings.

A huge, gilt-framed mirror, at least ten feet tall and five wide, stood amid stacks of weaponry—swords, shields and lances. A spearhead with a single drop of blood on its nicked point rested on a table.

The center and corners of the floor was crammed with exhibit after exhibit, artifacts from every possible time, every culture—Incan, Mayan, Chinese, Egyptian and others Sloan could not begin to identify. But each and every item appeared to be in perfect condition. The huge room was an archaeologist's wet dream, but in reality it was a sampling from every human culture ever influenced by the Tuatha de Danaan, the Annunaki and the race known as Archons.

Sloan went through the far door and the passageway subtly changed. The floor became smoother and the square-cut blocks of stone on the walls gave to way smooth, seamless expanses. They glittered dully with inestimable flecks of all colors, providing a soft light. The rounded ceiling wound gently in an ever widening curve. The floor, gleaming to the eye like oiled slate, gave a solid footing.

The corridor suddenly opened into a vast, domed space. Sloan took off her sunglasses and swept her eyes around the natural cavern. The unfinished stone of its ceiling gleamed here and there with clusters of crystals and geodes.

The floor dipped in a gentle incline, and at the center, surrounded by a collar of interlocking silver slabs, was a pool. The inner rim was lined with an edging of crystal points that glowed with a dull iridescence. At first glance, the pool took up the entire chamber floor, except for a walkway around it, about five feet wide. The pool was about fifty feet in total circumference and light shimmered within it, but it was not water. Sam called it the Heart of the Earth, a nexus point of geomantic energy, a hub of Earth energies.

The surface of the pool pulsed with a ghostly phosphorescence, and by its glow, Sloan saw the tall, slender figure standing at the rim. He wore a robe of a saffron hue, and his features were hidden by a cowl. She rocked to an unsteady halt as mist began to swell out of the throat of the pool, bulging upward. A shimmering sphere the diameter of the rim slowly rose, like a hot-air balloon made of a semitransparent substance. Sloan could almost but not quite see through it. Her flesh prickled with a pins-and-needles sensation, as if she were standing near a low-level electrical field.

In a serene voice the robed figure said, "This is an interesting if minor bit of synchronicity, Mother. Here I am communing with the forces of the Earth Mother, and you arrive for the first time in months."

Sloan saw how the crystals overhead pulsed with a purplish-black light that was beyond dark. The angle of tilt and the tuning of the facets against one another formed a balanced matrix, which drew out and suspended the energy globe. Sam had described the pool within the pyramid as a cardinal point in the world grid harmonics, a part of a network of pyramids built at key places around the world to tap the Earth's natural geomantic energies, what the Hindus called *prana*.

But Sloan wasn't thinking about such esoterica. She gaped at Sam, astonished into speechlessness by his appearance. She knew his metabolism was geared to a far faster rate than a human's, or rather she had accepted that concept.

"Sam?" she inquired hesitantly.

"Mother?" His voice, though muffled by the cowl, came out as a sardonic drawl. "Nice of you to visit at long last."

Sloan didn't answer for a long moment. She

couldn't answer. The last time she had seen the boy, barely three months ago, he was the size of a twelve-year-old. Now, judging by his height and the deepness of his voice, he had matured to the midteen years. And she sensed something else about him, as well, some subtle quality that pimpled her flesh and set her heart to thudding frantically within her chest.

At length she said haltingly, "There's been a change."

"Really?" He sounded disinterested, almost bored. "In you, me or in Cobaltville?"

"In me." She stepped closer to the pool, eyeing the bubble of mist floating above it. Images swam across its surface, or within it, but she could make no sense of them.

Although his back was turned to her, Sloan touched the gray streak in her hair. "I'm aging again... regressing."

The hooded head nodded. "That was to be expected, Mother. I can only turn back the hands of your biological clock so far before it begins keeping the correct time again."

"Yes, but—" She stopped herself, trying to smother the quaver of fear in her voice. "My concern is for my legs. What if I regress back to the state of only a few months ago? I'll be a cripple again, of no use to you or your program."

"That will not happen. The loss of your legs was

due to neurological damage inflicted by your cybernetic implants. I repaired that. It can't be undone."

Sloan was not relieved by the nonchalant assurance. An awkward silence stretched between them. Sloan was dismayed and distressed by how distant, even dismissive Sam seemed. Finally he asked, "Is that all?"

She lost what was left of her patience and her temper. "No, it's not all!"

She marched across the cavern to the rim of the well, reaching out to grab Sam's arm. "Look at me when I'm talking to you, damn you!"

She tried to spin him to face her, but it was like attempting to twist a granite statue on its pedestal. Sloan was too consumed with anger to wonder about his immobility. She pushed herself between him and the floating orb of mist. Sam bowed his head and turned away, and Sloan heard a dry, harsh rustle beneath his robe, the light friction of scales against cloth.

Plucking at his sleeve, Sloan demanded, "Is something wrong? Are you sick? Let me look at you!"

Sam paused and his hooded head swiveled slightly toward her. Most of his face was cast in the shadow of the cowl, but she saw his eyes gleaming there like two chunks of ice. The breath seized in Sloan's lungs. The eyes were young with an alien sort of youth that was not of the physical. In them glittered a cold wisdom—and a power that awakened the primitive in her heart.

They were the eyes of a dragon, hungry and superior. She wanted to run, to hide away. Every cell in her body recoiled, every instinct blindly backed away in a xenophobic cringing.

Sam spoke to her, his voice soft and sibilant. "Not yet, Mother. I have yet to make the change. When that happens, you may look at me."

Sloan realized he was manipulating the timbre and pitch so the vibrations would resonate sympathetically to the inner ear and stimulate the neuroenergy system. Her reason spinning like a child's top, she asked, "Make the change to what?"

"I'm not sure yet of what I will be. A child of the hidden places, the perfect offspring of another great order of life, the living legacy of the Serpent Kings…the last of which enters into extinction this night."

Horror engulfed Sloan. In that first overwhelming shock of revulsion, she was hardly aware of Sam taking her hands and pressing them between both of his own. She glanced down and cried out. She had grown accustomed to the faint pattern of vestigal scales that had glistened dully between his fingers. But the delicate coating of scales had spread across the backs of his hands. Pearly nails tipped his fingers, and they might have been pretty if they hadn't curved downward like claws.

"Annunaki?" she shrilled. "You're changing into one of them?"

Sam laughed softly as if he found her wild question

amusing. "Something far greater. Remember what I once told you—that hybrids take on all the positive attributes of their parents, becoming the most exceptional specimens?"

Sloan closed her mouth on a scream. She squeezed her eyes shut, not wanting to even glimpse the face that might be leering at her from the beneath the cowl. "I will not know exactly how exceptional," Sam continued, "until my change is complete. Then you will either take pride in the blood that runs through your halfing or disown me as a changeling."

Sam paused, and his grip tightened around her hands. His fingers were as strong and as cold as tempered steel. Sloan cried out in pain, but she didn't try to struggle.

"And you come to me because of a trivial, cosmetic matter. You are vain, Mother, and I have no sympathy for such a flaw." He chuckled again, but this time it sounded forced.

"Here is the truth behind your restoration. You have failed me. I charged you with the task of enlisting Mohandas Lakesh Singh to my cause. Instead, you squandered the youth I restored to you by glutting yourself on physical passions and flaunting your power in Cobaltville. I expected you to only succeed Baron Cobalt, not replace him with your own vainglorious ego."

His voice drooped to a low, gloating croon. "The gift of youth and the gift of power were always intended to be transitory. You enjoyed both only at my whim. And as you are now in terror of losing those gifts, the man Singh is also aware of the temporary nature of his restoration.

"If he experiences only a fraction of your own horror, then he shall be easy to recruit. When you bring him to me, I shall, as in the Sumerian tale of Gilgamesh, return you to the condition of your youth."

Sloan's mind seemed as trapped as her hands. It could not think or speculate, pressed between the heavy weights of fear and desperation. She strained for breath, her lips parting.

Suddenly, Sam set his own lips against her. They were dry and rough, as if they were chaffed from long exposure to cold winds. There was no love, no tenderness in the kiss. It was a gesture of contempt. Then he released her, thrusting her from him. He heeled away from her. "Do as I bid, Mother."

His parting whisper was as sibilant as the hissing of a serpent. "Remember—if you fail me, you fail yourself."

Chapter 14

Fear, like love, took time to develop, and Brigid Baptiste's compulsively ordered mind was in danger of being consumed by utter terror.

The prospect of Saladin or Maccan marching in and shoving Megaera's severed head into her arms didn't disquiet her particularly—it was the waiting for whatever was going to happen that dried up all the moisture in her mouth, made her heart trip-hammer and twisted her stomach into acidic knots.

Her memory kept flitting back to the day, nearly two years ago now, when she waited naked in a bare-walled cell to be brought before Baron Cobalt's tribunal. She was certain she would die that day. She had no problem recollecting the terror she had felt, the almost suffocating sense of doom. She'd had no plan, except to die without shaming herself. To weep and beg for mercy would not have accomplished anything or delayed the inevitable.

Brigid cast a glance across the room at Kane and Grant, envying their studied ease as they lounged against the curving consoles, speaking to Cleve about the location of weapons and EVA suits. Judging by their relaxed postures, they didn't anticipate anything more taxing than eating a hearty dinner.

She supposed both men had been through so many harrowing experiences, as Magistrates and after, that life-threatening situations no longer upset their emotional equilibrium. But she knew her assessment was a false one, despite the fact that they were hardened veterans of dozens of violent incidents. They had been raised to be killers, after all—to kill anything or anyone that threatened the security of Baron Cobalt.

She surreptitiously looked at Grant, who at that moment was stifling a yawn. Grant, like Kane, had been through the dehumanizing cruelty of Magistrate training, yet they had somehow almost miraculously managed to retain their humanity. But vestiges of their Mag years still lurked close to the surface, particularly in Grant. He presented a dour, closed and private persona, rarely showing emotion. He was taciturn and slow to genuine anger, but when he was provoked, his destructive ruthlessness could be terrifying. And though he didn't yet show it, she knew he was very provoked.

Nora, Philboyd and Cleve, on the other hand, showed their emotional states by pacing restlessly, going to the door, pressing their ears against it, then pacing again. More than once they bumped into one another as they circled the puddle of blood on the deck, now tacky and congealed.

Cleve approached Grant hesitantly and said, "Presuming any of us get out of this—"

"Nobody's given up yet," Grant interjected gruffly.

Cleve nodded. "In that case, allow me to apologize for kicking you while you were helpless. It was the act of a coward, of a bounder, and I can only offer a reason, not an excuse."

Grant angled an eyebrow at him. "Which is?"

Cleve gingerly touched his bandaged head. "One of Saladin's men bashed me around yesterday, because Janiesch had left the area without permission. He asked me where he went and he didn't care for my answer—which consisted of two words—and he whacked me with his rifle."

Grant nodded gravely. "I believe your friend is dead. He saved me from a carnobot, but he'd already been tagged by a Fury." He jerked a thumb toward Megaera's head. "She came along and completed the job."

Cleve swallowed hard. "I was afraid of that."

Nora sighed sadly. "So many of us dead now...I hope Eduardo, Neukirk and Mariah are still alive."

"Me, too," Philboyd said earnestly. "We always managed to stick together."

Kane shifted position. "If they're still alive when this is done, I expect all of you to come back to Earth with us."

Cleve regarded him distrustfully. "It's not a radioactive cinder?"

"Parts of it are," Kane put in. "Some parts aren't. But it's sure as hell better than here."

Philboyd threw him a bleak grin. "That wouldn't be too much of a stretch."

Nora sighed again, running her hands through her tangled mass of hair, then pursing her lips in disgust. "I haven't had a decent shampoo in a year or more. I certainly hope there's still some available where you're from."

Brigid decided to join in the conversation, if nothing else but to divert her attention from fearsome memories. "There's plenty of it in storage. Enough to last a lifetime."

Nora's eyes flickered with interest. "Really? What about cosmetics?"

Brigid nodded. "Those, too. Plenty of everything you'd ever want or need."

"Oh, for God's sake," Kane grunted in exasperation. "With what's facing us in the next few hours, I think our time is better spent discussing tactics, not lip gloss or panty shields."

Everyone fell silent. Kane presented the image of pondering a problem for a thoughtful second, then said, "Anyhow, some of that mascara in storage has turned to cement over the past couple of years. But you can mix water with it, stick in the microwave and make it as good as new."

"How the hell would you know that?" Grant asked suspiciously.

Kane grinned. "To be honest, I saw DeFore doing it a couple of months ago. That's all there was to it."

"I'll bet," Brigid drawled, then flashed him a sly smile to let him know she meant no offense.

For a long time at the beginning of their relationship, it was very difficult for Kane and Brigid not to give offense to each other. Both people had their individual gifts. Most of what was important to people in the postnuke world came easily to Kane—survival skills, prevailing in the face of adversity and cunning against enemies. But he could also be reckless, high-strung to the point of instability and given to fits of rage.

Brigid, on the other hand, was structured and ordered, with a brilliant analytical mind. However, her clinical nature, the cool scientific detachment upon which she prided herself, sometimes blocked an understanding of the obvious human factor in any given situation.

Regardless of their contrasting personalities, Kane and Brigid worked very well as a team, playing on each other's strengths rather than compounding their individual weaknesses. It had taken her several months to grudgingly admit she learned a great deal from Kane, and from her association with Grant and Domi.

She had learned to accept risk as a part of her way of life, taking chances so that others might find the ground beneath their feet a little more secure. She didn't consider her attitude idealism, but simple pragmatism. If she had learned anything from her friends, it was to regard death as a part of the challenge of existence, a fact that every man and woman must face eventually.

She could accept it without humiliating herself, if it came as a result of her efforts to remove the yokes of the barons from the collective neck of humanity. Although she never spoke of it, certainly not to the cynical Kane, she had privately vowed to make the future a better, cleaner place than either the past or the present. She suspected he knew anyway.

Cleve stroked his beard contemplatively and turned to Brigid. "You seem to know a great deal about the Annunaki and the Tuatha de Danaan."

She shrugged. "Mainly only the old legends. But we've come across sufficient evidence over the past couple of years to prove—at least to me—that the myths had a strong foundation in reality. The secret history of humanity."

Nora smiled lopsidedly. "I can't say it does anything for my ego to know that the human race was genetically engineered by a bunch of scaly aliens, to be manual laborers."

Brigid returned her smile, feeling some of her fear ebbing away. "That's only one part of the story. Evidence of alternate biospheres for unknown aspects of the one in which humanity lived has been part and parcel of mythology since the dawn of history.

"For example, the legend of Cadmus tells of a battle with a dragon that rose out of the Earth. He killed it and buried its teeth in the soil. From the planted teeth grew a host of armed warriors, who fought one another until all but five were dead. These men served Cadmus and helped build the city of Thebes. From these five 'dragon-born' were descended the five noblest families of Thebes—families who ultimately were descended from the dragon. The symbolism is obvious, representing a link between the human and nonhuman.

"Ancient Chinese mythology gives us the tale of the dragon husband, where the dragon took the youngest daughter from a farmer. Here the girl witnessed the dragon-king dancing with delight, curling like a ribbon or a DNA helix and transforming into a human being.

"These are universal motifs, occurring regardless of race, culture or location. The UFO-abduction scenario of the twentieth century was just a new mask for an old player, a new cover story for forces that have plagued and deceived humanity for thousands of years."

Philboyd nodded. "I can handle the idea that the Annunaki contributed to human cultures…but it's the notion they created the very concept of gods that I don't care for."

"So you're a religious man?" inquired Grant.

Philboyd shrugged. "Tough for a scientist to admit, but yeah, I tried to be. So it's unsettling to think we deified a bunch of extraterrestrials who viewed us as slave labor."

Brigid said, "I think they looked at us as more than that. At some point, the Annunaki reached the conclusion that they needed intermediaries between themselves and the masses of humanity. As a bridge between themselves as the gods and humankind, they introduced the concept of the god-king on Earth, appointing human rulers who would assure humanity's service to the gods and channel their teachings and laws to the people.

"Therefore, the Annunaki chose to create a new dynasty of rulers, known as demigods or god-kings, because of their exalted bloodlines. That situation has been revived now on Earth, through the baronies."

Cleve's eyes widened. He looked toward Kane and said in derision, "And you say Earth is better than here?"

"Our thirty acres of it is," he retorted. "But after this is all over, you're welcome to stay here and provide fuel for the carnobots, if you want."

Philboyd laughed, quickly stifled when Cleve shot a glare in his direction. He opened his mouth to say something else. He closed it almost immediately when the lock solenoids on the door snapped open loudly.

Chapter 15

The door rumbled aside, taking so long to slide into its double-walled slot that Kane wondered if it were malfunctioning. Distantly, he understood his time perceptions were distorted by tension slowing everything to a crawl. It was the mind's perfidious way of postponing a horrific inevitable. Recognizing the symptoms of stress, he began taking deep, regular breaths, forcing himself to relax.

He stood and gazed at the door, noting that Grant hadn't stirred from his sitting position on the curving console. At the periphery of his vision, he saw Brigid starting to rise to her feet, but he gestured to her, indicating she would stay where she was. Let them come to her, he told himself grimly.

The door opened all the way. Kane's belly turned a cold flip-flop when he saw Maccan standing framed in the portal, eerily backlit by the lights of the hangar. Saladin stood on the catwalk behind him, hefting his plasma rifle.

Extending a lean-muscled arm, Maccan pointed to Philboyd, then to Megaera's head against the far bulkhead. He swung his arm toward Brigid and beckoned to her with a forefinger. Before she stood, Kane stepped forward. "Maccan—"

"As you were," the tall man said sharply.

Kane ignored the command. "We know what you have planned, even if we aren't sure why. But there's one thing I am sure of—if you detonate DEVIL, you'll be obliterating people on Earth who still carry the Tuatha de Danaan bloodline."

Maccan smiled mockingly. "That's rather the point, isn't it?"

His soft voice had in it the bite of contempt, and Kane felt sweat form at his hairline. Maccan's casual revelation set the blood to thundering in his ears.

Philboyd retrieved Megaera's head and shuffled forward, holding it between two hands as if it were plutonium. He did his desperate best not to look at it. Maccan gestured imperiously to Brigid again. Slowly she stood, face composed. Kane sidestepped in front of her, putting himself between her and Maccan.

"I don't know what made you so crazy with hate," he said between clenched teeth, "but if you're hell-bent on suicide, why don't you just take a long walk outside without a space suit? You'd save everybody a lot of time and trouble."

Maccan stood very still, regarding Kane dispassionately. In a bland, neutral voice he said, "You are an arrogant one, aren't you? Don't you know I could kill you where you stand?"

Kane showed the edges of his teeth in a humorless,

wolfish grin. "You're welcome to try, Peter Pan." He watched his eyes, alert for a color change.

"You seek to provoke me and thus distract me with this empty posturing." Maccan uttered a short laugh. "That's all you humans could do. Posture, strut, proclaim. Once your kind venerated us, then you loathed and scorned us."

"Yeah," Kane replied in a drawl. "So I've heard. But there was probably a good reason for that. What did you want from us?"

"We required only a modicum of obedience and respect. Yet you hated and cursed us in the end."

"Yesterday's news," retorted Kane, aware that Grant was carefully shifting position, watching for an opening. "Humanity would welcome you now."

"Your repentance comes too late." Maccan's voice was remarkably soft. "Now stand aside."

Kane shook his head. "No."

"No?" Maccan repeated it as if he didn't understand the word.

"You heard me."

"Oh, I heard you. I just couldn't believe my ears."

Maccan's eyes suddenly flared with yellow fire, as if the interior of his skull were blazing with flames and his eye sockets only apertures into the inferno. The sudden psionic assault jolted Kane so hard he doubled over. The shock was so unexpected, so terrible, he nearly collapsed.

Time, space, the universe darkened and turned. His surroundings shattered into a kaleidoscope of flying fragments. He drifted among them, and the sudden terror of it dragged a scream up his throat. He clamped his jaws shut on it. A rush of unbridled emotion swept over him, nauseated him. For a shaved sliver of an instant he felt what Maccan felt—and it was terrible.

Life was eternal agony without purpose, and he was weary of living it. Life, memory, emotion, all were torments. He wanted only to sink beneath the waves of peace, as gentle as drowning in a sea of oblivion. He craved nonexistence as he had craved nothing else in his exceptionally long life.

His hunger for new experiences, for new knowledge and even love, had long ago been satiated. He could not forget all the places he had seen, all the battles he had fought, all the lovers he had lost. Nor could he drive away the memory of bitter betrayal and humiliation. His desperation to forget was intense, but he could never forget—not as long as a single entity with Danaan blood existed. And those memories fed the fires of a fury unquenched.

Kane didn't glimpse or receive so much as a hint from which far world the Tuatha de Danaan had originally come. But he felt that long, long ago the Danaan had gone out by a road that led to the distant ends of the universe, to cosmic regions forever outside human understanding.

It seemed he heard voices, very faint, thready whispers that skittered along the edge of his consciousness. Grayed images penetrated his mind, and he felt his own mind merge with them. Layers of thoughts, of recollections about an unknown people, plucked at his mind, and he glimpsed the pictures and emotions and textures of thousands of years of existence. He could make no sense of them, it was all flying fragments of remembrances and experiences.

It was as though he were tumbling headlong down a black tunnel, buildings, green fields and faces flashing by in kaleidoscopic images. He plunged through a thousand memories so fast, he couldn't comprehend any one of them.

Then it was over and Kane found himself on his hands and knees, making noises like a dog trying to dislodge a bone from its throat. He was only dimly aware of Brigid Baptiste kneeling at his side, attending to him.

"What did you do to him?" she demanded angrily.

In a ghostly whisper Maccan said, "A man is born in one world, and there he belongs. But my world is dead. Age and death came at last to everything there. I cannot live with the dreams of my world haunting me at every step. I would be rid of this life, as it would be rid of me, as of lifting then lowering a veil."

Maccan paused and added, "That is what I did to your insolent friend. I lifted the veil."

Brigid glared up at him. "You're insane."

Maccan nodded in agreement. "More than likely."

He reached down and closed a hand over Brigid's shoulder. His grip tightened, and she set her teeth on a groan of pain. It felt like the jaws of a vise were inexorably tightening around her shoulder socket. She didn't resist when Maccan pulled her to her feet. The orange glow of his eyes faded to little more than embers.

Kane staggered erect, wiping at the clammy film of sweat on his face. Maccan inquired gently, "I trust I have made my point?"

Kane was too numb to answer, and Maccan smiled at him patronizingly, almost fondly. "You are a brave man, I'll give you that. Courage was the quality of your race I most admired. But here it will do you no good."

He beckoned to Philboyd. "You. With her."

Philboyd's eyes blinked spastically behind the lenses of his glasses. Beseechingly, he asked, "Why me?"

Maccan's scarred face contorted in a macabre grin. "Why you, indeed. A very existential question. Perhaps you will find an answer to it in the hours to come."

Kane stepped forward, extending a hand to Brigid. She took it briefly, but Maccan pulled her away, so it was more of a swift, parting caress. In a hushed voice, barely above a whisper, she said, *"Anam-chara."*

It was the name they had for each other, learned during the op to Ireland long ago, but only rarely used. The old Gaelic term meant "soul friend." Memory of the hallucinations they'd shared during the mat-trans jump to Russia flooded through his mind. That hallucination suggested that Brigid and Kane had known each other in past lives. Morrigan, the blind telepath

from the Priory of Awen, had told Kane that their
souls were inextricably bound.

At her whisper, Maccan regarded her with startled
eyes and then an ironic smile tugged at the corners of
his mouth. "The language of the Gaels. The tongue
of the betrayers. I haven't heard it spoken in a very
long time."

His smile became a savage writhing of the lips and
his eyes flamed up again, more red than orange. He
covered her mouth with a hand, his inhumanly long
fingers reaching out to almost encompass the entire
lower portion of her face, thumb and forefinger nearly
meeting at her nape.

Coldly, with a deadly sincerity, Maccan intoned,
"And I will never hear it spoken in my presence
again. Do you understand?"

Kane took a quick half step forward and delivered
a lightning-fast double hammer blow to the small of
Maccan's back, right over the kidneys—or where a
human's kidneys would be located.

Maccan stiffened, throwing his head back and voic-
ing a gargling cry of surprised agony. Kane felt a
surge of satisfaction at the sound. The man could be
hurt and if he could be hurt he could be beaten—

Maccan moved. He was so fast, to Kane's eyes it
was as if he had transmogrified into a multicolored
blur. Kane felt a rush of air on his cheeks, then he hit
the deck flat on his back, the impact knocking his
breath out through his nostrils and mouth. He lay

where he had fallen, in the drying puddle of blood, trying to cough, trying to breathe, trying to move.

He squinted up at constellations glittering on the other side of the domed roof. His stumbling thoughts replayed the almost subliminal image of Maccan whirling and smashing a forearm across his upper body, the back of his fist catching him on the jaw.

Kane's mouth filled with the salty tang of blood as a deep boring pain settled in the center of his chest. He managed to hike himself up to his elbows as Philboyd, Maccan and Brigid went out through the door.

"Hey!" Grant shouted, rushing toward it. "Hey! How about some food or at least some water? It's been hours."

The door panel rumbled shut, but not before Kane caught a final glimpse of Brigid's stricken face, eyes gleaming with fear out of a face drained of all color. The door sealed with a hissing thud.

Nora, Cleve and Grant clustered around Kane, helping him to his feet, lifting him clear of the blood puddle. "Well," he managed to husk out, "I won't win any good-judgment points for that last decision."

He weaved unsteadily and leaned over a console, using his tongue to carefully probe the laceration on the tender lining of his cheek. Her face a mask of anxiety, Nora asked, "Are you sure you're all right?"

Cleve muttered in awe, "He moved so fucking fast—"

Kane turned his head and spit a jet of scarlet into the pool of Megaera's blood. "Very fucking fast."

"What did he do to you before, when his eyes changed color?" Grant asked.

Slowly, Kane pushed himself away from the instrument panel. He touched his forehead. "A psionic attack—or a communication. I don't really know which. But I know one damn thing—he's been waiting at least three thousand years for a final judgment that was never levied. So he's arranging it for himself."

"He would be rid of this life as it would be of him," Nora said in a faint, trembly contralto.

Cleve sat down heavily on the display boards, burying his face in his hands. "Oh, my God. All of it is over. All of it."

Kane winced as he straightened, squaring his shoulders. "Not quite. Survival first."

Grant squinted at him curiously. "Then what?"

Kane spit out a little more blood and said quietly, "Then revenge."

Chapter 16

Brigid and Philboyd followed Maccan down the steps and into the cavern. She felt a creeping numbness in her arms and legs and a queasiness in the pit of her stomach. It was fear, but she looked around with her usual air of calm, if for nothing else but to provide an emotional anchor for Philboyd. He shuffled along beside her, clutching Megaera's head. His complexion was waxy, and his quivering, ashen lips made him look like a drowned corpse.

None of Saladin's people came with them, but Maccan kept his back to the two people, walking with a peculiar grace that was almost a swagger. He was confident they wouldn't dare attack him from behind, certainly not after they saw how easily he had swatted Kane aside.

Maccan followed the same route she and Kane had been forced to walk after they were captured. They skirted the noisome sewage drain and a bare-walled, well-lighted corridor. The floor was a raised disk of a translucent, plasticlike substance about four feet in diameter. From beneath it emanated the faintest susurrus of electronic hums. A vertical shaft, the same size as the disk, extended up into shadows. Their vision couldn't penetrate the distance and darkness.

Maccan stepped aside and gestured for Philboyd and Brigid to step onto the disk. "You remember the message you are to convey?" he asked.

Brigid only nodded. Her eidetic memory would never allow her to forget it, no matter how hard she tried.

"When the lift stops," Maccan told her, "you will relay the message to any you might meet. Once you do, they will not hinder you."

Brigid narrowed her eyes in suspicion. "Who are you talking about?"

Maccan smiled. "Those called Furies, most likely. There are a handful who act as Enki's attendants and bodyguards. They take care of him."

"Do you have him trapped up there?" she demanded. The blurred image of Enki transmitted by the remote vid probe was what had triggered the mission to the Moon in the first place.

"No, he's not trapped at all. He chooses to sequester himself there, but he has ways to come and go as he pleases. But always he returns to wait."

Philboyd, fingers hooked in Megaera's hair, ventured falteringly, "Why haven't you just killed him, then? Your faction is well armed and probably outnumbers the Furies."

Maccan shook his head in pity, as if a mentally challenged child had asked him why the sky was blue. "Whatever gave you the idea I want to kill him? I want him dead, true enough, but that's not quite the same thing as killing him, is it?''

He started to turn away, then muttered, ''Oh, I almost forgot in all the preparations—''

From the sash about his lean waist he pulled the combat knife and presented it pommel first to Brigid. The dark blade was sticky with Megaera's blood. She looked at it impassively, but made no move to accept it. ''You want him dead but you want me to kill him with a knife?''

Maccan tossed his hair back and laughed. The shivery, sobbing sound did not warm the blood. ''Of course not. This is for you and your companion.''

Brigid slitted her eyes. ''What?''

''There is a possibility,'' Maccan retorted smoothly, ''that your minds will become so unhinged before the terms of the pact are fulfilled that you may wish to end the strain. I do not trust you with firearms—therefore, I offer you the most expeditious means to free yourselves. A bit crude and messy I cannot deny, but it's not as if anyone will have to clean up after you.''

Brigid hesitated, then took the knife, surreptitiously eyeing the carotid artery in the slender column of Maccan's neck. The idea of slashing his throat was only a fleeting impulse, but Maccan's eyes suddenly darkened, as if thunderheads skimmed across a clear sky. Brigid let the big knife dangle at the end of her arm, and the Danaan nodded approvingly. ''Very wise.''

"Wise enough to know you can't get the drop on a telepath."

"I'm not a telepath, not really." He cast her a self-deprecating smile. "A number of my people were quite adept in the art of mind manipulation. The human mind was childishly easy to trick, feeding it illusions of invisibility and shape-shifting.

"Like anything else, it was a learned skill and required much time and concentration. I found the effort was beyond my interest in the subject."

"You preferred to hang out in your fortress on the Boyne, strumming your harp and dallying with the women of the Celitc tribes, I suppose." Brigid did not try to soften her sarcasm.

"Ah, you have done your research," Maccan said with a disarming grin. "However, I do have the ability to interact with brain-wave patterns. I can sense emotional states, intercepting intent. A form of empathy."

"So you're not actually peeking into other minds?"

Maccan fluttered a dismissive hand through the air. "I receive flashes of insight. For example I know you are deliberately stalling, optimistically hoping something will happen to avert the next few minutes, much less the next few hours."

He smiled sourly, almost sadly. "You're hoping your friends will stage a miraculous and melodramatic rescue at the proverbial last second."

"It's happened before," she replied stolidly.

"Contraindicated by your attitude. But I assure you it will not happen. You are on the road of fate, trapped in destiny like a fly in amber. I suggest you adopt the fatalism of your companion.'' Maccan nodded toward Philboyd. ''He's resigned to it all.''

Philboyd finally showed some spirit. He glared at Maccan through the thick lenses of his glasses. ''Thanks to you and Megaera's madness, I've had a lot of time to get used to the idea.''

Maccan regarded him with an expression that was almost sympathetic. His eyes lightened. ''If our children had followed our edicts, set down so long ago, if they had circumscribed your development, this situation would not have come to pass and this moment would not exist. Earth, if not a paradise, would at least not still be suffering the effects of your last war. Your kind is paying the price for our own failure, and that is regrettable. However, once the final codicil of the pact is executed, you will be beyond madness.''

Brigid stepped to the edge of the disk. ''You can put a stop to the madness,'' she said urgently. ''It's not too late.''

Maccan's eyes darkened again. ''It's three millennia too late.''

He made the abrupt, intricate gesture with his left hand near his heart, but there was a bitter mockery to it. ''On your way.''

The disk hummed softly as it floated them upward. A sinking sensation in Brigid's stomach replaced her nausea, at least temporarily. She heard no mechanical noises from beneath the disk, so she guessed it operated on principles different from the hydraulic piston system used in the Admin Monoliths.

As if sensing her thoughts, Philboyd said quietly, "It's powered by a localized antigravity field. These shafts already existed and we just put them to use for the antigravs. Experimental and damn expensive, but what the hell, the government had money to burn." His lips twisted in an attempt to grin. "I guess the government and all the money is burned now."

Brigid didn't respond to the comment. "This isn't Danaan or Annunaki technology?"

Philboyd shook his head, inhaling deeply. He glanced down at the head in his hands and then looked away, his grin molding itself into a mask of revulsion. "I'm starting to believe that everything humanity thought they invented was Danaan or Annunaki technology."

He tittered suddenly. Brigid looked at him, her flesh crawling. The man was teetering on the brink of hysteria, if not a complete psychotic break. "What's so funny?"

Philboyd tried to stifle another giggle. "What Kane called Maccan." He laughed. "Peter Pan. I bet Maccan really is Peter Pan. Maybe the guy who wrote that based the story on Maccan—he probably met him when he was a kid or something...."

Brigid smiled at him wanly. "I suppose that's a possibility. But this isn't Never Never Land."

Philboyd swallowed another giggle, a reflex action that looked almost painful. "Fucking A."

Hundreds of feet of smooth, featureless shaft wall went by before the disk bumped to a gentle stop. An oval-topped portal opened before them. Incised into the top of the arch, Brigid saw the cup-and-spiral glyph.

Both people stepped off the disk. At first there wasn't much to see, just the perfect smoothness of ancient walls with ceiling light panels shedding an electoplasmic illumination.

Philboyd took several steps forward, then his entire body was racked by a shudder and he came to halt. He turned pleading eyes to Brigid, hands trembling violently around Megaera's head. "Let me get rid of this."

Brigid replied compassionately, "It's not up to me. The decision is yours to make."

"Make it for me!" he blurted. He looked ill, his eyes darting wildly, like some frantic animal's. They were fevered, tormented. "I'm sorry, but I can't go through with this. I'm liable to lose it, to go nuts and be of no use to you. Take your knife and kill me."

Brigid's lips tightened. "No."

"We'll be dead in a few hours anyway. Kill me now and I won't have to subject myself to this—depravity any longer!"

Laying a steady hand on the man's quaking shoulder, she pitched her voice to a calm, unemotional level. "Don't go simple on me, Dr. Philboyd. If you do, I won't kill you, but I'll make you wish you were dead, at least for a few minutes."

Philboyd clenched his teeth and a high wild, keening issued from beneath them. Tears crawled down his face. ''Please—''

Brigid slapped him, not an attention-getting cuff, but an openhanded blow that twisted his head on his neck and sent him stumbling into the wall. ''You claim you're a scientist,'' she said, slipping a steely edge into her voice. ''Prove it.''

The man blinked at her, shoulders sagging. ''How?''

''By acting like a rational human being, not a terrified animal. We'll get through this if you use your mind.'' Brigid packed every word with conviction. ''I'm scared, too, but I've been in enough jams like this to have learned that giving in to fear only makes the problem worse.''

Philboyd nodded, then slowly pushed himself away from the wall. He threw her a shamed, jittery smile. ''I've lived with fear for so long, you'd think nothing would bother me now.''

Brigid returned his smile with one she hoped was reassuring and understanding. ''You never can tell what'll crawl out of your psyche when you're not looking.''

Philboyd took several deep breaths and started walking. The foyer of the lift shaft opened into a big tunnel of softly gleaming alloy. It was like a rectangle with a triangle on top in cross section, at least fifteen feet across. There were no features, no friezes or glyphs of the type she had seen in the base of the citadel.

Philboyd wrinkled his nose. "The air is bad up here."

Brigid nodded. "It's thin. We'd better not exert ourselves unless absolutely necessary."

As the two people walked, their feet made echoes in the passageway and the reverberations sounded ahead and then behind them. Brigid stopped twice to look around, under the impression of following footsteps.

The passageway was only twenty yards long and it debouched into a vast, vaguely lit space. It was closed in by towering walls of black stone that rose to a high, arched vault, lost in the darkness overhead. Suspended from the apex of the arch, a single large globe lightened the heavy shadows, but only barely. It was little light for human optic nerves.

Brigid waited at the mouth of the tunnel looking around the gloom, then took a careful step over the threshold. "Let's take it slow."

"You're the boss," Philboyd whispered.

She smiled wryly. "That'll be a novel change."

Then she heard the faint sound of stealthy footfalls again, but not from within the passageway. The rapid, scuttering noise did not sound like human footsteps. They stopped for a second, then began again.

Brigid sensed Philboyd stiffening beside her. Tensely he murmured, "Oh, shit—"

"What?" she demanded, fisting her knife.

The sequence of scuffs and scutters began again, swelling in volume. A pair of crimson orbs stabbed out of the gloom. Philboyd struggled to speak, then managed to husk out in a breathless bleat, "Carnobots!"

As the mechanoid advanced farther into the light spilling out from the tunnel, Brigid saw it was only a single carnobot, but that didn't make her feel any better. Her heart was beating hard and fast in her chest, but she kept her breathing from becoming erratic.

The carnobot extended its head, and its maw opened with a faint whir of servo motors. The alloy-coated teeth looked as vicious as any teeth Brigid had seen on any living creature, mutated or not. But even worse than the teeth were the red photoreceptor eyes. The glow they exuded was almost hypnotic.

"It's smelling us," Philboyd breathed, "trying to match us up in its fuel data files."

The long segmented neck suddenly retracted into the dull gray body, and the lethal automaton backed away into the shadows.

"Why did it retreat?" Brigid whispered.

Philboyd shook his head. "I don't know."

Brigid's legs kept trying to tremble, but her mind kept them under control. "Let's ease on out. We'd better stand back to back, though."

Philboyd obeyed and the two people edged out of the tunnel mouth, taking small steps. The concept of leaving even the feeble illumination of the passageway's light panels caused Brigid's spine to grow cold with dread. No matter which way she looked, she felt certain the carnobot was creeping up on them from another direction.

"Do they act like this often?" Brigid asked lowly.

"Only one of it, two of us," Philboyd replied in the same hushed tone. "Maybe a single droid isn't programmed to attack multiple targets. It could be transmitting a signal to bring others here."

Brigid nodded. "Sounds reasonable."

The carnobot leaped from the shadows, hurtling toward them, head and neck at full extension, jaws gaping wide. Philboyd shouted wordlessly and shouldered Brigid aside. He went down under the heavy metal weight amid a crash, a clatter and wild flailing of legs.

Brigid yelled and kicked the robot's rump. Its head swiveled in her direction, and the jaws champed to expose sharp teeth. They were wet and red.

Brigid closed the distance in two quick strides. Her hand came down with the knife, driving it deeply into the carnobot's right eye. The blade split the malevolent crimson of the orb and filled the ruined socket with a brief flash of sparks. She felt it scrape against the back of the droid's skull and she viciously twisted the blade, hoping to spear through critical circuitry.

The carnobot sprang from Philboyd, and she yanked the blade free. Brigid felt the floor quiver from the predator's weight and she turned to run. She heard the clatter of its feet as it hurtled after her.

She never glanced over her shoulder. She heard the click of jaws opening and closing and in a brief, fear-crazed moment, she wondered if she had enraged the thing. The carnobot leaped and she reacted instinctively.

She fell back on the floor, twisting as she did so. She slammed her open hand against the mechanoid's lower jaw, popping the fangs together. Then she twisted hard in the other direction, driving the knife between the juncture of the robot's neck and its head.

The droid came down on her hard, nearly driving all the wind from her lungs and banging the back of her head against the floor. A mixture of oil and synthetic bile sloshed over her shoulder when the carnobot's heavy head slammed down on it, its jaws closing around it. A shrill yelp escaped between her teeth as pain ripped through her shoulder, but its fangs didn't penetrate the fabric of her shadow suit.

Brigid struggled against the metal predator's weight, trying to push it off as she twisted the knife between the automaton's neck and skull, widening the hole. Its jaws opened and closed against her stomach, but they lacked the strength to tear open the protective material and the flesh beneath.

Lying on top of her, the carnobot gave a final stem-to-stern shiver and went still. The glow from its single eye went out with the suddenness of a candle flame being extinguished. From within its body she heard faint mechanical tickings and drones, then those sounds faded away.

Breathing rapidly in big gasps, Brigid elbowed the robot's body aside. It wasn't easy, and afterward she lay on her back for a moment, stunned that she was still alive. Then, heart racing, she forced herself up and into motion. Her knife hand, arm and shoulder were covered in thick viscous fluid.

She returned swiftly to Philboyd, who lay in a limp, boneless heap. Megaera's head had rolled away from him, but his eyes were masked by blood flowing from a deep gash in his forehead, covering the lenses of his glasses with a scarlet film.

Kneeling beside him, Brigid removed his glasses, sluicing the blood away from his face. "Philboyd," she said loudly, "wake up."

His eyelids fluttered and his mashed lips stirred. She bent down in order to hear. "Broke something inside of me." His voice was a strained, aspirated whisper. "Did you get the damn thing?"

"I got it."

He tried to grin. "One tough babe. Tell me, babe…are there trees where you're from?"

Brigid smiled, but it felt stitched. "Lots of them. You'll get to see them."

"I'd like to, I really would."

She cradled his head in her arms. "Can you stand up?"

He coughed rackingly and liquid scarlet flowed over his lips to mix with the blood already coating his face. His face screwed up in pain. "I'll do my damnedest…but maybe you can ask them for help."

Brigid gazed down at him uncomprehendingly for a moment, then she swiveled her head so fast her neck tendons twinged in protest. Two of the black-clad, faceless Furies loomed out of the murk, light winking dully from the silver spheres tipping their Oubolus rods.

Frantically, Brigid reached out and snagged Megaera's head by the hair. She pulled it to her and held it aloft, turning the ruined features toward the Furies. They didn't react, only stood as silent and as motionless as ebony statues. She wondered if Megaera's face was so maimed they didn't recognize it.

Brigid announced, "Maccan gives you a last gift and final message. It is time to pay the devil his due."

She enunciated each word clearly and precisely, then she waited for a response. When none was forthcoming, she almost repeated the message, but then the Furies lowered their batons. One stepped forward and extended a hand to Brigid. A hollow voice emanated from the blank face.

"Our god has long waited for that message, as we have waited for your gift."

Chapter 17

Cleve looked at Nora, Nora looked Grant and Grant looked at Kane. He didn't immediately notice the visual scrutiny because he was leaning over the display boards, trying to reason out all the glowing icons. Finally, he sensed the pressure of three pairs of eyes and turned. "What?" he demanded.

Nora spoke up first. "We need a plan."

"Yeah," Cleve agreed. "It's all well and good to talk about stealing a TAV and flying up to the DEVIL platform—"

"But," Nora broke in, "we need a proactive bridge between the theoretical and the practical."

Kane regarded her with narrowed eyes. "By that I take it to mean we need to figure out how to get out of here. Is that why you're all looking at me?"

"Actually," Grant replied, "they were looking at me and I looked over at you, since you're usually the one who comes up with all the strategies."

"Which you usually say amounts to me making up shit as I go along," Kane reminded him acidly. "When they pan out at all."

Grant nodded. "As much as I hate to admit it, your track record for plans is pretty good."

Kane sighed in frustration, running his hands through his hair. "Hell of a time for you to finally tell me that."

Grant lifted the broad yoke of his shoulders in a shrug. "It's on my mind at the moment, that's all."

Kane started to pace around the dome-roofed chamber, encountered the leading edge of the blood puddle and changed direction. "Instead of food and water," he muttered, "I wish they'd send in a mop and bucket."

Grant grunted. "I don't think they're worried about us starving to death. They expect us to die of old age long before that happens."

Kane smiled, then winced. He touched his bruised cheek. Grant asked, but not at all sympathetically, "You sure you're all right?"

"Yeah. The suit pretty much absorbed the worst of it. I bet he has about five times my strength, so if he had hit me full in the head..." His words trailed off, eyes going vacant. He gazed down at the pool of dark blood.

Grant noticed the faraway sheen in his eyes and completed Kane's sentence. "If he'd hit you full in the head, you'd be dead."

Kane murmured, "Very much so."

"Yeah," Cleve interposed gruffly, impatiently. "But Mac didn't hit you in the head. We all know that, right?"

Grant stepped toward the door. "Right. But Saladin doesn't know Mac didn't hit him in the head. He was out on the catwalk. He saw Mac hit Kane and knock him on his ass.''

"On my back," Kane corrected.

"On his back," Grant conceded. "But he didn't see you get up."

Nora's eyes widened, darting back and forth between the two men in confusion. "What does that have to do with anything?"

Cleve snorted out a laugh. "I see. You'll play dead, lie doggo in here. We try to get somebody to open the door and fetch your body."

Grant nodded approvingly in his direction, tapping the side of his head with an index finger. "Now you're getting it."

Cleve glowered at him. "If I can get it, so can Saladin."

"Not necessarily," Kane retorted.

"Why should any of Mac's boys give a damn about a dead man locked up with live ones?" Cleve shot back.

Nora said, "You've got a point, Cleve. But they carted Megaera's body away, right? And Saladin is human even if Mac isn't. There's such a thing as morbid curiosity."

"Exactly," Kane stated vehemently. "Saladin or whoever may be interested in seeing the kind of damage their demon prince did to the outlander. They sure seemed to get a kick out of watching him decapitate Megaera." He glanced questioningly at Nora. "Where would they have taken Megaera's body?"

"Probably to the drainage ditch. It flows to the hydroponic-garden section of the base and as she decomposes, she'll serve as fertilizer."

Kane nodded. "Appropriate."

"You'll have to lie down in the blood again," Grant said.

Kane hesitated, then shrugged diffidently. "All part of the employment contract. Let's do it."

Sitting down on the deck and scooting backward, Kane followed Grant's instructions and carefully arranged his body in a position approximating where it had been in after Maccan hammered him off his feet. Grant dipped his fingertips into the blood and smeared it over Kane's face, trying to make him appear to be the victim of a fractured face. Kane squeezed his eyes and tolerated the daubing without protest, but Nora hugged herself and shuddered. "Disgusting."

"You only have to watch it," Kane told her, lowering the back of his head into the puddle.

Grant examined him, made a couple of suggestions, then went to the door and began pounding on it with his fists. He punctuated his drumming blows with bellows. "Hey! Saladin, anybody! We got a dead man in here! That pointy-eared psycho of yours killed Kane! Open up!"

Cleve and Nora moved to the far wall of the chamber and stood shoulder to shoulder while Grant continued banging and kicking on the portal. For several minutes he shouted, cajoled and finally begged.

"Please get him out of here—we can't stand it! His brains are leaking out of his ears!"

Finally, out of breath and hoarse, he stopped, turning to face Kane, Cleve and Nora. "He's not buying it."

"Maybe nobody is out there," Nora suggested.

"Or maybe they just don't give a shit," Cleve said gloomily.

Kane lifted his head slightly. "That's probably the most likely explanation. But let's not give up yet. It's the only plan we have."

Cleve mumbled, "There's no point to it. We're dreaming. We need to accept the reality that we're all—"

The locking solenoids clacked so loudly and unexpectedly everyone in the room jumped. Even Kane's legs jerked in startlement. The thick panel slid aside a few feet, then stopped. The sectionalized barrel of a plasma rifle poked in between the edge of the door and the frame. The barrel terminated in a long cylinder, reminiscent of an oversize sound suppressor.

"Back away," Saladin ordered curtly.

Grant did as he said, raising his hands. "Kane's dead. I think every bone in his skull is broken."

The door opened all the way and Saladin stepped in. Without being obvious about it, Grant looked beyond him. The catwalk behind him was empty. Waggling the barrel of his weapon meaningfully and menacingly, Saladin said, "All the way back, Grant. You know the drill."

Grant shuffled backward, talking as rapidly as he knew how. "Maccan killed him with one blow, never saw anything like it, just pow!"

As he passed Kane, he saw his friend lying as he had seen corpses lie, arms and legs bent unnaturally and stiffly, head slightly to one side. Saladin wasn't immediately gulled. He approached Kane warily, cautiously, shifting his gaze constantly from Grant to Kane.

When Saladin reached Kane's splayed legs, he nudged his feet with a boot. The corresponding loose wobble was satisfactory and he moved closer, scrutinizing Kane's blood-streaked face.

"He hemorrhaged like hell," Grant offered helpfully.

Saladin's lips twitched, either in a brief smile or a grimace. "Your friend seems very dead," he concluded. "If it means anything, I'm sorry. He wasn't our enemy, but he was very foolish to attack Mac."

"Are you going to cart him out of here?" Cleve asked.

Saladin peered at him contemptuously. "Why should I bother? The sight of death may disturb you, who was born on Earth in a different time…but it's all part of my existence."

"You took Megaera's body," Grant told him stiffly.

"I had help then." Saladin sighed and shook his head. "No, he must stay where he lays. But I'll do you a favor and make him less of an obstacle."

Saladin pointed his plasma rifle down, training the bore on Kane's midsection. "It'll stink in here for a few minutes, but at least he'll be out your way."

Through slitted eyes, Kane waited, watched and then he gathered himself. With all the speed his years of training and honed reflexes had given him, his right hand lashed up and tightened around the weapon's barrel. He sprang up, first to a squat, then to a crouch. Saladin roared in wordless fury and surprise. He reacted almost instantaneously, pulling back on the rifle, trying to wrench it from Kane's grasp.

Kane wrestled with it, forcing the barrel straight up toward the dome arching overhead. Grant lunged forward and Saladin, snarling in a language neither man understood, pivoted at the waist, putting Kane in Grant's path.

Kane resisted the maneuver, hands tight around the weapon. For a long second he and Saladin stood eye to eye. Kane grated, "Drop it. You fire that thing now and you'll—"

Saladin drove his head forward, butting Kane in the forehead. Kane staggered, but retained his grip on the plasma rifle. Then, either by accident or intentionally, Saladin depressed the trigger plate. A crackling fountain of blue energy flared out of the barrel and splashed against the underside of the dome.

Saladin's face twisted in shock, his mouth worked, but whatever he had to say dissolved in a prolonged, screeching rumble. The dome exploded into fragments, but none of the pieces fell into the chamber.

Propelled by the atmospheric pressure within, all the shards ballooned upward and outward into the hard vacuum of the lunar surface. A great, cyclonic wind gusted all around them, trying to sweep them off their feet.

Kane released the plasma rifle and grabbed the edge of a console. Legs flailing, Saladin clung to a panel with both hands, his body in a straining, horizontal posture as he struggled desperately against the relentless drag of depressurization. His fingers slipped and as if jerked by an invisible wire, Saladin plunged up, feetfirst into the cloud of frozen oxygen and half-slagged dome shards at the apex of the breach.

Kane felt a giant's hand snatch him, wrenching him upward. He braced his arms and fought the powerful, incessant suction, dragging himself along the curving instrument console toward the open door. Throwing himself headlong, he jammed and hooked his fingers into the narrow slot of the door frame. His legs kicked, still drawn upward by the maelstrom of decompression.

He felt a hand close over the toe of his left boot. Kane hazarded a glance over his shoulder and saw Grant latched on to his foot with one hand while the other gripped Nora's forearm. Cleve wrapped both arms around Nora's waist, and his lower body bobbed toward the shattered roof. All of their faces were twisted in a rictus of strain, pain and sheer terror.

Kane laboriously dragged himself forward until he was able to brace his arms against the door frame.

Grant lunged desperately, shifting his grip from Kane's foot to his ankle. He pulled, slowly starting to climb Kane's leg like a rope, his fingers digging deep. Arms trembling with the effort of keeping himself braced in position, Kane waited until Grant was able to clasp on to the door frame. Both men performed slow horizontal chin-ups, struggling to lever themselves out of the chamber.

With his longer reach, Grant managed to grab a crossbar off the catwalk's guardrail and with a muscle-tearing effort, jerked himself free of the epicenter of decompression. Hand over hand, he pulled out Kane, Nora and then Cleve. Before Cleve's toes had fully cleared the threshold, Grant slapped the control buttons and the portal slid shut.

Gasping, Kane kicked Cleve's feet out of the way as the door sealed with a muffled thud. The four people only dimly heard it. Their ears felt as if they were stuffed with soggy cotton wadding. For a moment, they crouched on their hands and knees just outside the door, hanging their heads, panting, wheezing and hurting.

Blood trickled from Grant's left nostril, and he dabbed at it with a sleeve. Very distantly, they heard the jangling of a bell. Nora raked the wild tangle of her hair out of her eyes and gasped, "Decompression alarm. Mac's people will be here in any second—"

Setting his teeth on a groan, Grant hauled himself to his feet by the crossbars of the guardrail. He looked down into the hangar at the array of Manta ships.

"Which one of you knows how to launch those crates?"

Cleve, his complexion shockingly white, pulled himself up. Hoarsely he replied, "Not difficult. But you'll need somebody to operate the roof hatch."

"Let's go," Grant snapped brusquely, looking for a way down. He spotted the metal rungs of a ladder affixed to the wall near the door and swung over the rail. Cleve followed.

"Stay with them," Kane told Nora as he got to his feet.

She cast a worried glance in his direction. "Where are you going?"

"To find Brigid—and Philboyd. You said I could the reach the top level of the citadel by the antigrav lift, right?"

Nora nodded. "But the whole area will be crawling with Mac's crew."

Kane broke into a jog, feet ringing on the grilled floor of the catwalk. "Do what you can to help here."

"Kane!" Grant's voice lifted in an aggravated bellow.

Kane paused, leaning over the rail and looking down into the hangar. Grant, halfway down the ladder to the floor, stared up at him peevishly.

"What now?" Kane demanded.

Grant slowly lifted his right index finger to his nose and snapped it away in the wry "one percent" salute. It was a private gesture he and Kane had developed during their years as hard-contact Magistrates and re-served for undertakings with small ratios of success.

Kane returned it gravely, then pushed away from the railing and started running again. His chest ached, and the muscles in his lower back and thighs throbbed every time he moved his legs, but he kept sprinting, dashing through the circuitry tunnel to the hatch that led out to the cavern.

His fingers stabbed at the keypad on the wall, and the slab of metal began to rumble aside. Before the door was a quarter open, he squeezed through and bounded down the stone stairs, taking two at a time.

As Kane hit the cavern floor, still running, he glimpsed a cluster of EVA-suited men running across the stone bridge from the opposite side. They shouted when they caught sight of him, but he couldn't hear what they said. He figured it didn't really matter when streams of flaming plasma lashed out toward him. They struck the rock floor, leaving wide scorch marks in their crackling wake.

Without breaking stride, legs pumping furiously, Kane raced toward the lift alcove. Before he covered half the distance, a tall, lean figure stepped out of it. The light was too uncertain to discern Maccan's ex-pression, but there was no mistaking his gait. He approached Kane with the self-assured manner of a tiger stalking its wounded prey.

A projectile hit the floor very near Kane's left foot, and he felt stone chips pelting his leg. He didn't know if a standard-issue bullet or a tungsten-carbide-steel pellet had been responsible, and he didn't give much of a damn.

Kane came to an instant and borderline insane decision. He swerved sharply away from Maccan, sprinting full speed toward the drainage channel. More guns were triggered and the cavern walls magnified the reports, making it sound as if an entire battalion fired volley after volley. He heard Maccan shouting angrily, probably imprecations at his men. Kane guessed the rounds were coming too close for comfort.

The massed fusillade tapered off, but shots were still fired at him. Kane heard a little whump of displaced air as a projectile passed to the right side of his face, fanning his cheek with a swish of warm air.

He reached the bank of the channel and came to a halt, looking back and forth. From his left came Maccan and from his right rushed at least a dozen weapon-brandishing men. He bent his knees, then straightened them as he dived into the channel.

Kane had only time and thought enough to close his mouth and eyes as he struck and disappeared beneath the slowly moving flow of filth.

Chapter 18

To Grant's almost overwhelming relief, locating the canopy catch release for the Manta's cockpit was no more difficult than the one on Philboyd's flitter-gig. While he raised the canopy, Nora and Cleve entered a small glass-walled booth beneath the catwalk and sealed the door.

Grant slid down into the pilot's seat, giving the cockpit a cursory examination. A bronze-colored helmet with a full-face visor was attached to the headrest of the chair. A pair of tubes stretched to an oxygen tank at the back of the seat. He saw that the chair and helmet were a one-piece, self-contained unit.

He studied the instrument panel, dismayed by its simplicity. The controls consisted primarily of a joystick, altimeter and fuel gauges. Quite fortunately, all the labeling was in English, not Sumerian cuneiform as he had half dreaded.

When he slipped the helmet over his head, he realized the simplicity was something of an illusion. He heard the whine of an internal power source juicing up immediately. The interior curve of the helmet's visor swarmed with a squall of glowing pixels. When they cleared a nanosecond later, he had CGI icons of sensor scopes, range finders and various indicators.

At the same time he felt a peculiar shifting pressure around the base of his neck and realized the helmet was automatically extending a lining and seal. As he strapped himself into the chair, he heard a hiss of static and Nora's voice spoke into his ear. "Can you read me?"

Turning his head slightly, Grant saw Cleve and Nora within the cubicle. Cleve brandished a control box attached to a thick cable that stretched from the ceiling. "Loud and clear," Grant replied.

"I'll open the roof hatch with this," Cleve said. "We'll be safe from decompression in here."

"That's nice to know," Grant muttered, trying to make sense of the images glowing on the visor's surface. "But it might be a wasted effort since I don't know how to power up this crate—"

He experimented with the joystick, pulling it back slightly, then pushing it forward. As he did so, it caught and clicked into position. The hull began to vibrate around him, in tandem with a whine that grew in pitch. On the inside of his helmet flashed the words: VTOL Launch System Enabled.

"I found it," he said. "Do you hear me?"

Instead of an affirmative, loud frantic voices shouted into his ear. Twisting in the seat, he saw a group of space-suited men descending the ladder from the catwalk above. Cleve and Nora yelled at him to close the canopy and take off.

Grant did as they said, pulling down the canopy and latching it tight. Through the tinted shield, he saw Saladin's men rushing across the hangar floor, firing at the glass-enclosed control booth. The sound of gunfire echoed through the vast room. Bullets smashed into transparent walls, striking a white pattern of stars.

Nora ducked, but Cleve still stood with the control box in his hand. The two great leaves of the hangar roof swung upward on a complex arrangement of hinges and pivots. The sky above gleamed with brilliant starlight. As Grant pulled back on the joystick, he hazarded a quick glance toward Cleve. The man gave him a cheery wave just as a storm of bullets struck the glass wall.

He was hit in the chest, bright crimson blossoming against the faded green of his coverall. He jerked sideways, but he kept his grip on the box. He clung to it, his head drooping and blood spilling from his lips. A faint cry from Nora entered Grant's helmet, then it dissolved in a hash of static.

With a stomach-sinking swiftness the Manta lifted upward. The humming drone changed in pitch as the aircraft rose to the open hangar roof. Despite the situation, Grant couldn't help but be impressed as the TAV ascended smoothly, as if drawn by the attraction of a celestial magnet. The helmet's heads-up screens offered different vantage points of the ascent, and Grant's eyes darted from one to another. The Manta's vertical climb felt nothing like that of a Deathbird.

He watched as the lunar plains and rocky crags receded so quickly they became mere ripples of contrasting texture and color. High mountain peaks appeared, then shrank to little cones of pumice.

Grant pulled back on the control stick, and the acceleration of the lateral thrust smashed down on him, slamming him hard against the back of his chair. The speed-gauge icon scrolled with numbers.

He pushed the stick forward and then to the left. The Manta's velocity slowed and it banked to port. Through the cockpit it appeared that the tumbled, rocky wilderness of the tightly clustered craters wheeled crazily around him. The TAV handled far easier than Grant had expected, much smoother than Philboyd's customized, cobbled-together craft.

He ran through the inventory of all the dials, switches, gauges and fire controls. His memory went back to the long training sessions involved in learning the operation of the Deathbirds. The principles were the same, but the applications were vastly different.

Grant pushed the Manta onto a tangential course, heading for space. He had difficulty dividing his concentration between the helmet displays and what lay out in the star-speckled blackness, so he missed the first warning of attack. He didn't realize he was being pursued until a streak of fire lanced past his starboard wing.

Instantly, Grant upped the craft's velocity and pulled back on the stick, slamming the Manta into a screaming climb for altitude. He felt the bones in his face seeming to crack under the stress of acceleration, but at the verge of tolerance, inertia dampers kicked in.

He eyed the flashing sensor icon and interpreted the symbols and scrolling digits to mean an enemy craft was climbing into space after him, roaring up from below. He recalled the pilot's slow reaction time in the first TAV he had encountered, but a Fury had been in the cockpit then. He assumed one of Saladin's people, probably better trained, jockeyed this pursuit craft, so he couldn't count on the same kind of incompetence.

Under Grant's guidance, the Manta performed barrel rolls, loops and wide, swinging yaws, trying to lose the other ship. He alternated the burn times of the port and starboard steering jets, causing the TAV to leap and skitter wildly. The fabric of the ship moaned, quivered and shuddered. In an instant of terror, Grant thought the craft was breaking up and prepared himself for the whistle of air through ruptured hull plates. But the Manta held as Grant put it through its paces.

The other ship climbed after him in a whipping spiral. Grant put the TAV into a sharp dive, pulled up equally sharply, reversing an old Deathbird maneuver he called the peel up pop down. The same tactic had worked to confuse the pilot of the TAV he had encountered the day before.

The pursuing Manta ship zipped up and across his course. For the briefest of seconds, the TAV was outlined in his helmet sights, past the crosshairs, and he thumbed the trigger button on the control stick.

A missile flamed from its pod sheath on his starboard wing. He felt the craft shudder slightly with the explosive release of the projectile. The missile inscribed a fiery trail, bright against the black backdrop of space, but he saw no explosion. Instead, he saw the flare of incoming fire. He sent the Manta straight up, engines at full thrust and over on its back, a half roll. The rocket sketched a wavering track well below him.

Shoving the joystick forward, Grant dropped the ship in a sharp feint and came rushing up on the enemy Manta from below and behind. The sensor scope targeted the TAV and he launched two missiles.

Hit! he thought savagely. Hit!

Neither one did. He traced the projectiles' paths out beyond the range of the scope and snarled in self-disgust. He now faced a double problem. He had only two missiles remaining and he couldn't afford to waste both of them on the enemy craft, nor could he take the time to engage in a protracted dogfight.

He craned his neck around, looking for the enemy vessel, and caught a fragmented glimpse of it at least a mile to the northeast. He couldn't be sure if the pilot knew his intended destination, but he figured he had some kind of idea—otherwise, he wouldn't have bothered coming after him. All right, asshole, he thought grimly, let's give you something bigger to play with.

Grant pulled the control stick backward, and the sudden surge of acceleration slammed against his chest. If not for the oxygen filtering into his helmet, all the wind would have been knocked out of his lungs. When he saw the next missile coming, a bud of destruction loosed by the enemy craft, he dropped his ship's speed a fraction. The projectile blazed across his bow, missing it by a fractional margin, then he veered up, opening full throttle.

Within a minute, the mass-detector icon began flashing. Grant changed course a few degrees, one eye on the computer-generated image inside his helmet and the other on the starlit tapestry beyond the port. He saw something ahead of him, solid and dark, a blacker blot against space.

He nudged the control stick to starboard and then he saw it clearly, its rough curves highlighted by the Sun. The DEVIL platform loomed before him, a plate-shaped mass of ancient, rust-pitted slabs of metal, crudely welded together. It hung there like a de-formed, negative image of the Moon far below.

Grant edged the Manta closer, wondering what the enemy pilot had to be thinking. He figured the sight of the DEVIL device must be something of a shock to him. He prayed he knew nothing about the plas-moid defense array Philboyd had talked about.

Maneuvering his craft in wide-swinging orbit around the hulk, Grant's belly turned tight and cold. He expected a blaze of fire from the rusty mass at any second, but as he completed the first circuit around it, nothing happened. It occurred to him that the plat-form's armaments could have gone off-line many years before, unbeknownst to anyone. As it was, the huge hunk of slapped-together debris looked about as fearsome as some old junkyards he had seen.

He dropped the speed and the nose of the Manta so he could fly beneath it and locate the generator. As he did so, he saw the enemy TAV cleaving a path on a direct course toward him. The ship was so close, Grant thought he could almost make out the shape of the pilot behind the sweeping curve of the canopy. He struggled frantically to align the craft in his targeting scope.

Space was suddenly laced with a hellish web of pure energy, deadly beams stabbing out in a hellfire barrage.

AT FIRST KANE COULD NOT touch the bottom. He clawed the slime aside, floundering more than swimming until he entered the tunnel in the cavern wall, almost wishing Maccan's men hadn't stopped shooting at him. If one of them had scored a lucky hit, at least he would have been put out of his misery.

He kept his head above the surface, trying not to breathe any more than was necessary. The darkness was total. Slimy objects brushed him, clung to him, and now and again he took a breath. Kane dry heaved, nearly vomited more than once, but he wasn't ashamed. The sewer, the cloaca for a dying colony, was as near to his notion of hell as he ever wished to come.

The current, sluggish at first, began to quicken and bear him along. He floated through the quagmire of putridity, rounded a bend and saw a glimmer of light just ahead, but it was light only in the relative sense. It was patch of gray against the absolute dark seeping down from above. A heavy weight bumped into him and he pushed it away, recognizing it as the headless body of Megaera.

Kane's toes touched bottom and he could now walk more or less, keeping his chin above the slime. Within a few moments he was only shoulder deep. He kept a hand on the rock wall as he waded. He rounded a bend and looked at the pipeline stretching away before him. In was far narrower than the channel, but far, far away he saw the source of the light.

Standing shoulder deep in the ghastly brew of human waste and corpses, he decided he had no choice but to enter. He walked in a stooped posture, and the bruises from the crash of the TAV and those inflicted by Maccan pained him. The tube curved ahead, featureless expect for water dripping from its circular walls. The smell of rotting vegetation was very strong.

Kane didn't allow his thoughts to dwell on Grant or Nora and Cleve. He could only hope everything had gone according to plan, but he doubted it had.

Within a minute he came to the junction with another sewer pipe. Water flowed out of it in a rushing current around his body. It smelled comparatively clean, and it swept him and the stinking sludge along. A deluge of water poured through the adjacent tube, the current dragging at his legs.

He fell down and was pushed along, rolling with

the flow. He did his best to keep his head above the water, staring up at the tunnel's roof, looking for the light source.

When he saw the iron-rimmed circle through which light shafted, Kane stroke furiously for the side of the pipe. He seized the bottom rung of the short, rust-eaten ladder and hooked his arms through it. Water spumed and splashed around him, the level rising fast. The water rose against him, trying to force him up to the ceiling of the pipe.

Hand over hand, Kane scaled the ladder. The current suddenly doubled in speed and force, sweeping his feet out from under him. He managed to retain his grip on the ladder, but the flood tide caught him, pulling him into a horizontal position, his back bumping the top of the tube.

Kane fought the rush of water with flailing legs, dragging himself up the ladder, fearing that he would lose his grip and be washed out onto the lunar surface. Another surge of water, this one eddying up from below, slammed him upward. He doubled over as if he had received a punch in the stomach, but his hands still gripped the rungs of the ladder.

He was swept up, and he burst out the tube. His shoulders scraped against the edges of the opening. The rim of the opening fetched him a painful crack across the crown of his head as he was forced up and out. Water spumed, sprayed and foamed all around him, his body buffeted by the surging upward current.

Kane felt himself being hurled full tilt, head over

heels, then he lay on yielding ground, spitting out water and drinking in great lungfuls of air. He sensed warm, humid air touching his skin like soft hands. Slowly, he pushed himself to his hands and knees, blinking at his surroundings.

The air was still and thick, hung with veils of steamy mist. The mossy ground was dotted with algae-covered puddles all around. Vegetation grew on all sides of him, and Kane realized he was in one of the hydroponic farms established by the Moon base colonists.

He got to his feet, looked up and saw nothing but a high roof, half-cloaked by steam. He set off through the undergrowth, hoping he was heading in a useful direction.

Kane had not gone more than a score of yards when from somewhere ahead of him came the steady swish of vegetation being pushed aside. Instantly, he sank into a crouch, tilting his head, straining his ears. He heard nothing for a handful of seconds and was about to stand up again. Then he detected the stealthy pad of footsteps. He tensed himself to spring up and run.

From behind him, Maccan's voice said mildly, "Far too late for the harvest."

Chapter 19

Brigid Baptiste and Philboyd went forward, step by step into the darkness of the hall, flanked on either side by the Furies. Monolithic slabs of stone stood in two rows, arranged to curve around and meet in a circle. They were hung with tapestries worked in multicolored threads that depicted scenes from ancient times—ziggurats from which sprouted terraced gardens, animals long extinct, human and nonhuman faces. They offered brief glimpses into a world lost millennia ago, when the Annunaki were the gods of the Earth.

In the center of the monoliths rose a dais. It seemed at first to be some strange work of sculpture, but as Brigid drew nearer she saw with a quiver of dread it was more akin to a throne.

Directly above the platform revolved a huge globe made of a softly gleaming alloy. Continents and landmasses rose in relief over its curving skin. At least ten feet in diameter, it hung in a supporting web of slender metal girders. Sprouting from its smooth surface were dozens of delicate crystal rods, shimmering, twisting, turning, stretching out, bending in on themselves at right, then left angles. She had seen something like it once before, and though it might resemble a work of art, it wasn't.

Inscribed on the floor at the foot of the dais were dozens of the spiral-and-cup glyphs, each one three feet in circumference. The Furies directed Philboyd to stand within one, while the other black-clad figure pushed Brigid into its mate, an equal distance from it. Bolted to the stone inside each of the glyphs were manacles of a dark metal. The Furies fastened these about their ankles.

A moan of panic bubbled past Philboyd's lacerated lips, but Brigid said sternly, "Stay with me, Philboyd."

A Fury took Megaera's head from Brigid's hands and marched to the foot of the dais, where the shadows swallowed him. The second Fury stood motionless between Philboyd and Brigid, his blank face turned in the direction his companion had taken. He seemed to be ignoring them, so Brigid returned the favor.

"Philboyd," she called, "are you keeping it together?"

He nodded, touching his chest and wincing. "Trying to. If I lose consciousness, it doesn't mean I fainted from fear...it means I passed out from pain. So don't call me a wussy."

She smiled in appreciation. "So noted."

Philboyd craned his neck, studying the big globe hanging overhead. "What the hell is that thing?"

"I believe it's a Danaan map. Or so I was told when I saw one like it in Ireland."

"Map of what?"

"Quantum pathways," Brigid answered. "Interphase junctures, which we now call parallax points. According to what I was told, thousands of years ago, the Tuatha de Danaan and the Annunaki mapped them out. If you look at it closely, you'll see the patterns are three-dimensional depictions of the cup-and-spiral markings."

Philboyd cocked his head from side to side. "Yeah, I think I see it. They're oriented to cardinal points on the Earth, mathematical correlations of landmasses and regions."

He turned his head toward her. "If it's a Danaan artifact, then what's it doing here?"

She shrugged, then tried to lift her leg, testing the manacles. The Fury shifted position, pointed his Oubolus rod, and she subsided. She said, "There apparently are a lot of things I don't understand about the relationship between the Annunaki and the Tuatha de Danaan. But before I leave this place, I intend to."

Philboyd made a wheezing, gargling noise, and she looked toward him alarmed, fearing he was hemorrhaging internally. Then she realized he was trying to chuckle. "Even if it's the last thing you do?"

She nodded. "Exactly."

They heard a slow shuffling of feet from the dais and both people tensed. The Fury appeared, but he didn't carry the severed head. He assumed a guard position beside Philboyd, but the shuffling went on. Brigid and Philboyd stared, waiting. Brigid found herself laboring for breath as if she had just run a three-minute mile. She feared, yet was desperate to see who or what approached them from the gloom. Despite her best efforts, she felt the cold beginnings of terror. Maccan's suggestion about the knife seemed less patronizingly facetious now. She wished she hadn't left it in the carnobot.

A man-shaped figure moved slowly into the dim light, limping as if crippled. A sound like wet lips trying to whistle preceded it. A faint, dry rustling sounded in Brigid's ears. Gradually, the figure moved closer. The dim light gleamed dully from an intricate pattern of tiny, glittering scales.

Brigid bit back a cry of shock and revulsion. Even seeing Enlil's preserved corpse in New London had not prepared her for the flesh-and-blood vision of Enki, last of the Serpent Kings, the final dragon lord, as he slowly crept out of the murk.

He stood taller than Grant, erect upon great, houndlike legs. From downsloping shoulders dangled long arms, the four fingers tipped with spurs of discolored bone. Within his hands he clasped Megaera's head, holding it close to him as if it were a precious treasure.

His neck was longer than a human's, the head blunt of feature with a wide, lipless mouth. The narrow, elongated skull held large, almond-shaped eyes, black vertical slits centered in the golden, opalescent irises.

The eyes were almost invisible under knobbed brow ridges.

Mind wheeling and reeling, Brigid recalled her discussions with Lakesh about how the similarity between Balam's folk and the traditional images of demons may have accounted for the instant enmity that sprang up between humans and his people.

Lakesh opined that since ancient depictions of imps, elves and jinn were more than likely based on early encounters between Balam's folk and primitive man, humans weren't capable of reaching an accord with creatures who resembled archetypal figures of evil.

Upon seeing Enki, Brigid realized that Balam's people, those known as the First Folk and then later the Archons, were adorable cherubs compared to the utterly alien, inhuman aura this entity radiated. She forced herself to look full upon his face. Pride was stamped there, as well as a dark wisdom. She sensed loneliness, too, and understood dimly that he was old, so old that his soul wearied of trying to dredge up memories of youth.

Enki continued to shuffle forward, dragging a deformed, three-toed foot behind him. The leg was twisted, gnarled at the ankle. He stopped and his head swiveled slowly from Brigid to Philboyd, then back to Brigid again.

He breathed heavily, laboriously. When his voice came, it wasn't the liquidy, snakelike hiss Brigid had half expected. It was soft and quiet, cold and clear. "Children, I would have you know I am not your enemy. I make no war on your kind, but a battle must be fought nevertheless.''

THE FLURRY OF PLASMOIDS reminded Grant of giant phosphorescent bees, swarming from their hive and converging on him like a blizzard. He maneuvered the Manta in a fast bank, tipping the craft up on its portside wing.

The cockpit suddenly flared with a burst of almost blinding white light. A plasmoid skated past, less than a yard above the canopy. He put the Manta into a tight, corkscrewing spin, spiraling down toward the bone-white, pocked face of the Moon's surface. More bursts of light flashed into the cockpit. Each burst was followed by blackness as the TAV continued to spin, the plasmoid barrage following him down.

When the flashes ceased, Grant pulled back on the joystick, steadying the ship and climbing out of the dive. Even as he did, he saw a missile etch a trail of flame against the background of stars. The projectile seared past his fuselage very close, but not as close as the buds of destructive energy loosed by the DEVIL platform. The missile continued on its downward arc, impacting with a puffball of flame and smoke in the center of a crater far below.

Grant swung around in a sharp loop. He glimpsed the enemy Manta ship banking off his starboard side, trying to achieve a parallel course. Grant accelerated, arrowing back toward the hulking sphere of the

DEVIL device. It hung above him like some dark god, untouchable and omnipotent.

The other TAV kept up with him, edging ahead to cut him off. Grant allowed him to advance, reducing his speed and then pushing the Manta into a shallow dive. The craft soared past overhead and triggered the mass-proximity sensors aboard the platform. The plasmoid battery let loose, peppering the path of the enemy ship.

The pilot pushed his craft into a steep climb, almost standing it on its tail assembly. He performed a wide barrel roll, came out of it as twin missiles flamed from the ship's wings. Grant slid his Manta as close as he dared to the outer border of the plasmoid. The globes of energy intersected with the missiles' paths and both of the projectiles exploded, washing Grant's cockpit with a flood of orange light.

Grant pulled up sharply to avoid flying through the expanding, roiling ball of fire. He swung the Manta around and down again, coming in from below and behind the enemy vessel. It veered away, climbing fast. The pilot seemed to have finally caught onto to his strategy of luring him close enough to the DEVIL platform so its self-defense measures would either drive him off or destroy him.

A coruscating white globe swelled in Grant's view port. In a fraction of a second he noted how swiftly the plasmoid rotated, little tongues of flame tearing off from it. The closer it came, the more it seemed to elongate, until it resembled a shimmering cylinder, not a ball.

Grant jerked back on the stick, but the ship shook from stem to stern as the plasmoid struck the fuselage a glancing blow. Static discharges crackled inside the cockpit and he felt them even through his suit, as if a million ants crawled along his body. Despite the helmet's faceplate and his own impaired sense of smell, the sharp sting of ozone cut into his nostrils.

He curved the Manta away from the platform just as the plasmoid batteries were triggered again. He felt the ship shudder beneath multiple impacts, before he was able to whisk the craft down and away. A pattern of scorch-mark holes had appeared on the port-side wing. He twisted the stick, kicked the rudder and the Manta gained speed.

Grant made the ship descend, and he kicked up the speed to maximum. He made an almost vertical bank, and the Manta plunged directly back toward the platform. The craft vibrated dangerously as he continued to push it at peak speed. He kicked the rudder and waggled the wings, tilting the craft from side to side in a controlled yaw as he lanced beneath the platform, tipping up one wing, then the other to present a smaller target for the plasmoid salvo. As he roared beneath the underside of DEVIL, he craned his neck upward and saw the top cube of the fusion reactor protruding from between the plates of rust-streaked metal.

As he came out on the far side of the platform, the

enemy Manta was waiting for him. A missile sprang toward him, but a swarm of plasmoids surrounded it and intercepted its course. For a second it looked like two swords of light crossing in the night, then the missile vanished in a billowing cloud of flame.

Grant saw the fireball spreading out toward him and there was nothing he could do but grit his teeth and plummet through it. Beyond the view port he saw fiery veils curling past, whipped like radioactive sea mist over his onrushing bow. Something struck the ship, most likely a fragment of missile casing, then he was in clear space again.

He gusted out a relieved sigh, ignoring the beads of sweat collecting between his temples and the helmet's lining. Grant looked around for the enemy TAV, glimpsed it hovering no more than a hundred yards away, and banked toward it. To his surprise, he saw how the pilot mimicked the maneuver, trying to maintain a wide distance between the two ships. He guessed the craft was all out of missiles, but some compulsion kept the pilot from retreating.

Grant debated whether to ignore him and devote his full concentration to taking out the reactor or chase the ship off, perhaps even risking one of his two missiles on removing his adversary from the equation altogether.

Before he made up his mind, the pilot took the decision out of his hands. The enemy Manta performed a fast hard-about and plunged toward him, as if the ship were the head of an arrow loosed from a compound bow. It pitched up on its starboard wing, slashing through space like a flying ax blade. It followed an unmistakable collision course.

AT THE SOUND of Maccan's voice, Kane didn't hesitate. Balancing himself on the palms of his hands, Kane thrust his legs backward, slamming a reverse heel kick into the back of Maccan's ankles.

As Maccan went down, crying out in surprised anger, Kane sprang to his feet, put his head back and his chest out, and ran as he had run very few times in his life. As he plunged among the crops of the hydroponic farm, he realized he had no problem admitting to himself that Maccan scared him—badly. Whatever he was, Danaan, human or something in between, Maccan was definitely mad with an undeniable taste for murder.

Kane ran through the sluggish, humid air, splashing through puddles of stagnant water, trampling what appeared to be stalks of corn. He squinted through the mist, trying to get his bearings and chart his escape.

The steam was too thick for him to see the source of the light, but he sensed it wasn't far overhead, and therefore he figured he'd reach a bulkhead or a wall before long. Suddenly, he stumbled and threw out his hands to grab the stalks. They snapped and he fell heavily. He remained on his knees for a moment, listening, measuring the noise he had to have made. He doubted it was much, but then Maccan's hearing was far more keen than his own.

Almost as soon as the thought registered, Kane heard Maccan's habitual sobbing and blood-chilling laugh float through the mist. He couldn't determine its direction, so he continued to crouch among the plants.

"Clumsy as most humans," Maccan said. "As much as I admired your breed's courage, I found your gracelessness almost intolerable."

Kane wanted to remind him of who had been the recipient of a leg sweep, but he elected to remain silent.

"I don't understand why you're fleeing or where you hope to flee," Maccan said pleasantly, almost conversationally. "There's nothing you can accomplish. You're like a half-drowned rat trapped in a maze, a crazed monkey entangled in a net. I suppose I should just leave you alone, let you stumble around, but there's always a chance—however remote—you could do something to cause me problems. All humans eventually caused me problems, even the ones I married. Especially the ones I married."

Maccan paused, then said cheerfully, "Besides, this is a spot of fun to brighten up an otherwise dismal day. Rather like the foxhunts I used to enjoy back when your kind kissed my ass instead of trying to set it on fire."

Kane crept forward very slowly and carefully, not even daring to breathe hard, using Maccan's voice to cover the sounds of his progress. When he stopped speaking, Kane stopped moving. There was a long pause and Kane tensed, expecting to see Maccan towering over him out of the steam.

However, when he spoke again he didn't sound any closer. In a clipped and clinical tone he said, "I understand your fright, but what will happen is actually for the best, you know. It wasn't an easy decision for either Enki or I to reach, but factoring in even the most extreme variables, we had no other choice."

Maccan sighed heavily, regretfully. "Do you know that out of all the other races in the galaxy, the human race is actually the most recent? That's why you were organized in the manner you were, to keep you safe. By the time my people arrived on Earth, we had four million years of accumulated history to reflect upon and we found much of it wanting. We were able to identify our mistakes.

"Of course, by then we had reached the limit of our development. When we met your kind—ah, we were so delighted with you. We adored the immensity of your potential."

As Maccan spoke, Kane crawled forward, only half-listening, more alert for the times Maccan paused than his actual words.

"In all the stewardship arrangements with the Annunaki, we were the happiest with this one. We decided not to rule you from afar as Enki's folk had done, but to go among you—maintaining a certain distance, of course. So we put aside our machines, our instruments and weapons, and tried to make you believe we were essentially the same as you. We became examples to inspire you, to instill in you aspirations to exceed your Annunaki-bred limitations.''

Ahead of him, in between the plants, Kane saw the flat gray expanse of a bulkhead, glistening with moisture. He crawled swiftly to it, touching it, looking to the left and right. A score of feet away he saw the steel collar of a circular hatch protruding from the wall. Swiftly he made his way toward it, found a keypad control and pressed one colored green. Lights danced within the keys, and a gasketed pressure lock separated with a shuddering clank he felt through the soles of his boots. Kane winced at the sound.

The hatch irised open, releasing a puff of cold air and an eerie whistling sound. He saw a chute stretching away at a gradually inclining angle. Regularly placed light rings on the chute's ribbing cast a sickly, yellow-green illumination.

Kane entered the tunnel, pushed the keys on the inner wall and the hatch cover closed. With a breathless curse, he realized immediately the interior of the cylinder held an atmosphere but only a rarified gravity. The inner walls of the chute came equipped with staple-shaped rungs, by which he pulled himself along. Behind him he heard the clanking hiss of the hatch opening, and he twisted his head as the iris widened.

Maccan dived through, his scarred face split by a grin. "Tallyho," he said by way of a greeting. His eyes gleamed against the pallor of his face like a pair of blood-drenched rubies.

Chapter 20

"Battle?" demanded Brigid. She pitched her voice low to disguise the quaver of fear in it. "With whom? You?"

Enki did not reply. Slowly, he turned Megaera's head in his hands so her blistered face and sightless eyes gazed up at him in silent worship.

"Which one of you," he asked softly, "did this to her?"

At the periphery of her vision, Brigid saw Philboyd sag with the weight of horror. He apparently expected Enki to exact vengeance at any moment, and she wasn't at all sure he was not correct.

"Neither one of us," Brigid replied, an edge of defiance to her words. "It was Maccan's doing."

Enki nodded as if the answer was no surprise. His ophidian eyes were full of sorrow. "Just so, just so. She was mad, yes, I know. As was her grandmother who first found me. She went mad with the knowledge I imparted to you and passed both the insanity and the knowledge down from generation to generation. My final legacy to humanity.

"Yet, for all of that, she was loyal to me. It was the one quality you humans possessed that was beyond our understanding. We placed little value on it then."

Brigid forced herself to stare directly into Enki's inhuman face. "Were you the one who inspired her to go out and pass judgment on sinners? Were you the one who commanded her to grant salvation through pain and terror?"

Enki's lips stretched in what she hoped was a smile. "Megaera—all three of them—did as she did of her own free will. I did not inspire or command her to use Annunaki tools for her own crazed ends. Free will was an inborn trait your kind exhibited even in the earlier protoform of your development. My brother, Enlil, wanted it bred out of you, but I opposed him."

Brigid stood very still, too fascinated for the moment to be afraid.

"He thought me a sentimental fool," Enki continued in a whisper, "and time proved him right. I learned of my own folly too late, learned that the pupils to whom we gave the seeds of knowledge had grown too clever."

"Enlil is dead," Brigid declared matter-of-factly.

Enki's eyes flickered with a touch of emotion. She could almost have called it envy, and when he spoke, there was wistfulness in his voice. "Yes, Enlil is dead. They are all dead. Ninurata, Ninhursang, Shamash, even grand and glorious Ea…only I remain."

Philboyd finally spoke, in a voice so low Brigid barely heard him. "Why?"

Enki turned slightly toward him with a sound like the rustling of dry leaves.

Philboyd coughed and asked in a stronger voice, "Why do you remain?"

"It was my duty. I was charged to remain until Nibiru completed its orbital cycle."

"And then?" Brigid pressed.

"And then make it young again, as when my race stood tall and proud." He paused, and a surprisingly human tongue darted from his mouth to dab at his lips. He added contemptuously, "Tall and proud and arrogant."

"You've been here on the Moon for over three thousand years?" Brigid asked.

Enki nodded thoughtfully, then shook his head. "I can no longer be sure of anything in regards to the passage of time. When we were released from stasis two centuries before the preappointed time, without the proper reconditioning, our minds were confused."

"'We'?" Philboyd echoed quizzically. His scientist's training was slowly but surely pushing back his human terror.

"Maccan." Enki pronounced the word in such a way that it came out almost as a sardonic drawl.

Enki made a guttural sound in his throat and turned away in a slow, painful shamble. Brigid glimpsed the short, vestigial tail dangling from the base of his spine. "Unlike me, Maccan was banished here by his own people. And like me, he was weary of abiding by the terms of the pact and sought to change them."

Enki limped toward the shadowed dais, a silent signal the conversation was over. Brigid shifted position, rattling her manacles. "Enki, wait!" she called after him.

Enki continued limping away. Brigid raised her voice. "Enki, I've got to know."

The tall, scaled figure paused, not speaking or turning his head toward her. "Enki," she repeatedly urgently, "I have to know about you. Even if I'm fated to die in the next few hours, you must tell me about your race. You must share your knowledge."

A peculiar sibilant hissing came from Enki. He turned back around to face her, his throat pulsing strangely. If Brigid could have recoiled in fearful revulsion, she would have. Then with a start of surprise she realized Enki was laughing.

"Knowledge," he echoed bitterly. "Oh, yes, I have much knowledge. I know everything my race knew, no matter how trivial. Or shameful. I've suffered with it for centuries piled upon centuries. When your kind labored to build pyramids in the Nile Valley, I suffered. If I could forget all that I know and thus end the suffering, I would happily do so."

Enki moved closer, dragging his crippled foot. "I'll share my knowledge…and perhaps a bit of the agony my soul suffers because of it. You would like that?"

Brigid swallowed hard and said. "I would."

Without preamble, Enki began speaking of a race that had grown to maturity on a world already in its death throes. In planetary terms, Nibiru was drawing its final breath. Its wild orbit caused it to be unusually variable as to heat and cold and caused drastic weather changes, geological upheavals and gravity disruptions.

But in biological terms, Nibiru's final breath was long enough for the Annunaki to evolve from a race of saurian bipeds into a prosperous, even magnificent civilization. If life on any planet in any solar system was a rigorous, merciless test of survival of the fittest, it was on Nibiru, and the Annunaki passed. They did not allow nature to stand in their way. As on Earth, adaptability was the primary key to survival.

They conquered their wild environment, but they were not conquerors by nature. They were organizers first and foremost and they tamed Nibiru by organizing themselves, learning to subsist on the resources of a nearly depleted world.

When the Annunaki mastered space flight and then the secret of hyperdimensional travel, they turned to the other worlds in the solar system to supply the deficits of their own.

Brigid knew that part of the story, or at least the Danaan version of it, as imparted by the Speaking Stone of Cascorach. Her eidetic memory was prodded by Enki's words to bring forth the images telepathically impressed into her mind on that day.

By human standards, the Annunaki were cold of heart. They viewed Earth as a vast treasure trove of natural resources. Their technology depended upon it, and labor was their scarcest commodity. The little blue-white planet, third from the Sun, provided both in abundance. They set about redesigning Earth and its primitive inhabitants into models of maximized potential.

Again she saw the images of shapes moving across the smoky, sooty sky of ancient Earth—boom arms swinging in slow circles, black objects crawling along glistening tracks, buildings and factory complexes, the foundations of which stretched deep beneath the surface. The Annunaki tapped the core of the planet itself for the generation of pure energy.

Once Earth was modified, the indigenous protohumans were remolded. They were graded at rough intellectual levels, classified by physique, agility and dexterity. Once the selection of the best of the best was completed, the process of creating a kindred yet superior species began. The Annunaki scientists unwound the dextro-rotary helix, wrapped it around some of their most desirable genetic characteristics, dabbled with the cerebrospinal fluid and rewrote the chromosomal codes.

Brigid saw strange creatures, some slender with wings, some burly and furred, others one-eyed and ugly and some so bizarrely shaped she could not even guess at what the bioengineers were hoping to achieve. They were the lost races of man, the mistakes, the chimeras that served as the foundation for creatures and monsters of myth.

The first generation of slave labor was only a step above the indigenous hominid species, and they were encouraged to breed so each successive descendant might be superior to the first. Also, children made the best slaves, because they knew no other kind of life. The brains improved and technical skills grew. And so did cogent thoughts and the ability to deal with abstract concepts.

Sluggish mental activities increased exponentially in speed and depth, prompting the construction of ideas that eventually led to the formation of restlessness and dissatisfaction.

The Annunaki failed to notice this expansion of cognition on the part of their slaves. As an essentially peaceful race, they viewed violence as unproductive and a waste of resources. They were exploiters, not conquerors.

Eventually—because revolution was the product of frustration—rebellion came. Even Earth turned into an unprofitable enterprise, so the Annunaki arranged for a catastrophe to destroy their labor force. The catastrophe was recorded in ancient texts and even cultural memories as the Flood.

But this was not an easy decision to reach among the Annunaki, and they factionalized over it. Enlil, ever the persecutor of humanity, was opposed by Enki. Although he took covert steps to insure there would be human survivors of the catastrophe, he had no choice but to leave Earth with the rest of his brethren.

Enki and a small group of supporters had become attached to Earth and its inhabitants and were overwhelmed with guilt and remorse. They could not return to Nibiru or any of their outposts on the other planets and live in peace with Enlil and the others who had approved and engineered the near genocide of humankind.

Over the course of the centuries on Earth, their perceptions about life had changed. They acquired a new need, a new passion that sent groups of them across the widest gulfs of space. They had stopped seeking power and even knowledge, and found themselves driven by a motivation grander than the simple survival of their race—a motivation to aid the development and fulfillment of all sentient life.

Quietly, without particular emotion, Enki said, "We could not undo what had been done to your kind, nor could we keep to ourselves what we had achieved. So we thought to share it. We thought of life-forms springing into being all over the universe, evolving races that needed our knowledge, and even the vast distances between the stars could not hold us back.

"Having acquired all the skills and technology that we were capable of acquiring, we spread across the galaxy, driven by a need to rectify our crime against humanity."

Enki paused, his eyes briefly veiled by his deeply wrinkled lids. He shook his blunt-featured head as it trying to rid of it ugly memories. "And then," he said hoarsely, "the worst disaster imaginable befell my people. We met the Tuatha de Danaan."

Enki opened his eyes, jerking his head back as if surprised to see Brigid and Philboyd standing before him. From his mouth issued a stream of jumbled consonants.

The Furies immediately dropped to their knees but not in benediction. Swiftly, they opened the manacles around Phiboyd and Brigid's ankles. Both people were too shocked to speak.

Enki turned toward the dais, pivoting on his good leg. "Humanity has been in shackles long enough. You will come with me."

THE TWO SHIPS WERE almost on top of each other. According to the measurements scrolling madly within Grant's helmet, they were. Swearing coarsely, he jerked the control stick and veered out of the path of the approaching Manta. Its edge-on wing missed cleaving through his cockpit canopy like a butcher knife by less than a yard.

The two ships sprang apart, swerving right and left, up and down, circling the DEVIL platform in a wide arc as if it were the hub of a wheel.

A grid of hairlines glowed inside the visor of Grant's helmet, and a tiny bead of light, a digital copy of the enemy ship, zipped to and fro through the little computer-generated opticals.

The DEVIL platform continued to spit plasmoids, but their frequency seemed to be tapering off and Grant wondered if the batteries were close to exhausted. Twice his craft shuddered under the impact of glancing hits, but they did little more than shake him up a little. The energies they contained seemed weak, little more than electrified snowballs.

The pilot of the other Manta ship posed a far more immediate threat. He seemed to pay no heed to the pulses of energy, fixated as he was on crashing his craft into Grant's. It was no longer a dogfight—it was a protracted game of tag and Grant wasn't enjoying it one bit. With an angry reluctance, he realized he had no choice but to sacrifice one of his two missiles to blast the pursuing ship out of space.

As it approached him again on another suicide run, Grant threw his vessel into a dizzy corkscrew spin, right between the DEVIL platform and the nose of the other ship. The blazing volley of plasmoids missed him entirely but tracked the enemy craft. The ship veered sharply away from the salvo, looped and returned to engage Grant again.

A flurry of plasmoids streaked toward both ships like a glowing sleet storm. The enemy vessel began an evasive turn, but two bolts struck dead on target amidships. Another ball from the DEVIL platform touched the Manta's rear guidance assembly, fragmenting it and all but shearing it away. The ship spun helplessly, its stabilizers obviously knocked out.

Grant didn't hesitate. He lined up the wobbling ship in his helmet's crosshairs and thumbed the launch stud. The missile roared out of the starboard side wing pod in a flare of flame. It streaked in a straight line to impact against the Manta's topside fuselage, right where the curve of the cockpit canopy spread out to merge with the wings.

It exploded in a bloom of flame and metal fragments. The Manta ship flipped into a crazed sideways wing-over-wing roll, strewing space with flying shards of canopy and engine parts. The craft tumbled in a careening barrel roll. The fuel tank ignited on the fourth roll with a detonation that swallowed the bodywork in a mushroom of roiling flame. The ship disintegrated in a shower of hardware, both of its backswept wings wrenched loose and cartwheeled in opposite directions.

There was no sound, for sound does not travel in a vacuum, but Grant's ship shuddered and shook from the shock wave. He repressed a snarl of savage satisfaction, turning it into a sigh of relief instead.

Manipulating the joystick, he flew straight up, standing the Manta on its tail, then dropped the nose, plunging back down toward the DEVIL platform, intending to fly far beneath it then come up directly from below. Several of the plasmoid batteries appeared to be exchausted. Only two had fired at the enemy vessel, but the energies were at full strength.

He completed the maneuver perfectly, pulling out of the dive with the same smooth, effortless grace of a hawk skimming across the surface of a pond. He soared upward, thumb hovering over the trigger button on the joystick. Carefully, he nosed the ship into a ninety-degree angle relative to the postion of the DEVIL platform's underbelly.

Just as carefully, he aligned the protruding cube of the generator with his helmet's optical-targeting system. His eyes were fixed on the cube as it loomed larger and larger in the center of the canopy. His thumb rested on the missile stud, waiting, holding his breath.

Then, when the image of the cube completely filled the crosshairs on the inner curve of his helmet's visor, he depressed the button. And nothing happened. He snarled out a curse and pressed it again and again, receiving only a series of impotent clicks for his efforts.

In a fraction of a second he realized the plasmoid strikes had disrupted the circuitry to the missile launch commands. His thoughts rolled loosely in his head like dropped marbles, but he didn't alter course or decrease his speed.

Then lightning flashed in a jagged arc from above him and his Manta shuddered brutally and rocked. He pulled back on the stick but the ship kept to its course, the controls locked and frozen. A crack spread across the canopy and as he watched in horrified, breathless fascination, the crack became a spiderwebbed network. For a microsecond, he heard grisly jangling and crunching noises and the canopy blew outward, showering him with razor-edged shards.

Grant thought of Shizuka and her Bushido code and wondered if she would think this particular death was an honorable one. He decided to forestall that judgment as long as he could.

When the Manta was only two hundred yards away from the top of the cube, Grant wrenched at the lever beneath the pilot's chair. The explosive pop of the eject rocket lasted only a shaved sliver of second. A giant boot seemed to kick him in the rear and catapult him out and upward. He found himself plunging toward the floating debris of the enemy ship.

The Manta continued on its upward course, on a direct heading with the generator. Grant watched as it plummeted into it, its nose flattened, turning up on itself, the hull splitting like a banana skin. The resultant flare from the engines was so bright that he averted his face. Then the missile, its warhead already armed, detonated with a rolling billow of flame, draping the underside of the DEVIL platform in a blanket of fire.

For an instant it appeared to Grant that even the stars themselves took flame.

Chapter 21

Kane clambered hand over hand along the chute, kicking himself from the floor as he dragged himself forward by the metal rungs. He clenched his teeth so hard his jaw muscles ached. Behind him he heard Maccan's similar progress. The lighter gravity enhanced Kane's speed, but didn't give him much of an advantage since his pursuer was similarly blessed. He guessed they were entering an area only tangentially affected by the artificial-gravity inducers.

Kane knew the obvious option was to turn and face Maccan, but that tactic would provide only amusement for the man—and result in Kane's death. Out of the many things in his life he hated, being pursued, forced into the role of prey, topped the list. It didn't come naturally to him.

Maccan didn't exhort him to stop or give up, but he laughed occasionally, evidently enjoying the chase immensely. The chute curved slightly upward, so Kane couldn't see what lay at its far end. He dreaded what he might find there, fearing it would be only a closed and locked hatch cover. He imagined bumping his head in stupid futility against it, like a bug that had made an arduous crawl inside a pipe, only to find the drain plugged.

He didn't look behind him but continued pulling and kicking himself along, hating Maccan with an intensity that surprised him, and hating himself for allowing the red-eyed madman to frighten him so. He tried to remind himself of all the enemies he'd faced and bested, and how, despite their frightful aspects and supreme confidence, they were gone while he still lived.

The light grew stronger ahead, and with a surge of strength and tendon-straining effort, Kane doubled his speed. The chute terminated in a round opening, framed by a rivet-studded steel collar. Without hesitation, he stretched up his arms and wriggled his body through.

Staggering to his feet, he spared his surroundings only a single, swift glance. Sunlight flowed down from a round skylight in the high, arched roof, glinting from stacked metal crates and long trestle tables. Symbols and letters were visible on some crates through the cargo netting draped over them. Kane walked casually on an oblique course that brought him close enough to read them. Some of the cases bore the acronym NASA, and others strings of indecipherable letters that seemed like a deliberate jumbling of the alphabet. Several read DEVIL/Manitius Base.

The walls, ceiling and floor of the chamber formed one continuous surface, making a huge, hollow ellipse measuring out to a hundred feet in diameter. It was as if he were within the center of an impossibly gargantuan ball.

From the curving walls of the chamber jutted platforms connected by a series of cage-enclosed lifts and crossed girders. Tall, Y-shaped induction pylons sprouted from the floor, but their ceramic surfaces were blackened, soot-smudged. Between two of them stood a pair of oblong pedestals, nearly seven feet tall. Four small pyramids crafted from pale golden alloy were placed equidistantly around them. Resting on their points were smooth, crystalline ovoids, made of some translucent material.

The small, calm and cool part of his mind identified them as stasis units, larger versions of the one he had seen in the crashed Archon mother ship beneath the Black Gobi nearly two years before.

Kane ran among crystal-and-metal mechanisms that had no meaning for him, looking for anything he could use as a weapon. He found a three-foot length of metal that resembled a piece of rebar with a coating of golden lacquer. Hefting it in one hand, he was disappointed by its light weight, but he attributed it to the lesser gravity. Besides, he had no time to search for anything better.

Maccan's head and shoulders rose from the opening in the floor. His crimson eyes shifted back and forth, seeking out Kane, and when they fixed on him, he grinned jauntily. "Ah, so there you are!"

"Yeah," Kane replied flatly, slapping the bludgeon against the palm of his right hand. "Here I are."

Maccan heaved himself lithely out of the chute. "Tired of the game so soon?"

"I'm tired of running, if that's what you mean."

Maccan's face arranged itself in a moue of mock hurt. "That's a shame. I was quite enjoying myself. I'm very disappointed."

"I know," retorted Kane. "And I intend to disappoint you a lot more."

Lines of anger appeared in Maccan's high forehead. "Whatever do you mean?"

Kane took a slow forward step, balancing himself on the balls of his feet. "Let's dance, you fused-out fairy."

Kane plunged forward, swinging the length of metal toward Maccan's head. He leaned backward, one long leg shooting upward and outward in a murderous kick. Kane didn't get out of the way completely. A booted heel, heavy and hard, plowed into his stomach and waves of pain washed over him.

He managed to keep from doubling over and bobbed left and right, avoiding more kicks. Maccan circled him, lips twisted in a feral grin. "Do you have any idea of how many of your kind I have killed in these quaint hand-to-hand contests? Jealous husbands, warriors seeking to add to their legend or simply arrogant little turds like you who earned my wrath due to one transgression or another."

Kane didn't waste his breath with a reply. He swung the club again, feinting first at Maccan's eyes, then jabbing it toward his groin. Maccan backed away warily, circling. Another foot lashed out, and Kane was caught a glancing blow across his forearm.

Maccan performed a graceful pirouette on the toes of his left foot and swung his left in a spinning crescent. Kane managed to duck and hook his heel with the rod of metal, then grabbed his ankle with his free hand and spun savagely.

Maccan went down on his back, his face expressing more shock than pain. Almost instantly he levered himself up by his hands. Kane followed through, roundhousing with the rebar in a short arc that cracked into the side of the Danaan's skull. Maccan received the full force of the blow. It knocked him sideways to the floor, long legs and arms asprawl, and lacerated his temple. Red blood flowed down the side of his face, contrasting sharply with his blue-white complexion.

Maccan turned his sprawl into a roll and swiftly came to his feet. He started to charge Kane, then checked the movement. Cautiously, he touched the wound on the side of his head and examined the blood shining on his fingertips. Kane noted distractedly his blood was a lighter shade of red than his eyes.

"That actually hurt," he said wonderingly. "I underestimated you."

"A lot of assholes do," Kane said quietly. "That's why most of them are dead now."

Maccan affected not to have heard him. "I'll be damned. You actually hurt me." His voice held no anger, only bewilderment.

Kane grinned, but there was little humor in it. "Remember when you said I reminded you a Celtic warrior of the old days—the one who interfered with the Danaan?"

Maccan nodded absently, frowning at the blood.

"If you were thinking of Cuchulainn, it might interest you to know that I've been told I have his soul."

Maccan pursed his lips thoughtfully. "It's possible. Fand always said he was something special, but he just seemed like another unwashed barbarian to me, smelling of donkey feces. But then she always was a whore."

Maccan lunged in a blur of speed, the lesser gravity turning his leap into a catlike bound. Kane was ready for him and dodged easily. As the Danaan went by, he struck him twice across the upper and lower back with the length of metal.

Crying out, Maccan halted, instantly reversed his body, and his left arm slashed out and down in a scything sweep, the edge of his hand catching Kane's right wrist. He felt a flash of agony burning a zigzag course up his arm and his fingers reflexively opened. The bar clattered to the floor.

Kane backpedaled rapidly, pistoning his left fist into Maccan's face in a short, fast jab, straight out from the shoulder. His aquiline nose spurted blood, but he only grinned, snorting out a spray of scarlet.

Magistrate martial-arts training borrowed shamelessly from every source—from tae kwon do to savate to kung fu. The style was down and dirty, focusing primarily on the aspects of offense rather than defense. Magistrate doctrine taught never to be defensive when any opportunity presented itself to go on the attack. Most Mags had no idea when, or even how to back off.

Maccan launched a roundhouse kick at Kane's midriff in a lightning-swift semicircle. Kane couldn't evade it so he moved into the arc, striking down with his right elbow an instant before the man's foot made contact.

Kane's arm rebounded, a hot flush of pain spreading through his arm. Maccan cried out angrily and retreated, favoring his leg. As much as he wanted to, Kane didn't massage his elbow or allow his astonishment to show on his face. The last time he had executed that maneuver, he had literally crippled his attacker. Apparently, Danaan bone was made of a denser substance than human.

Limping only a little, Maccan closed with Kane, trying to exchange punches with him, but his flailing fists missed their weaving target or rebounded from his forearms. Kane realized that although Maccan's strength was immense, his reflexes little short of superhuman, his combat acumen and skills weren't even up to the levels possessed by Baptiste.

Kane took ruthless advantage of him. He kicked him, he clawed him, he head-butted him, bit him and tried to gouge out his crimson eyes. Maccan stumbled and staggered from the battering. Kane had about half a second of triumph before he felt an agonizing vise-like close on his upper left arm.

Kane glimpsed the scarred, silently snarling face of Maccan just as the Danaan yanked his 180 pounds up from the floor and tossed him three-quarters of the way across the room. He slammed down on the concrete floor chest first near the stasis units, and all the air went out of his lungs in an agonized bellow.

Gasping, Kane forced himself to one knee, but not before Maccan delivered a kick to his belly that lifted him completely clear of the floor and dropped him on his back ten feet away. He lay there, writhing in agony, unable to move or even breathe.

Through the blood thundering in his ears, he heard Maccan say in a voice swimming in a pool of contempt, ''Humans. Too stupid to know when you're outmatched. Didn't you know I was just playing with you?''

Kane managed to drag in a shuddery breath, half-filling his lungs. Blinking back the pain haze from his vision, he saw Maccan standing over him, blood-streaked face twisted in a cold smirk.

''That's all we ever were to you,'' he managed to choke out. ''Playthings, toys. When you got tired of us, you tossed us under the bed of history.''

Maccan's lips peeled back from his teeth in a snarl of maniacal rage. He roared, ''Toys? Toys?''

He screeched words in an unintelligible tongue, and though he didn't understand a single syllable, the blazing fury he directed at Kane's presumption hammered him.

He bent and his hooked, rigid fingers sank into Kane's throat in a crushing grip meant to keep him from speaking, meant to break bones, to snap cartilage, to tear through any muscles that got in the way.

Kane caught his wrists, noting fearfully that despite their slender appearance, they felt like two bars of tempered steel. He bellowed into Kane's face, spraying him with blood and spittle. "We loved humanity! We loved you so much and for so long, you took it for granted. We nurtured you, cherished you, *protected* you! Yet you spit in our eyes, hunted us down, tied us to posts and set us on fire!"

Kane pounded at him with his fists, but it was as if Maccan were made of steel and bone. He gritted his teeth and took the blows with little grunts.

"We fought wars for you!" Maccan shrieked. He shook Kane ferociously, as a terrier shakes a rat. "Thousands of us perished—all for you!"

What little oxygen remained in Kane's lungs was depleted. The lights overhead began to swim, and with a twinge of horror, he thought he heard his own vertebrae beginning to collapse under the throttling grip.

As his thoughts clouded, he recalled the first morning at the Magistrate Division—when he was twelve—and how he had awakened on his bunk before dawn, cold, frightened, yet strangely eager for the day to begin.

The twenty years since that morning had condi-

tioned all childish fears and frailties from his mind
and body, particularly the day of his final examination.
He was sixteen, a day that marked his last day as a
recruit and his first day as a badge-carrying Magistrate. There was no such thing as failure of the examination—those who survived it were the ones who
didn't fail.

The test had no true name, but everyone called it
Blood Stomper. As he hung within Maccan's crushing
hands, Kane recalled that day with a painful vividness.
Already possessed with a near inhuman ambition to
win at any contest, the young Kane was a ferocious
opponent. Even the larger recruits tended to give him
his due, and tried to keep from being run down when
Kane had the ball.

Blood Stomper mixed elements of predark American football with European soccer, but what few rules
were in place served to drive home the object of the
game—get your team's ball from one end of the playing field to the other, and damn the consequences. The
ball was only out of play when it went out of bounds,
or the carrier was stopped in his tracks by almost any
means possible.

The concept of being fouled was not one of the
rules. Also missing from Blood Stomper were protective helmets, padding and gear. The recruits played in
little more than loincloths. There was no protection.
Rarely did an examination end without multiple injuries, ranging from bloody noses to fractured skulls.

Deaths, although not particularly commonplace, were not by any means rare.

Kane had taken the ball that day and run like the winds of a hellzone, face flushed, feet pumping, the sound of his overtaxed lungs rasping in his ears. Blockers on his side did their best to clear the way, but Kane was moving too fast and dealing with his encroaching foes in two ways—he either outmaneuvered them and kept moving forward, or he went right through them. He was confident in his speed and reflexes, and so became careless, if not downright cocky.

That day, his drive and speed were not adequate to keep him safe. He took an elbow to the throat and fell down fast and hard, flat on his back, gagging from the blow and gasping to regain the wind that been shoved out of his lungs when he slapped down on the hard ground beneath the grass.

The opposing team then used their fists and feet to keep him from ever getting up again. There wasn't anything personal in trying to beat him to death—it was part of the examination. He would have done the same to a fallen member of the opposing team.

He remembered his strategy from that day, how he not only managed to survive the vicious beating, but also scored the winning point. With nothing to lose, fueled only by desperation, he employed the same tactic now.

Kane let himself go limp and let his tongue protrude from his mouth, hoping against hope Maccan would misread the signal as had the opposing team all those years ago.

Maccan shifted his grasp, meaning to pull him upward. For a split second the grip loosened and Kane jacked up a knee, hammering it into Maccan's back. At the same time he rammed his arms up and outward between Maccan's wrists, breaking the killing prison of his hands.

Before the Danaan could reapply the stranglehold, Kane lifted his right hand, wrist locked, fingers curled, and smashed a leopard's-paw strike toward his opponent's nose.

Maccan swiftly lowered his head so instead of crushing the cartilage and driving bone splinters into his brain, the heel of Kane's hand bounced painfully from the Danaan's forehead. Still Maccan's head jerked back and Kane managed to buck him off.

He tried to shamble to his feet, but Maccan latched on to one leg and dragged him back down. Kane twisted his body so he landed on top of him.

They tumbled over the floor, locked in each other's arms, tearing at each other.

Kane battered at the pale face with both fists, pounding it repeatedly with hammering downward jabs from the shoulder. His mindless fury made him oblivious to the pain searing his knuckles and streaking up his wrists.

Maccan flung him aside and scrambled to all fours. Kane achieved a half-crouch and both combatants glared at each other, breathing hard, faces moist with sweat and blood.

Hoarsely, Maccan said, "Your holy men, your church men turned us into devils...humans with whom we made contact were tortured and killed. Even our children—" He bit back the last word, lips compressing tightly as if to keep himself from ever uttering the word again.

Kane, in between pants, demanded, "Who are you, Maccan? Who *are* the Tuatha de Danaan? Devils, angels or aliens?"

Maccan inhaled a long breath. "We were your caretakers. We entered into a pact with the Annunaki to watch over you until they returned. But by the time they did, our lives were so intertwined with that of humanity, with your glorious loves, your petty hatreds, your territorial disputes...we could not simply hand you back over to those reptiles and walk away."

He squeezed his eyes shut and shook his head sorrowfully. "No, we could not. We should have, but we did not. We were fools. We had become...dependent on you."

He uttered the word as if it were most appalling thing imaginable.

"What the hell are you talking about?" Kane snapped impatiently.

Maccan's arm whipped up and around, catching the side of Kane's face with an openhanded blow. His head twisted painfully on his neck and he fell heavily onto his right side.

"Who are you to question me?" Maccan demanded, infuriated.

Kane struggled back to his hands and knees. He felt blood flowing from both nostrils, tasted its salty tang as it slid over his lips. He swung his right arm in a looping blow, planting his fist solidly on Maccan's prominent chin. The Danaan didn't fall like Kane, but with the meaty thud of impact, a glassy sheen covered his eyes.

"I'm one of the human beings you fought wars for," Kane half growled, half gasped. "That's who I am."

Maccan shook his head, narrowing his eyes to slits. When he widened them, their bright crimson hue had faded to a pewter gray. In a halting, strained voice, Maccan said, "We were a race who had fought our way to the stars…we always fought. We were warriors, we were conquerors. But when the aeons of time pressed down, we realized we could not maintain our empire. We pulled in our colonies, our outposts and left them to those we had conquered. We abandoned it all."

"Why?" Kane demanded.

"Knowledge was our godhood," muttered Maccan. His eyes were vacant, as if he gazed not at Kane but into the dim past. "Godhood was our knowledge. It was our form of unity."

Kane's nape hairs tingled at the utterance of the word.

"Then that unity repudiated itself," Maccan whispered. "We met the Annunaki. They were stronger than us, but they did not make war on us, try to conquer us. They sought peace, sought an accord, wished us to help them wash out the stain of genocide. They sought to make a pact with us. They were capable of peaceful coexistence with all things. We thought we were, as well. It was a better dream than those of empire."

Biting back a groan, Kane slowly pushed himself to both knees. "I don't understand."

Maccan voiced his high, sobbing laugh. "Of course not!"

He struck Kane with a knotted fist, knocking him back down.

"Of course not! How could you possibly understand—how can you know what it's like to be an exile on the world of your birth?"

Kane gingerly fingered the side of his face where Maccan's blow had landed, then lunged forward, butting the Danaan squarely in the forehead. The impact sent shivers of pain all the way to the base of his spine, but he bellowed in fury, "I know what it's like! Now it seems like it was all due to you and this bullshit pact thousands of years ago to curtail humanity's development."

Maccan cupped his forehead with both hands, resting on his elbows. As if he were quoting a text he intoned, "The scientific quests of humanity will lead them to extinction. We have extrapolated from their current level of curiosity, it will lead them to extinction...the knowledge we gave them makes it clear that within three millennia humanity will leave its planet and venture into space. They must not be allowed to go forward, for that way lies the extermination of their race.''

Kane's mind swam. This was not what he had expected to hear.

''The concept of progress must be repressed within them,'' Maccan continued in the same flat voice. He lowered his hands from his forehead and pushed himself up to a crouch. His lips curled in a disdainful sneer as he spoke as if mocking someone. ''There must be no purpose in any field of knowledge. The human race must remain as they are. You will help them consolidate what they have and live in peace with them. It is up to you to insure they present no threat to us, either now or in the future.''

Kane felt an anger rising in him. ''Who are you quoting?'' he snapped.

Maccan's body shook, and for a moment Kane wondered if he were suffering from a seizure. Then Kane realized he was laughing silently, his mouth open, spittle and blood forming bubbles on his lips. He struck at Kane again, but this time he shunted the blow aside. ''Who are you quoting?'' he repeated in a fierce shout.

''Me!'' Maccan howled fiercely. ''Myself! No other! It is what I said to Lam, to Los, to Urizen during our first council. They agreed wholeheartedly— then.''

Kane watched, stunned into speechlessness as Maccan slowly and painfully staggered to his feet. Blood streamed all over the battered mask of his face. He touched the laceration on his temple, frowned at the crimson wetness on his fingertips and said, "Instead of rectifying our error, they repeated it."

"Who is 'we'?" Kane asked.

Maccan laughed scornfully. "Enki and I, representatives of our two peoples. We made a fitting pair, godfathers of a new race that was designed to be greater than the sum of its parts. A fitting pair indeed—a prince without an empire and a god without worshipers."

He turned toward the pair of stasis canisters. "And to our royal beds we retired, to sleep until the time came to fulfill the final terms of the pact."

Casting Kane a sour smile over his shoulder, he murmured, "Imagine my surprise, both of our surprises, when we were awakened long before the pre-agreed time—roused by none other the curious little monkeys we had tried to confine to their compounds."

Kane rose stiffly, wincing at the flares of pain igniting all over his body. "Who were you expecting?"

Maccan turned fully around, facing him. "No one," he stated flatly. "Nobody at all. And therein lies the crux of the problem. But at least that one has a solution."

With that, Maccan lunged toward Kane, hands outstretched, reaching for his neck. Kane did not retreat. He launched into a *tobi-geri* flying kick, and aided by the lighter gravity, he sailed across the distance separating them. He slammed Maccan under the chin with his extended left foot and smashed his right heel into his sternum.

Kane's ferocious double kick sent Maccan spinning backward, toward one of the open stasis units. The back of the Danaan's thighs struck its raised rim, and he toppled directly into its cushioned interior. He seemed stunned for an instant. He opened his mouth to voice a berserker's howl, but before he could propel himself out of the container, the humped, crystalline cover slid over him, cutting off his enraged scream as if an Off switch had been flicked.

His respiration labored, hair damp with sweat, Kane walked over to the canister. It seemed filled with a cloudy, smokelike substance. He touched the crystal surface, the vapor within the ovoid immediately cleared. Within it he saw Maccan, fingers curved like talons, the tips pressed against the inside of the lid, his eyes wide and wild, but unseeing all the same. His expression was locked in a contortion of maddened fury. All the color seemed to have been leached from his body. His form had the appearance of pale blue ice, not only in color but composition. Even the blood on his face was black, like splashes of ink.

Kane took his hand away from the humped crystal form, and the smoky vapor within it immediately swirled around the figure of Maccan again, obscuring it from view. The stasis unit was an encapsulated survival system that froze a subject in an impenetrable

bubble of space and time, slowing to a stop all metabolic processes.

"Sleep a little longer in your royal bed, Mac,"
Kane whispered. "Sleep forever, prince without an
empire."

As he stepped back, a flicker of light overhead
caught his attention. He looked up through the skylight. A tiny red spark gleamed against the black backdrop of star-speckled space. Kane squinted as the
spark slowly expanded like a flare, like a matchhead
flaming up. It did not fade but continued to glow.

Kane felt his heart begin to pound within his chest
like a bird trying frantically to escape a cage. The
explosion wasn't of the kind he expected from a fusion generator and he hoped—he prayed—if Grant
was responsible for it, he had left himself an avenue
of escape.

Chapter 22

For the first handful of seconds, Grant couldn't see anything approximating an avenue of escape as he drifted through the debris field. Still securely strapped to the pilot's chair, he pushed the blackened fragments of the two Manta ships out of his way, barely able to see the white patches of the Moon between them.

Turning his head, he saw the bloom of fire unfolding its coruscating petals. Only vaguely could he discern the silhouette of the DEVIL platform above the flower of flame. He couldn't understand what was happening, or what was feeding the conflagration since there was no oxygen.

Nor did the phenomenon resemble a breach in the combustion chamber of the two-tiered fusion reactor. Twice before he had been uncomfortably close to generator meltdowns, and the effects both times had been little short of apocalyptic.

A chunk of wreckage smacked into his chair, jarring him and sending him skittering sideways. He returned his attention to navigating through the debris. The pieces and shards of the TAVs bobbed and swept past him steadily, and he assumed he was making good progress to get himself clear of it. Then his heart gave a painful jolt as he realized the white curve of Luna below him was not growing in size but receding.

Choking back a curse of fright, Grant twisted in the seat again, slitting his eyes against the glare shimmering from the underside of the platform. He saw the wreckage funneling toward it, as if caught in a swift current of force or drawn by a giant magnet or even by a—

Singularity.

The word popped unbidden into his head, and with it came the chaotic memory of the artificial black hole created by Lord Strongbow in his New London fortress.

Gritting his teeth, Grant leaned his body outward, straining against the harness as if he hoped his head would be caught by the gravity well of the Moon. He knew if he freed himself of the chair he would have to jettison the helmet, as well. Exposure to the vacuum of space would probably be a swifter and less painful death than being sucked into the imploding inferno, but he preferred not to find out.

Tightly he gripped the lower edge of the seat and was barely aware of his fingers depressing a flat toggle switch inset into the metal. A burst of flame spit from the rear of the chair, and he felt a kick against his back. He shot forward, hurtling through the outer edge of the debris field at an accelerating velocity.

With a surge of relief, Grant realized the pilot's chair was equipped with more than a life-support system and a parachute. A parachute would be of no use if a man was forced to eject into space. He silently thanked the long-dead designers of the TAV for their foresight.

Grant jetted straight downward and his fingers carefully explored the keys and switched studding on both sides of the chair. He didn't depress any of them, but suddenly the jet pack ceased flaming. His body rolled over, and he felt the tug of increased speed. He was falling now, caught by the gravity of the Moon. The white pumice deserts and jagged mountain ranges spun crazily, rushing up at him with an appalling suddenness.

He pressed another toggle switch and glimpsed pinsized spurts of blue flame licking out from the underside of the chair. It was as though a giant hand checked his fall for a moment, then he tumbled on downward again. His fingers played desperately over the buttons and he suddenly swung upright, at least in relation to the Moon's surface. He knew he had touched an attitude control and now that he was no longer plummeting headfirst, his eyes scanned the area spread out below him. The gravitational pull was so weak he had plenty of time to look around and pick an appropriate landing site.

He was fast approaching the Manitius colony, the base built in the regolith of the crater. It was a collection of towers and radar dishes and bulldozed flat planes bisected by terraced channels with concrete-paneled sides.

He saw four smooth cylinders, each with a chute

type of tunnel leading to them. Each one was half-dug into the side of the crater, presumably for shelter from radiation. Atop some of the towers were small directional dishes. From others, stairs on elevated girders climbed to pyramidal structures that were part of the solar-cell energy array. The entire expanse was interlaced with thick power cables and conduits stretching along forked pylons.

The cylinders were the life hutches, habitats constructed to offer emergency aid to people who found themselves in difficulty out on the surface of the Moon. Grant decided to make them his landing point. He knew once he touched down he would have to disengage from the chair and therefore his supply of oxygen. Then he would have to run to the nearest life hutch and hope he could get into one of the habitats before he suffocated. Even though no one could hear him, he muttered, "Oh, I really love this, I really get a big fucking kick out of this."

The stark light shed above and behind him by the DEVIL platform suddenly dimmed. Grant hitched around in the chair to give it a final look. A shade crossed the face of the blaze, like the shadow that preceded the coming of a storm. He found the effect subtly terrifying and couldn't help but wonder if concocting a survival plan wasn't a waste of time, since it might prolong his life by only a few minutes.

He pushed this fatalistic thought from his mind and concentrated on gauging speed and distance. His pulse raced with grim determination. When his trajectory began to wobble, his chair tilting from side to side, he pulled the cord attached to the harness.

Grant couldn't hear the whip-crack of the parachute deploying, but he felt the spine-compressing, teeth-clattering shock of the canopy popping open above him. Reaching up behind him, he grasped the guide cords and tugged, trying to achieve a stable attitude. Looking above him, he realized the chute was more of an expanding sail, made of a very thin, lightweight material that he guessed was aluminum-coated Mylar. With no atmosphere to buoy it, a conventional parachute would have been useless on the Moon.

He drifted down, extending his legs. He struck the ground at an angle, a puff of dust mushrooming up around his feet. He bounced high, then sprawled heavily on his right side, the chair plowing a furrow through the pumice. He lay for a moment, taking inventory, a little surprised but very gratified that he wasn't dead or even injured. If he had made the same kind of landing on Earth, he had no doubt he would have died.

Squirming around, Grant saw the cylinder of the nearest life hutch sprouting from the lunar soil fifty yards away. It would be a long walk with no oxygen, but he was certain he had faced more daunting tasks in the past—he just couldn't remember them offhand.

Grant breathed deeply, saturating his lungs with oxygen as he unlatched the harness from around his body. Carefully, he shucked out of the straps, then reached behind him to find the couplings for the air hoses feeding into the rear of his helmet. He gripped the sockets, inhaled a final breath and twisted them free. He heard a high-pitched whistle inside his helmet, then he sprang to his feet and bounded in long-legged leaps to the life hutch.

His heart pounded and his temples throbbed with the exertion. He kept his mouth tightly closed. Within moments, his eyes began to water. He continued his leaping progress, like a crazed kangaroo. He stumbled a time or two when he came down, sending up explosions of pumice dust.

By the time the outer decompression hatch of the module was in sight, his lungs felt on the verge of bursting and his vision was swimming with amoeba-shaped floaters.

Grant staggered against the hatch, putting his hands out to catch himself. He could feel the frigid metal even through the insulation of his gloves. He scrabbled his fingers over it wildly, not finding any keys, buttons, levers or even a wheel lock. His darkening mind flashed back over his life now that it seemed about to be extinguished. He wasn't satisfied with the memories.

His dimming senses became aware of a vibrating motion on the hatch and through the blur of his vision he saw it iris open. He fell inside rather than stepped.

Grant was only faintly aware of thrashing on the floor, gagging and gasping like a fish stranded in the middle of a desert, clawing madly at the collar seal of his helmet.

His hands were grasped and pinned against the deck, and he felt a fumbling pressure around the base of his neck. Then helmet was tugged up and off his head, and half-conscious, he gulped air into his starved lungs.

Finally, when his chest no longer burned, he raised his head and blinked around. Three figures swam into focus and when he jerked away, a familiar female voice said soothingly, "Relax, Grant. It's only us."

Clearing his sight with the heel of a hand, he saw Mariah, Neukirk and Eduardo kneeling around him. He looked around at the interior of the hutch. It was a cylinder, just like the exterior. He noted the relay machines, the computer terminals, a medicine cabinet clamped to the bulkhead and a refrigerator.

"You look like hell," Mariah said.

Grant stood up stiffly. "Nothing that won't pass with a little time, providing we have any left."

He scanned their faces. Mariah wasn't beautiful or young. Her chestnut hair was threaded with gray and cut painfully short to the scalp. Deep creases curved out from either side of her nose to the corners of her mouth. Dark-ringed brown eyes gazed at them from beneath long brows that hadn't been plucked in years, if ever. Her teeth, though white, were uneven.

Neukirk, wearing a gray coverall, was a short, chunky man with weather-beaten features and a white crew cut.

Eduardo was slightly below middle height, wearing a dark brown coverall. His complexion was of a similar hue, and his long black hair hung in lank strands, framing a deeply scarred face.

Despite the three people's contrasting appearances, they all appeared to be gripped by a soul-deep terror.

"You're not looking so grand yourselves," Grant retorted.

"We've been hiding out in here since you and your friends left with Philboyd." Eduardo's voice was bleak, hopeless. "This is the hutch we modified to be the central control analog for DEVIL."

"But it's dead," Neukirk said. "All of the enabling codes get bounced back."

"We don't know what the hell is going on," Mariah put in. "Do you?"

Grant sighed heavily, happy he could perform that small act at least. "I have a general idea, but I doubt it'll matter a whole hell of lot. Ask me again in a few minutes."

Chapter 23

Brigid and Philboyd followed Enki into a long corridor at the base of the dais. The walls were severe but beautifully crafted out of a dark stone, like the exterior of the citadel itself.

Philboyd rubbed his chest and grimaced with every step. Brigid side-mouthed to him, "You're doing fine."

His lacerated lips started to stretch in a smile, but the pain was too great. "That's because I'm a tough geek. Tough geek with a tough babe. I like the dynamics."

Brigid smiled at him wanly as if she knew what he was talking about. Her mind was swirling, functioning in a matrix of fear, elation and wonder. Her mind toyed with images, of what ancient technical marvels and alien works of art Enki would reveal to them.

When Enki led them into a small antechamber, Brigid's disappointment was so profound she almost blurted out a cry of annoyance. In the center of the chamber a metal shaft rose straight up to the shadow-shrouded ceiling. Brigid guessed it was the support post for the crystalline structure she had glimpsed at the uppermost point of the citadel.

There were no furnishings at all, only a four-foot square of ground glass inset into the wall. It was a copy of the big VGA monitor screen in the Cerberus operations center. The image it displayed routed her disappointment and a cold fear caught at her, deep inside. A seething, brilliant mass boiled there, like the open mouth of an inferno or the core of a star.

Enki absently caressed Megaera's head as he murmured, "Quite possibly a very impious action. Possibly not."

"What the hell is happening?" Philboyd sounded as if he were strangling on a bone. "That's the DEVIL platform, but it's not undergoing the entropic process—it's not even the reaction you'd get from a breached fusion chamber!"

Enki nodded slowly, then just as slowly shook his head. "You are right. Even nuclear reaction, from fission to fusion, is potentially unstable. I surmise the combustion chamber is feeding off the energies of the particle accelerator."

"What will happen?" Brigid demanded.

"I really could not say with a degree of certainty," Enki replied softly. "I can only speculate. And I find not knowing is in itself a little exhilarating."

A strange pathos touched Brigid's heart. "What did you really have in mind for the DEVIL process? What was its point?"

Enki's reply was a low, rustling whisper. "Everything has an ending...and from that a new beginning."

Philboyd cocked his head toward him. "You mean entropy is like a circle, like the spiral-and-cup symbol you have all over the place here?"

Enki did not reply. He only smiled cryptically and Brigid stared into his strange eyes, the wise, inhuman but loving eyes, and a shudder shook her. "Are you using the DEVIL process to wipe out your people—and the Tuatha de Danaan—to rectify what was done to humanity thousands of years ago?"

Enki's nostrils dilated as he exhaled a long breath. Brigid guessed it was his form of a sigh. "When the Annunaki left Earth, our main force returned to Nibiru. I and others did not wish to do so. So we became explorers, not exploiters. We learned that all life was growing. There was no limit to what life could be. Individuals and races have their limits, of course, but the process of life itself was unlimited.

"Every living, sentient creature could contribute to its growth. Individuals and even races might perish, might be forgotten, but what they had accomplished could never be extinguished. It would echo for eternity because it became part of the evolution of all life."

Enki paused and glanced down at Megaera's head in his hands and a deep sorrow gleamed in his eyes. "In the infinity of possibilities, there was only one restriction. No race can know the potential of another race. Hard as it was to realize, the older races had to allow the younger races to make their mistakes and not interfere.

"We tried to share that philosophy with the Tuatha

de Danaan when we met them. We believed they believed it. They were searching for a new home, a new challenge, and we were searching for a way to help humanity reach its true potential. My group could not intervene, to help them overcome the disaster wrought by Enlil, so we struck a pact with the Danaan. They were to watch over you until my people's internecine strife was settled.''

Enki shook his head sadly. ''Eventually, my faction returned to Nibiru and after time and torment, we were once more a united people. When Nibiru's orbit brought it back into this sector of space, we returned to Earth.

''We found the Tuatha de Danaan were totally entrenched, emotionally dependent on humanity and directly guiding their development. The Danaan viewed us as invaders and broke the pact. We offered them other options, but they were refused. And so, inevitably came war.''

''And it ended,'' interjected Brigid, ''only when you agreed on another pact, a compromise of sorts. Both of your peoples would leave Earth and turn the reins of stewardship over to a new race, one that combined the best qualities of both.''

''Yes,'' Enki said. ''A number of Danaan and Annunaki did not abide by the pact, but they were disorganized and scattered over the face of the Earth. We told the custodians, the watchers, to be alert for their interference in human development.''

"Where did the rest of you go?" Philboyd asked. "The Tuatha de Danaan and your people?"

"The far realms. What your science refers to as hyperdimensional space." Enki nodded toward the caldron of light blazing on the monitor screen. "I believe what we're seeing here is a rift into one those, an interdimensional event horizon."

"You still haven't told us the purpose of the DEVIL process," Brigid said a trifle impatiently.

"The Tuatha de Danaan understood the far realms more than my people," Enki replied. "They had unlocked the mystery of entropy. They proposed we use that mystery to restore both races in the future. And so, the so-called DEVIL process was created."

"What?" Philboyd demanded raggedly. He clutched at his chest and winced but continued speaking. "Are you telling me you built DEVIL thousands of years ago?"

"The seeds of the knowledge were planted thousands of years ago," Enki answered serenely. "Given to our custodial children to be used at a future date. They disseminated those seeds over the long track of time…until your own science found them and nurtured the crop. It would be our way of changing the past in order to create a more reasoned future, by restoring Nibiru and therefore our people to the glory we once shared. And therefore, give an entire race a second chance. But I have learned a bitter lesson. I failed."

"You're talking antientropy," Brigid challenged.

"Entropy is entropy," Enki retorted. "A never ending circuit of birth, maturity, age, death and rebirth."

Brigid raised a skeptical eyebrow, but thought better of casting aspersions on Enki's honesty. She knew the Archons, the descendants of the First Folk, had been responsible for the most of the Totality Concept researches. The Totality Concept and the development of its many interconnected and related researches was the most ambitious and secret scientific project in recorded history. The Archons provided the crucial technology to translate and meld quantum and hyperdimensional physics with relativistic physics.

Enki seemed to sense her thoughts. "You believe the past is like a fixed object, immutable and unchanging?" His tone was chiding. "When today becomes yesterday, it subtly alters tomorrow."

Brigid nodded and said dryly, "So I've been told. But—"

"Oh, my God!" Philboyd cried. "What's going on?"

Brigid swung her head toward the monitor screen. On it, from the colossal crystalline structure topping the citadel, there leaped up a long lightning stroke of deep crimson light. The giant stroke darted toward the seething mass of the DEVIL platform, penetrating it with an explosive flare.

"The final fuel has been added," Enki said calmly. "Now we will learn if our future does indeed lie in our past."

Pale ectoplasmic waves shimmered out from the

curving contours of the platform. The pallid borealis seemed to creep in a fitful aura, fanning out slowly.

Brigid and Philboyd stared unblinkingly at the screen, incapable of movement. A strobing flicker ran across the blaze. The shimmer around the platform grew more visible, pulsing and throbbing as it advanced. In the center of it appeared a black blot. The circle of darkness swiftly expanded.

"God in Heaven!" shouted Philboyd, eyes wide and wild. "The DEVIL is disrupting space itself in that area."

The terrifying solution to the mystery of the DEVIL's power caused all of them to gape at the monitor screens. Brigid could not understand the scientific method of it, but she realized the DEVIL released a force that annihilated not just matter but space itself.

In a quavery voice, thick with awe, Philboyd murmured, "The space-time continuum of our universe is a four-dimensional sphere within the extradimensional void. The DEVIL destroys the fabric of the continuum, starting with subatomic particles. Electrons have been squashed against protons until the charges cancel and they become neutrons. There are no separate atomic nuclei anymore, just a spherical mass of neutrons like one giant nucleus!"

They glimpsed stars and space wheeling crazily around the black blot, convulsing and recoiling from the energy the machine released.

A thin blue halo crackled up and down the length

of the metal shaft. Brigid and Philboyd recoiled, pressing up against the far wall as lances of lightning and tongues of cold flame leaped from it.

With a throbbing like an invisible surf, the halo expanded and Enki strode purposefully toward it. Philboyd threw an arm over his eyes as the brilliant discharges grew in intensity. He began to whimper.

A tiny spark leaped onto Enki's head and it began to spread. It seemed to feed on his body and like wildfire it covered him in a shimmering cocoon. Brigid shielded her eyes, but she sensed the approach of other presences, other minds, grave and powerful but stricken with sorrow.

She knew she would never learn from what far realm, what dimension the Annunaki had come. But the DEVIL process had opened a doorway and dimly, she saw shadowy shapes, swirling around Enki as tenuous as smoke in the gloom.

Enki spoke to them. Brigid could not understand his words, but she recognized he was asking for forgiveness—and a desperate plea to join them.

The glowing fire covering Enki's body was suddenly drawn toward the shaft, as if it were a sponge absorbing the energies. It leaped back to the metal, and Enki seemed to go with it. One instant he was there, and the next, the last of the Serpent Kings was gone.

As the shimmering brilliance faded to a tolerable level, Brigid, mouth dry and her heart pounding, risked a glance at the monitor screen. The beam still played over the burning core of the platform, but now it was of a darker red hue as if streaks of black played along its length. Then it faded into insubstantiality.

The space around the DEVIL platform peeled back on itself. From the burning central mass came a wave of dazzling white flares and variegated lightnings that streaked and blazed.

The shimmering sphere of the platform, appearing to burn in space, became a bubble of quivering blackness through which shot coruscating particles of brilliance, like a fireworks display as seen from a vast distance. It exuded rolling multicolored clouds overlapped, engulfing it until they could no longer see it.

Philboyd and Brigid could only stare at the monitor screen in dumbfounded silence. It displayed only a slice view of star-speckled space. Finally, after two attempts, Philboyd managed to husk out, ''Well, that's what you get for investing in entropy. There's no future in it.''

Epilogue

There wasn't much to do after that. It required several hours before everyone was reunited and by then the most immediate crisis appeared over. The people who had followed Maccan were still presumably running free, as well as a handful of Furies, but no one molested the group of astrophysicists or Kane, Brigid and Grant when they met in the life-hutch module.

After everyone had told their stories, the scientists stared at a blank monitor screen as if it could explain what had really happened aboard the DEVIL platform. Philboyd could only speculate, rambling loudly about interdimensional rifts, the collision and synthesis of space-time and entropic gradients. His injuries had been treated by Mariah and though they were superficial, more unsightly than critical, he still needed recuperation time, which he refused to take.

He was far too excited and agitated to sit still. At one point he thrust his face close to Grant's and said challengingly, "I really don't know what you did up there, you beautiful bastard, but you very well might have saved the entire solar system."

"Yeah," Grant drawled. "Too bad there wasn't any money in it."

Kane sat down in a chair and propped his foot up on a computer desk. To Brigid he said, "Sounds like it was pretty rough for you two."

She eyed the bruises on his face. "Not as rough as it was for you. What do you think we should do about Maccan?"

He shrugged. "We could keep him cold storage and thaw him out when we want to ask questions about the Tuatha de Danaan. The son of a bitch likes to talk—too bad most of the time he doesn't make sense."

Brigid nodded and surveyed the collection of astrophysicists clustered together in the cramped habitat. "We've got a group of valuable new recruits for Lakesh to indoctrinate."

Kane smiled ruefully. "After the kind of aliens they've been dealing with, they'll probably find the barons cute and cuddly, not scary."

Brigid matched his smile. "Cerberus can certainly use their expertise, their brilliance."

"And their tech—especially those transatmospheric planes. There's lot of ordnance up here we can use." He glanced into her face and noticed a frown tugged at the corners of her mouth. "Sort of tips the balance of power a little more in our favor, don't you think? Levels out the playing field."

Brigid shook her head, then smoothed her mane of hair back from her face. "It's no longer a matter of power or games, Kane. If we learned one thing up here, it's that we have to find a way to end the bloodshed or we'll all die—not just the hybrids and the barons but humanity, as well.''

Kane met her glinting green gaze. ''I was under the impression that goal was what brought us up here in the first place.''

Brigid folded her arms over her chest and stared at him levelly. ''With what you were told—what I was told—do you think we'll ever know the real secrets of the Annunaki, the Danaan, the hidden history of humankind?''

''You might,'' Kane retorted.

Brigid smiled. ''I intend to.''

She turned away toward Philboyd. Kane reflected that he had never before noticed how Brigid Baptiste could, upon occasion, look insufferably smug.

DEATH LANDS®

Amazon Gate

Available in
September 2002
at your favorite retail outlet.

In the radiation-blasted heart of the Northwest, Ryan and his companions form a tenuous alliance with a society of women warriors in what may be the stunning culmination of their quest. After years of searching, they have found the gateway belonging to the pre-dark cabal known as the Illuminated Ones—and perhaps their one chance to reclaim the future from the jaws of madness. But they must confront its deadly guardians: what is left of the constitutional government of the United States of America.

Stony Man is deployed against an armed invasion on American soil....

DEFENSIVE ACTION

A conspiracy to cripple a sophisticated antimissle system—and the United States itself—is under way, fueled by the twisted ideology of a domestic militia group. Their campaign against the government has gone global, their terrorist agenda refinanced and expanded by a cabal of America's enemies: North Korea, Russia and China. Crisscrossing the North American continent, Stony Man enters a desperate race against time to halt this act of attrition…before America pays the price in blood.

STONY MAN

Available in August 2002 at your favorite retail outlet.